LISA

a chess novel

JESSE KRAAI

ZUGZWANG PRESS

Printed in the United States of America
First Printing, 2013

ISBN 978-0-9768489-0-5

Zugzwang Press

Jessekraai.com

THE JOURNAL

A ceremony once marked the completion of Lisa's journals. Her mother would take the finished work into her hands and hold it for a time with her eyes closed, as if she were giving thanks. But she would never look inside, for the journal was private. Then, together, Lisa and her mother would begin to craft Lisa's next book. They ran linen thread through wax. They bound the pages to one another with a Coptic stitch. Finally, her mother would bring forth a colorful postcard—once it was Renoir's *Banks of the Seine at Asnieres*, another time it was a bunch of colored tiles by a guy named Mondrian. Lisa and her mother glued a postcard on the cover of every new journal. And Lisa would often return to those decorations, wondering what her mother hoped her to find in the blank pages beneath them.

In those early days, Lisa's mother sometimes recited a small section of the Schmied family's *Tagebuchlied* or *Song of the Journal* that had been passed down through the generations:

> Know the earth your roots meet,
> Pushing down, with many feet
>
> Name the stones that you grip,
> Hold tight, and do not slip

Upward stalk in the wind,
Pass doch auf kleines Kind!

But her mother—whom everyone else called Jan—didn't know what the last line meant, nor could she remember the rest of the song that her mother—Lisa's grandmother, Lena—had sung to her.

Jan had always been too busy running her kitchen and home store, Domestique, to write in her own journal. And ever since she had expanded the business to four stores, she hadn't had time to sew the pages together. Lisa's new journals were from her mother's flagship store in Orinda. They were heavy, with hard covers and a clasping lock. A splatter of noble wood fragments gave each thick page a unique texture. And they all read "My Diary" in big curvy letters.

As Lisa grew older, Jan began to disapprove of the large amount of time she spent with her journal, as if it were a security blanket that her daughter needed to let go of. But she never admitted it. Jan would only repeat, over and over, that Lisa, now thirteen, needed to learn to face the world. And she let Lisa's stepfather, Ted, tease her about her journal. "Oh, go hide in your book!" he would say—or, "Must be some expensive thoughts you're writing on those woody pages."

But Lisa would not betray her journal, the one friend who offered her insight and loyalty. On January 30th she wrote, "The rainy season has come back. Like a forgotten memory, the wet darkness holds me. Thick clouds won't let me see. And I am left to myself, withering and whitening. The kids at school don't want to feel the rain. They hide their ignorance underneath facts: how long it's been raining, rain clothes, condensation, forecasts. And I'm rolled up like a burrito in their assembly lines all day long."

Lisa began to casually leave her journal around the house—on the long granite countertops of her mother's spacious kitchen, on the colorful tiles next to the sink of the downstairs bathroom, stenciled with native Californian plants Lisa had never seen—always with her entry from January 30th facing outward. But nothing changed. Jan continued to talk about Lisa's middling grades. She complained that Lisa didn't have any friends. And she sometimes even made odd remarks that seemed to refer to how fat Lisa was.

Lisa was supposed to be like the other girls at her small college-prep school, Mens Conscia Recti. They were so engaged with life! Together, they knew what they were supposed to do. And Lisa did try to join them, when she first arrived at the school a year before, in seventh grade.

Lisa thought her wit would have to come fast, before she lost her chance. Someone would interrupt her if she allowed any breath between her words. But her hurried sentences floated down like shredded paper in front of the other girls. And she soon found herself on the outside, staring at their lithe backs, their earrings and their perfect hair.

Lisa began to look down on their inane conversations about boys, makeup and clothes. She hated the way they always did what they were supposed to. Life was so easy for them, so thoughtless. Everything they did was about getting into Berkeley, or Stanford. That unoriginal goal—which wasn't really even theirs—was the only meaning their lives had. They are like cows, Lisa thought, trusting the rancher's prods to guide them down his corridors of barred steel to his cornmeal. They think he acts in their best interest.

Alone with her journal, Lisa became skilled at finding the tender wounds of the people around her. She stabbed at Ted's emotional ignorance, her teachers' slavishness and Jan's hypocrisy. With her fine blade of sarcasm and irony she cut through all of their intestinal muck until she felt the hard grimace of the backbone. Then she would pull violently to the head, and all of their squishy bits would pop out and ooze.

Like the Hercules beetle, whose gruesome black pincers grossly outsize its body, all Lisa could ever see was her own weaponry. And she had to drag that heavy load around with her wherever she went.

Through the journal, Lisa expected to know and manipulate the textures and patterns around her. Filling its pages, she expected to gain foresight, and carefully choose the friends and enemies who would define her. But she didn't feel in control. And there were many things she wanted to know, but could not discover—especially about herself.

Lisa needed to find Grandma Lena's journals. They would show her how to write in her own. But the house was huge, and there were any number of places where Jan might have hidden them. The rooms were cluttered with neglected stuff that Jan couldn't sell at her store, because of a chip or a scratch. The redwood dresser was full of clothes that needed to be donated. The fifteen hundred thread-count bedspreads in the guest rooms had suntan lines. And the stalks of once wildly exotic plants drooped over great clay pots like strings exhausted by a cat. "It's not a house. It's a home." That was Domestique's slogan. But Jan's own home looked more like a warehouse.

Lisa thought it wouldn't be so hard to find herself. After all, her own words didn't have to put on clothes or give themselves airs when they went about and talked with one another. But Lisa didn't know where to start. It seemed natural that she begin with her most elevating experiences, moments like the wet of January 30th, when her intimate connection to the world felt like a call to something higher.

It was such an exhausting task that Lisa had to fast from school. She did what her teachers asked, but with dull eyes and limp limbs.

She just needed to get through it, then she could be alone in her large room on the quiet side of the house. Everything outside that room became drowsy. And her classes, once overgrown with thorny bushes of failure and displacement, now thinned into featureless tundra.

Every night, Lisa expected the rain's chanting patter to allow her past the barriers that made the daylight so insensitive and cruel. And she did drop, as if into a well, briefly caressing leathery patches, sandy ridges and sections of lace as she fell. But she wasn't able to return from these pilgrimages of her soul with anything tangible that she could be proud of. She only found dinky trinkets, false souvenirs of herself. Like the kind of thing she saw on bumper stickers, or tattooed on the unfortunate arm of a young girl. They could hold a sentiment, but never her. And they certainly never encompassed her with the shrouding intimacy of the cold and dark rain.

School was not ending. It moved with the groping motions of a garden slug, slowly tearing windows in the thick greens for the coming sun. And as the rainy season extended, Lisa's nocturnal discoveries became more ghastly. She found herself naked in the middle of the girls from school. They laughed at her and wouldn't give her any of their clothes. Lisa broke all of the expensive wine glasses at Jan's store and made the customers walk over the shards with bare feet. And she killed Ted, with poison, knives and kitchen gadgets.

These images created a biting pressure, like one of the ballooning pimples on her face. And they had to be uncaged. It was a release to cut her arm with a razor, to watch the animal within her pulse its blood. And Lisa did feel free when she called her mother "Jan," like everybody else did. These violent acts were a revenge upon the darkness that wouldn't let her see herself.

♟

One very early morning, a faint light glooming through the thickly painted glass of the clouds, Lisa thought she was outside. Lying in wet, neither asleep nor awake, Lisa waited for the rain to deepen. Slowly, she began to fall and feel the puddle rise around her. Unseen men lowered her with thick ropes. As her descent accelerated, a woven script unfurled away from her, and stuck to the sides of her casket-sized plunge. Lisa felt called to awake and read the patterns on her fabrics, to see herself. But she could not. An alarm clock rang, and another day sulked through its sameness and small thoughts, for the reward of another evening to herself.

♟

For years, Jan had driven Lisa to activities. They were designed to turn Lisa outward, and integrate her into the world. Some were supposed to make her smarter. Others tried to make her more social. And even though Jan never said it, Lisa knew that many were designed to make her lose weight. Lisa suffered most of these patiently: horseback riding, swim lessons, story time, therapy with Dr. Frohlich. Lisa was usually happy to be alone. She could wait for friends. They would be older, and show Lisa something more than the small world she was forced to inhabit.

But the animal shrieking of young boys at chess class always made Lisa feel bitterly lonesome. Jan took her there every Tuesday and Thursday. Alone in a boil of unspanked violence, with no other girls in the room to pillow the boys' barking, Lisa was in the way. And she would discover herself looking and feeling paranoid, especially when she had to hold her hands up as if they were earmuffs, to protect her head and her glasses from the projectile weapons chess pieces can become.

Each chess lesson had a preamble. To Lisa, it always sounded like, "Get ready to smear our peanut butter all over this AMAZING obstacle course. It's gonna be great!" It was easy for Lisa to sit back and not care. Like at school, some boy would always be too eager to regurgitate the gluey cud when her turn came around.

The lesson never lasted very long. The slouchy man at the head of the class couldn't tame the boys. He would gently ask them to be quiet, to pay attention. But they would not. They talked back, and said things like, "But I got the ADD!" So they were allowed to play variants of the game. They played Bullet chess, where each side has one minute for the whole game. They played Atomic chess, where the most recently played piece explodes everything in its vicinity. And they played Suicide, where the boys raced to get rid of all of their pieces. These were all very loud.

On a Tuesday in April, Lisa awoke from her tired stupor. A boy was shouting at her: "GO! . . . I'M VERSING YOU . . . HEY! . . . MOVE!" A man came by to hush the boy, but Lisa could see the next scream filling the monster's eyes like a water balloon. The violent splash would come. The wave would recede, and Lisa would lie broken on the floor, as she always feared her glasses would be. It was unfair. What, after all, did the boy's pushiness have to do with her?

Lisa remembered the ropes pulling on her. The rooty mess of her puddle scratched her. The slime of seaweed slithered around her like snakes as she broke her fingernails on the stones she wasn't strong enough to dislodge from the sand. Why couldn't she clean it out? Where was the sublime between she had felt inside her drown of rain? It had been so simple and whole. Why was it so hard to find again? Lisa needed the closeness to save herself, a promise of a deeper world to hold against the cruel thoughtlessness of her waking day.

Several moves had already been played. Had she made those moves? The chaotic clump of the matte plastic pieces was like a small patch of ground that her face had been shoved up against. She felt that she was supposed to get up from that humiliated view. It was animal to be so close to the ground. But she saw no reason to get up. She knew the phony exhaustion of the world up there too well.

Lisa looked. An ant appeared. Soon, some friends followed its path. They had discovered a flower, and were harvesting something from its yellow calyx. A small spider was nearby, but she didn't seem to be interested in the ants, as if she were in a different world, concerned with something else. Glistening trails of some creature pointed their way to a different flower.

Softly, the pieces began to reveal their discussion. Unlike the braille around her, Lisa could see the friendship of her pieces. Rains would come, the geography would shift, and the group would have to foresee new ways to hold hands across the mounds, rivulets and pits. Lisa could feel her pieces warming each other, with the familial coziness of mammals, but without the mammalian need to turn on each other. They were consonant.

Lisa's immobile meditation punished the boy. The slap and bang of his pieces drifted off into the silence. And the waterslide of his quick decisions, rushing down to a splashy pool, was taken from him like a toy. He wasn't going to land in fun. His command was at first angry, "MOOOhoove, moWOOVVE!" But then it became a plaintive, bovine despair.

No, Lisa would not move. She sat. The moves she had already played on the board were not hers; they were sleepy decisions, unaware of themselves. Nor would she have her pieces coarsened by the boy. Her close view, pushed to the ground, able to see what everyone else walked over, was hers alone. All the other games were finished, and the boys huddled together on a nearby table to stack the pieces as high as they could. They hooked the heads of four knights onto the crown of a rook, building the base. They strategized ways to build something on top of the bishop's pointy head. Then, when the construction fell, and chess pieces were spit out into the far corners of the room, the boys shrieked "Jenga!" Delighted, they began their task anew, with a different set. Lisa continued her meditation.

♟

Thursday. Lisa watched the boys tumble into the after-school class that never started on time. One group of boys imagined themselves wizards, and cast down terrible spells upon their opponents with the fanciful cards of *Magic The Gathering.* "Treva is the voice of the ur-dragon, demanding cries of worship." "I'll rain down on you with the power of magic itself. Then we'll see who prevails." Some other boys were playing bughouse, a tag-team chess match, and a boy was already climbing up to the top rope of the wrestling cage he imagined himself in. He wore a red cape and a scary mask of curving black and white streaks. When he landed his knight he yelled, "Oh, OHHH, TAASTE MEEE!"

Lisa was awake now to the teacher. He had to speak quickly, and loudly, to meet the tyranny of the boys' needs. But Lisa expected chess to speak through the man. If she listened carefully, the game's powerful words would rise like invocations up into the cruder world she was forced to inhabit. But she could not discover any deeper meaning in his words.

♟

Lisa hadn't spent time in the living room in months. It was Ted's space—"the man cave," as he called it. But that night she wanted to explore the chess world on Jan's laptop. She wasn't allowed to have her own. They were dangerous. A big engine sound revved colorful cars around a track inside Ted's big screen. An empty carton of yellow curry poked out of the plastic bag he had brought it home in.

Gentle burps of beery satisfaction rose from his belly as he enjoyed the race. Ted worked hard all day, managing hotels or something. He had earned the right to rest his dirty socks on his glass coffee table.

Lisa had eaten Ted's take-out food. He liked his bites to contain the unexpected. He didn't want to know the names of the spices; he wanted them to bounce through him wildly, like a maniac shooting off fireworks in the sewer. He felt the same way about his eighty-inch flat-screen TV. He wanted to be dragged out into the unknown in a violent undertow of color and sound.

Lisa sat with Ted on his leather couch as Google led her to a Bay Area chess group for women on chess.com. There was only one event listed. Lisa imagined a sea of kindred seekers at the Northern California Girls Championship, girls who shared what she had found. There would be older girls there, high school girls. In them, Lisa would be able to see women she could become. In three weeks, they would share the conversation. And she would finally pursue something Jan wanted—she would play chess.

Jan was sitting on a table behind the couch, just outside the invisible boundary of Ted's cave, doing the numbers from her store. "Jan," Lisa shouted over the barrier, "I'm going to play in the Northern California Girls Championship."

Jan looked up from the concerns of an Excel spreadsheet she had printed out. "Championship? Of what?" she asked.

"Chess," Lisa said.

"You mean there's a separate tournament for girls?"

Lisa shrugged.

Jan put on her disappointed face and said, "I thought chess was supposed to be just a game, for fun?"

"I want to play, Jan."

It seemed like Jan did not want her to play, but didn't know how to forbid her. Instead, Jan asked, "Why does it have to be way off in

Fremont?" "Why does it have to last all weekend?" And, "Why don't you want to play with the boys?"

Elegant drapery hung from the tall windows of the man cave. The fabric was gauzy and thin, from Domestique. Lisa used to press her face up against the delicate texture, and look out to Jan in Ted's world. Then Lisa would blow, as hard as her young lungs could, to encourage the draft of the open window. The drapes would swallow Ted and all his stuff. But now Lisa felt the room collapsing around her, and the light drapes roughened into curtains underneath the undulating whine of Ted's car race.

The conversation became unpleasant, especially after Lisa realized she had a winning mantra. Again and again, Lisa repeated her shouting logic: "So, you put me in chess class, and now I can't play in a tournament? Do you want to take away my journal too? You're always complaining about it, saying I obsess. That I should exercise, and focus on my grades." Jan could only counter with complaints, saying that she didn't have time. Then Lisa threatened to take the train there herself.

♟

Lisa prepared for the tournament by playing against herself. She set up five boards throughout the large house—in the garage, the dining room, the blue guest room, the red guest room and on the verandah. Lisa marched a steady circuit through her positions and sought to cultivate her most elevating experiences, the embodied intimacy of the rain and the interconnection she had felt in her game with the rude boy. Before she had only seen what everybody does, that each piece only knows a geometric movement. Now she saw that each piece really only acquires meaning as part of an evolving conversation, that the individualism of each piece is clothed within larger, moving patterns.

Lisa knew only one stratagem: if she took all her opponent's pieces it wasn't that hard to figure out how to mate the lone king. This made her pieces greedy. They wanted to hold each in a thick embrace, as if their love were eternal. Lisa practiced feeling that interconnection, striving for a snug mutual defense. Then she would smell for weakness, awkward movements among the herd of opposing pieces. Like a wolf pack, Lisa's pieces sought to cut the sick and tired from those who might defend them.

Lisa strove to beat the boys in the few competitive games she was allowed to play at the Berkeley Chess School. But the boys' thoughts were crude. Their pieces had no sense of the herd. And their thoughts didn't have time to see the whole board. That's why they rushed their prettiest piece forward, prancing about without any help. Lisa would surround the errant young bull and stab him until he fell. Sadly, these violent eviscerations went largely unnoticed. The glory of Lisa's triumphs was masked underneath the playful atmosphere of the school, which seemed to insist that chess was just a game.

♟

The plastic chess sets in the tournament hall looked like test booklets to Lisa. Garishly shining in the fluorescent light, they marched in long rows upon the fold-down cafeteria tables. Lisa wanted to run away. But she found herself trapped, like a soldier in a forward-moving box of men, advancing to the front. Some of her peers might also want to run, but they would never be able to escape all by themselves. Fear moved everybody onwards.

Lisa was alienated by the hunger to prove themselves that she saw in the girls around her. It surprised her to see that they were not like her. They didn't come from the same place. It seemed like one bus full of girls had arrived straight from India, and another from

China. Lisa was imagining chess among women to be like a sacred ceremony, not a test. And she was ashamed to admit that she had been hoping to meet a white girl, someone like her.

But Lisa would have a whole hour to play her moves. No boy would shout at her. And she didn't have to play against herself—it would be a real conversation. Lisa found her seat in the anonymous hall. She prepared her scoresheet, carefully writing down her name and that of her opponent, Shreya Datta. Finally, her puddle would have rain and a chance to deepen itself.

But Lisa's first-round opponent moved too fast, like an anxious boy. Nor did she feel the bonds between her pieces, and Lisa began collecting them.

The scoretable to which Lisa and her opponent reported their result was the only place in the wide hall that seemed inviting and friendly. A light paisley cloth covered a circular wooden table of dark oak. And a bouquet of irises stood behind a sign that read "Wim Ruth Charing, Chief Arbiter." *What strange names people have here*, Lisa thought. The unsaturated colors of the older woman's clothes drew Lisa in. Heathered, they gracefully acquiesced to the darkness of the rainy season.

Lisa came up to this woman and said, "Hi Wim, my name is Lisa. Me and Shreya are here to record our result."

Ruth laughed and said, "Nice to meet you, Lisa. My name is Ruth. WIM stands for Women's International Master."

After each of her games, Lisa would come to sit down on the cold linoleum, underneath the paisley skirts of Ruth's table. She liked to be hidden, and listen to Ruth talk about chess with the players and adults who reported to her. Sometimes, when Ruth had a free moment from the administration of the tournament, she would tell Lisa stories from her life in the game. Jan was far away, using her cell phone to place orders for her store on the other side of the large cafeteria hall.

Lisa won rounds two and three in much the same way she had won round one. Two remaining games would be played the following day. Lisa didn't think too much about her wins, but she was surprised that her eager opponents could not see the threats their pieces stood under. As the room was being tidied, and Lisa and Jan were leaving, Ruth came up to Lisa and said, "I watched some of your third round. You're really good, especially for someone who has never played in a tournament before. And now you're tied for first place. I think you might have a chance! Especially since Emily Zuo isn't here."

Everyone, especially Ruth, had been talking about Emily at the score table. She was rated 1672, and was taught by some famous guy named Khmelnitsky. But Emily had to take the SATs that weekend. Lisa didn't know anything about ratings. It seemed like the kind of thing a boy would get excited about. They said that Emily had represented Northern California at the Polgar Girls Tournament the year before—that was where the winner of the Northern California Girls Championship got to go.

"Come on, Lisa, we have to go. I have to go to the store to clean up a mess," Jan demanded. Lisa felt she had always been tugged away by Jan. And she wanted to shout at her, like an insistent horn in a traffic jam: "Jan, can you wait a second?" But she calmed herself. Ruth, after all, was standing right there.

"Ruth," Lisa asked, "why does it matter if you win or lose?"

Ruth fell into thought, as Lisa felt Jan's impatience tightening into silence. "I'm not sure anyone has ever asked me that before, Lisa," Ruth said. "I guess it's because we can measure ourselves in the game. In real life, our thoughts flow out of us like water. We don't know if they will be understood, or where they will go. At some point they evaporate, like my voice in this room."

Jan pulled Lisa away. "Thank you very much, Ruth," she said. "I'll have Lisa here for round four tomorrow morning."

Lisa thought about what Ruth said about measuring yourself all night. In chess, you could see all the pieces and you knew how they moved. That's what made it honest. It wasn't like life. But what was the measure? Ruth talked about ratings all the time, as if a person's rating was somehow a reflection of the quality of their meditation. To Lisa, ratings seemed like birdcages suspended in an elaborate pulley system: however much someone went up, someone else went down. Those cages seemed like places for boys to hide, so that they wouldn't have to know the experience of the rain, or ever truly look at their pieces. But Lisa was flattered that Ruth had watched over her thoughts, and praised her meditation. She did want to please Ruth.

♟

The next day, after she had won her fourth round game, Lisa overheard the anxious complaints of a mother from her hidden linoleum cave. Lisa could only see the woman's legs from her place beneath Ruth's table. They were thin and muscular, so unlike the blue veins and thick ankles she was used to seeing in kids' moms. And her toenails weren't painted. "My daughter not pay tension," the mother shouted. "She not Con-cen-trate. I try tell her. I always tell her. But she not listen. I not know what wrong with her. You chess lady. You talk." In Ruth's most lofty vision of herself she was a volunteer for women's chess, but now Lisa could feel her squirming as a passive listener to all the girl's failings, repeated by her mother. "Tell chess lady why you not Con-cen-trate." Ruth was trapped behind the oak table that she had brought from home, not knowing what answer to give.

Did Claire Ho's mom want her daughter to know about the measure Ruth told her about yesterday? Lisa wondered. *Were Ruth's measure and Claire's mom's the same? Why doesn't Jan care about chess? Alone, hidden, the pieces know what they want, but the people who move them don't seem to know at all.*

Ruth gently pulled Claire to her. She stroked her shiny black hair and consoled her loss. Claire looked down at the floor, and repeated in the most plain American English, "I tried. I really tried." Lisa thought Claire must know that she was right beneath the table, behind the paisley cloth. Her downward eyes must see her. Lisa was about to jump up, out of her hidden place, and tell Claire about the ants, the spider, the interconnection and the text. Chess wasn't school! It wasn't some dumb obstacle course you had to run through to get a grade. Lisa didn't know how she was going to say it. It would all just spill out. But then Claire's mother furiously said, "No comfort, not deserve. Tell her Con-cen-trate!"

An assistant arbiter, distinguished by a piece of blue felt wrapped around her arm, came by the table to calm the distress. Playfully joking, she said, "Have you guys heard that Igor Ivanov talks to his pieces? They say he talks to them the same way I talk to my cat. 'Pebbles,' I say, 'what do you really want out of life?' Pebbles never says anything back. Sometimes he licks himself. But Igor says the pieces tell him all kinds of things." This vision of chess craziness lifted all three women, and they shared the bond of a condescending smile. Chess was, after all, just a game.

Once they were alone again, Lisa asked Ruth about Igor.

"Oh, Igor was a great talent," Ruth replied. "He came to this country years ago, but lost his way in drink. He's still the strongest player in the area, and wins whenever he plays. Chess is everything to him. I don't think he ever had much of a life outside it."

"Does he really talk to his pieces?" Lisa asked.

Ruth laughed. "Well, I've never seen him do it, but for him the pieces are like an extension of himself. He says he is his pieces. Totally crazy, huh?"

GANDER

Walking kale crowded the narrow path to the grandmaster's cottage. Eight feet tall, the perennial plant extended its many fronds like hands on long arms. Underneath them was a rich forest of annual kales, the frilly blackish green of dinosaur, the poisonous-looking bright colors of rainbow and the prickly stems of Siberian dwarf.

To get to the grandmaster's door, Lisa had to squeeze her body around a wooden cart of horse shit that was harnessed to an enormous steel bike. The bike's seat loomed behind her head like a fence post, forcing her on top of a dirty brown mat that said "Welcome." Lisa knocked and waited. She tried to push her tank top down over her belly. But her flesh rolled away from her; the stretchy piece of cotton never stayed. Her pastel blue shirt was a ribbon around a present no one wanted.

"Grandmaster Ivanov?" Lisa could barely hear her own voice. Then she spoke with more force, directly into the door she had just knocked on: "My name is Lisa. I'm a chessplayer." The floorboards squealed as the man came to his door. The right-hand side of his shirt had just been fisted into his pants. His belt buckle hung open, and soiled jeans slid down his lean frame.

The giant man finally looked down and found Lisa. He began to examine her. And it was then that Lisa first saw real chess eyes. They were cold and wet, like a healthy dog's nose, impolitely sniffing at all the things she couldn't smell herself.

Lisa's sentences began to jump. "I found you with Google. My parents will never know I'm here. They get home late. School is just two train stops away. I want you to teach me. I won the Northern California Girls Championship. I got some study money. From the Polgar Foundation. I need to train. For the Polgar Girls Tournament. At the end of the summer. I can pay you."

Lisa had waited for the shuttle with the other kids, just like every other day. The high wooden-shingled roofs of their private college-prep school were warm and ordered, like a summer camp. The boys jumped on each other, made the wave with their stomach muscles, and did the armpit fart. The girls stood aside, superior and mature. The rainy season was over, and school would end soon.

Lisa took the school shuttle to the train with them. She knew she could break the rules and simply walk the four blocks to the train station, through the dangerous traffic. But Lisa wanted them to know that she was going in the other direction. They would follow the customary path, and travel through the mountain to the suburbs on the other side, to Orinda, Walnut Creek and Lafayette. Lisa would go toward the water.

Lisa transferred at MacArthur Station. On the platform, a wrinkled woman yelled into the emptiness, "I've had enough of your candles! Purple, pink and black. I can't take it. GET OUT of here!" Lisa looked around for the candles, but didn't see any. After a while, it seemed like the woman wasn't real; no one noticed her.

Then Lisa rode to Ashby Station, close to where she had found Igor's house on Googlemaps. She saw a mangy rat precariously clutch a Starbucks cup in his big teeth and scurry off into the station's thick vines. Black people stood on the street corners she walked by. They asked her for money. And now she stood close to Igor's thick forearm hair. Purposeful veins travelled over a rippling network of muscles and tendons like elevated train tracks. Splotchy scars decorated his arm like tattoos.

Lisa maneuvered around the cart and backed away into the hands of the man's kale. "Aren't you going to say anything?" she asked. The man just stared at her.

Finally, he said, "I not teach American. No respect for game. Not since camp in Payson, Arizona. Is promise I make, to self."

"The Polgar Foundation will pay you!" she cried. "They gave me money for a teacher!" But this did not move the man. He stood in his doorway like a tree, waiting for her to go.

As if Lisa were looking for a friend, she dove into her backpack. A princely unicorn looked out from the plastic cover of the pack that Jan had bought for her. He was pure white with a wavy black mane. Lisa had once thought him wise and powerful. Now he just seemed childish, especially as bright pink and gold flowers fell about him. Lisa arose from her backpack with a book. She straightened her back. Armed with her journal, she was suddenly poised and articulate, and she began to read aloud:

"I know I'm not that good. It's not just that Emily Zuo wasn't at the tournament—she would have beaten me for sure—it's that I've never really studied the game. Chess was just one of those places my mom drove me to, some place where a teacher tries to lead us around, entertain us, always smiling. I don't know what chess really is. I sometimes feel like there is more going on. I can't see it. I only sense it. I win my games by taking stuff. I feel stuck there, even if I am good at it, like a beginning painter who only knows how to draw stick figures."

Igor was silent, and Lisa continued reading from her book: "Ruth said that Igor talks to his pieces." Here Lisa looked up at Igor, as if he should know who Ruth was. "She said it in a way that made him seem crazy. But I think I might understand what he means. Maybe I'm crazy. They say he won't teach anymore, that he's angry. The parents try to trick their children into concentrating with chess. They say, 'Chess is fun!' But he says that chess will hurt. I tried to friend him on Facebook. Nothing. I left a message on his phone. No response. So tomorrow I'm just going to knock on his door."

"What is book?" Igor asked.

"It's a journal."

"This journal, what is?"

Lisa looked down on the stupid book that the grandmaster pronounced "djurnaal." It was flimsy and girlish in the dappled light of his dark green garden. The cover had once been very pretty, a watery pink that seemed to expect a later bloom of luscious red. But Lisa had defaced that veneer with black roses and a thick tangle of spiky vines. She had drawn them with care and deep feeling, as if many other girls had not decorated their shields with the same bloodflowers. Inside, thick and woody pages expected the fine calligraphy of a curving hand. "It's supposed to tell you what's important," Lisa mumbled.

Igor turned around and went inside. He abandoned Lisa, without even giving her a chance. So she sat down. She didn't wait for his attention. No, this spot of ground was as good as any other. Like a goldfish swimming around and around in a tank, every place was equally meaningless.

Eventually Igor came out, to shovel the green-and-brown shit from the cart on his bike into his garden. The shit had swirls in it, like chocolate ice cream from a dispenser. White maggots squiggled out of the muck and tumbled down the pile. A feral cat hunted something along the side of the fence. Lisa imagined a rat, breathing heavily in the brush, afraid to move.

Then she felt a weight on her shoulder. It was the biggest book Lisa had ever seen. "Do first five hundred mate-in-two, come back tomorrow. Please give book respect, is old friend." Lisa stood up, but then had to stoop forward as she took possession of the overlarge black tome.

"You did what?" Ruth gasped. Lisa needed help, somehow, and had called the volunteer for women's chess right away, just a couple blocks away from Igor's backyard cottage. At first it had seemed like the mate-in-twos would be easy. You move, they move, and then zap, it's all over. But Lisa quickly saw that there was no way she could ever do five hundred by the following afternoon. And there was also no way she could get the book into her room without Jan asking questions about where she had been, and with whom.

Lisa sat down on the sidewalk to wait. About ten feet away there was a very large human turd, as if someone had wanted to make a proud public proclamation. The book held 5,334 black boxes. Each box held a position, and a demand to find a very efficient mate, a simple answer, a haiku. The pieces seemed random. Many problems had a lopsided material imbalance. Like:

What is the point of mating in two in a position like that? Lisa thought. She knew she would be able to mate, eventually. *And problems?* Chess had been about the conversation of the pieces. That's what she wanted. That's why she had come to Igor. The problems reminded Lisa

White to play and mate in two

of boys and their pointless math problems. Lisa allowed herself to doubt. And this comforted the failing she saw ahead of her. Maybe chess was bullshit, like everything else.

Lisa saw Ruth approach from a great distance, slowly pedaling up the gradual incline of the East Bay. Her great brown skirts bobbed up and down in the cavity of the old-style women's bicycle. Ruth arose out of the darkness of the rainy season to meet Lisa on an unusually bright and hot day. She sweat.

Ruth listened to Lisa's troubles and considered the great book she carried. "Copy shop," she spoke into her phone. On the walk there, Ruth told Lisa that Igor was a troubled man. He was not to be taken lightly. And, as far as she knew, he hadn't taken a student in a very long time.

"But," Lisa said, wanting to defend the man she didn't know, "aren't the people who suffer always the heroes?"

"What?" Ruth said. "No! No they're not. Listen Lisa: all Russian intellectuals have to choose, by the age of forty, between blunt racism and the notion that Jews conspire to control the world. But this age has passed Igor by long ago, and he still has not chosen his path. He is therefore a very confused man."

Ruth made Lisa photocopies. She paid for them. And as she worked, she explained that she and Igor had been at several events together, at the Olympiad Team Championship and at a couple US Championships. Ruth had played in the women's event while Igor played in the genderless equivalent. But, Ruth said, Igor probably wouldn't remember her. He and the other Russians didn't consider women's chess to be the real thing. And he had always been drunk.

Ruth said that Igor was a legend. For he had escaped. The Soviet authorities allowed him to play in the prestigious Capablanca Memorial in Havana after he beat World Champion Anatoly Karpov in 1979.[1] On the way back, the big Soviet plane had to make an

---

[1]Ivanov-Karpov: 1. ♙e4 ♙c5 2. ♘f3 ♙e6. 3. ♙d4 ♙xd4 4. ♘xd4 ♙a6 5. ♘c3 b5 6. ♗d3 ♗b7 7. castles ♘e7 8. ♔h1 ♘bc6 9. ♘xc6 ♘xc6 10. ♕g4 ♘h5 11. ♕e2 ♘e5 12. ♗f4 ♘g4 13. ♖f3 ♕h4 14. ♙h3 ♗c5 15. ♗d2 ♙g6 16. ♖af1 ♕e7 17. ♙a3 ♙f5 18. ♖e1 ♕f8 19. ♙b4 ♗d4

emergency refueling stop in Gander, Newfoundland. And Igor simply walked off. "It's not like he could have planned it, you see? He just grabbed his chance and jumped."

When the photocopies of the first five hundred problems were made, Ruth said, "Listen, Lisa. This thirty-pound book, it's a collection of the problems that Laszlo Polgar used to train his daughters, Judit, Zsofie and Zsuzsa. They all became champions. And Judit was the only woman to ever compete with the best men. I want you to learn from Igor. He can teach you in the Russian tradition. I didn't have that chance, and it's too late for me now.

"I will hold on to the book so your mom won't have to see it. Believe me, I know what you're up against. Just do as many as you can and then take what you have to him tomorrow afternoon."

Lisa snuck the problems back to her room on the quiet side of the house, where her journal had abandoned her. She solved all night, without sleeping. The next day, she placed the photocopies inside her textbooks, and pretended to study what her teachers wanted while she actually did the problems.

But Lisa wasn't even close to done. When the final bell rang she had only been able to do eighty-nine.

The many geometries of the problems felt like a cloth she was weaving together. They were her task. And she could not return to Igor until she was done. Yes, she had failed his test. But she would not go back half-naked.

Five days passed like this. She would have been a day earlier too. But one of the problems was incorrect. It was a great malevolence; a

---

20. ♙a4 ♖c8 21. ♘d1 ♕f6 22. ♙c3 ♗a7 23. ♙xb5 ♙xb5 24. ♙xf5 ♙xf5 25. ♗xb5 ♗xf3 26. ♕xf3 ♖c7 27 ♙c4 ♗d4 28. ♕d5 ♔d8 29 ♕d6 ♘f2+ 30. ♘xf2 ♗xf2 31. ♗e3 ♗xe3 32. ♖xe3 ♕e7 33. ♕d2 ♔e8 34. ♕d4 ♖g8 35. ♕b6 ♕g7 36. ♕xe6+ ♔d8 37. ♕d5 ♖a7 38. ♖d3 ♖a1+ 39. ♔h2 ♖a2 40. ♗c6 ♖a7 41. ♕c5 ♖c7 42. ♕b6 ♔c8.
black resigns

sloppy editor had miscast the problem, put some piece where it shouldn't have been. And Lisa was forced to suffer a great deal before she realized that it had to be wrong.

Lisa retrieved the big book of problems from Ruth that afternoon and then simply left it on the grandmaster's doorstep; tucked inside were several pages of her answers, written on thick paper that she had ripped out of her journal.

Igor caught Lisa by the liquor store. There he held her lower neck, backpack strap and upper arm in his left hand, as if she were a little plastic chess piece. She squirmed, for she had been taught that this was a very bad situation, but his grip was firm and easily prevented her from escaping.

"Come, Lisa. Let us sit for moment." Igor pronounced it 'momient,' and the liquor store exhaled the sticky smell of spilt beer like a sewage vent. They sat on the concrete ground, underneath a yellow sign that read A&I LIQUOR. It blinked quickly and erratically, like the heart of a young mouse with an arrhythmia. "Now, Lisa. Tell about your chess."

"One of the problems is wrong," Lisa complained.

"Where are pieces?" he asked.

"I don't have a set with me," Lisa answered. Down the street she noticed a sign that read, NO DRINKING NO LOITERING.

"No, I mean in problem that wrong you, where are pieces?" Lisa began to reach into the unicorn for her photocopies, but Igor pushed her hand away with his huge palm.

"Where are pieces?" Igor repeated.

"How should I know? I have to see the problem."

"Don't need for see. Tell where pieces are."

Lisa pushed her eyelids together tightly, trying to find the memory Igor pointed her back to. But she could only see black darkness. "I can't see it," Lisa said.

"Remember pain," Igor said. And he waited.

Lisa remembered how the pieces had not gotten along. The miscast problem was like her own family: someone was in the wrong place, but no one knew who it was. She recalled the disagreements she had overheard, then the pieces slowly arose from their box: "Queen g7, king e6, knight e2 ..."

Lisa watched the problem sink into Igor. It seemed as if he didn't rush to prove himself to the solution, but let the notational placement of each piece drop like a pebble into his carved space. He must also have to confront the blank nothingness of sixty-four squares and pieces whose only meaning was a place on a grid. Too much information to hold. But then, in the man's face, Lisa began to see the pieces talking to one another, each one looking to the others to find its role. Roles combined into alliances as the clatter of the street and its attendant smells faded. It was as if he saw possible mates before his mind thought to ask for the first move. The patterns were his old friends, and shortly after they bowed their greeting to one another they showed Igor the solution. Maybe there was a way to solve the problem.

Igor opened his eyes and moved away from the enemy king. "Queen c3," he said.

His answer was wildly wrong. It wasn't even on the right side of the board. Igor pointed to a woman across the street, entering a little shop called Sweet Cupcake. People sat outside on metal chairs and laughed underneath a smart blue and white awning. "This diabetes lady," he said with scorn. "She kill best friend. Other friend only have one arm left; legs gone."

He was insane. One step away from homelessness on the streets Jan and Ted had told her to avoid, like the crazy woman on the train platform. No one could listen to what he said.

Lisa unzipped her backpack and looked at the photocopies one last time. The offending problem was stamped with the word "Fuck" and crisscrossed with several angry lines. Igor's answer wasn't even close.

Ruth's photocopies made a crinkly sound as they brushed up against the flank of the plastic unicorn. Then Lisa shoved the stupid problems into the cavern of her backpack. She zipped and strapped her unicorn with the efficiency of a schoolgirl who has to make a class and began walking toward the train. But she didn't have anywhere to go.

From the daydream of wander—unaware of the exhaust from the cars, the grime in the sidewalk or the shouts of the drunks—announcements of a broader geometric vision began to fill Lisa's mind. The justice of the problem's geometric interconnection snapped her spine erect and she walked back to Igor, filled with the numbing wonder of a deeper truth.

Her thoughts had circled too intently on the squares housing the king, like a horde of nine-year-old boys crowding the soccer ball on a large field. After Igor's move, the king now had even more squares to move to, but Igor had foreseen death in each of his destinations. The variations had a dirty wit about them. They were fart jokes, laughing at all the phonies who pretended not to smell the world's flatulence. And Lisa was suddenly the construction worker whose callused hands can see past all the prettily painted facades and touch the cheap drywall behind them.

"Is nice zugzwang, yes?"

But Lisa didn't know this word.

"Zugzwang cruel inertia of the life," Igor said. "Must move, player cannot sit, must go into emptiness."

Jan had told Lisa that this was true. The cartilage of her nose had turned into bone in the months after her birth. The lower vertebrae of her tailbone would fuse when she stopped growing. She would lust. Someday she would experience something called menopause. Then she would die.

That evening, Lisa followed Jan around the big house. She watched Jan pause at individual pieces, all from her store: a ceramic coffee table, a great vase of blown glass, an ancient rocking chair. Lisa saw Jan ponder each for a moment, probably thinking about her business—but maybe also thinking beyond it. It was like following someone around a museum.

Lisa waited for Jan's meditative state to develop, and the moment her eyes crossed from the bamboo placemat to the solstice light in the long window, Lisa ambushed her with an introduction to some of the new and powerful words: *zugzwang, gegenspiel, zwischenzug.* In her reflective state, Jan did find their pronunciation charming. "Help me, Ted!" Jan cried to the distant sound of the TV on the other side of the house. "Lisa is giving me the zugzwang." She pronounced the a in *zwang* like "twang," Igor said it more like "song."

Lisa tried to get Jan to understand the words, without all the comic associations she was giving them. Jan said she couldn't understand; Lisa thought she didn't really try. These words, so alive and elastic when she was with Igor, now hardened. Like bricks, the words fell to the ground between Lisa and Jan and formed a small ledge. "Come on, Jan!" Lisa pulled on Jan, trying to get her over the little step. But she did not step over. Lisa tried easier words: "promotion," "gambit," "structure." But Jan only shrugged. These words also fell. And now a proper wall stood between the two women.

Jan would not see the brilliant theocracy in front of Lisa. Above her, Ruth stretched out her hands, and called Lisa forth like a priestess. Ruth had once been rated 1900. She had played in the US Women's Championship. Beyond her, Igor commanded the basilica. He had played with the best in the world. Their names hung like icons in Igor's cathedral: Polgar, Kasparov, Fischer. Everyone knew their place in this world, and where they wanted to go.

Lisa came to the wall, and proudly told Jan about Igor and the problems she had secretly been doing. Lisa's words and aspirations became quick darts and knives. She wanted to cut Jan, to make her bleed until she saw the truth. The conversation became loud. Jan said that Lisa had lost her trust. Ted came in and shouted about the crime and the unbelievable danger of Lisa being anywhere near Ashby Station. Needles, disease, and child-abductors clutched at his step-daughter there.

"Why don't you just say that I can't play chess?" Lisa shouted. "Isn't that what you really want to do?"

But it was as if Jan had learned from their last argument—she didn't care how right Lisa was. And all this stuff, about the bad neighborhood and the danger of unfamiliar men—it was like Jan and Ted weren't answering to the truth of what Lisa was saying. They weren't really listening to her. Chess was more fair. You either answered your opponent's moves or you got crushed.

Jan and Ted forbade Lisa from studying with Igor. She could use her money from the Polgar Foundation to get a teacher from the Berkeley Chess School.

Defeated, Lisa went to the kitchen and found her old journal. It was still open, to her entry from January 30th. On the granite countertop's white and blue-black swirls, Lisa's thoughts about the rain had stood about like undignified beggars. No more; Lisa picked up the book and put it in the redwood dresser, where she had once searched for Grandma Lena's journals, underneath the old clothes that Jan procrastinated giving away. She would study with Igor. She would find a way. And she was right. Jan stood with Ted on the other side of the wall with the rest of the chessless, with no access to meaning, stumbling from one superficial concern to the next.

Standing in his doorway the next day, Lisa told Igor about her plan: She would secretly arrive at his cottage, every afternoon, to study. Ruth would be the executor of the Polgar money. Ruth knew Zsuzsa Polgar personally, and could arrange everything easily. She wanted to help.

Igor contemplated the position for a time, and then said, "First Question: Father say no to chess; why?"

Lisa shrugged and said, "Cuz they're stupid. They don't even know how to move the pieces."

Igor looked out above Lisa, into his thick kales. "Not satisfy for explain. Why does Lisa make her plan?"

Lisa became eloquent. She told Igor how unfair it all was; how Jan had gotten her into chess and now wouldn't let her pursue it. And summer was coming; she should be free to do whatever she wanted. That was the bargain. Jan and the school always seemed to be saying, "just a little longer, then you'll be free."

Igor closed his eyes, as he had done when he solved the mate-in-two, and said, "Lisa think only about own pieces, injustice of their lives, about their intention and potential. But not think about opponent pieces. Lisa not sense danger. Lisa is right. Lisa is just. Gods smile to her. It not matter that position will not hold, that plan will be discovered. Light will fall upon Lisa's moves and everybody will see how good she is because she right." Igor laughed at Lisa. "Maybe Lisa think that everybody will dance around her and say how smart she is when plan is discovered." Igor let out a sharp jangle of a growl, like a Shostakovich chord from the far left side of the piano.

Red shame rose into Lisa's face. But she did not cry. And she did not run away. The garden light began to shift toward darkness, and the first evening breezes announced the cold summer fog. Softly, Igor began, "We must hinder plan of opponent. We call this prophylaxis. After all my years inside the chess, prophylaxis stay big surprise: We learn that stopping intention of opponent is for truth way for free own pieces. Is surprise because we wish for think our pieces are the movers and the shakers. But we must learn to move beyond own pieces. We cannot be trapped in their moods. We have to reach into pieces of opponent, and make for big understand that our pieces only know themselves inside of opponent wish for kill. We need to see him, opponent for us, like mirror. Big practice need to feel opponent, to feel man who wish for kill us."

Lisa considered herself from this flipped perspective: The rain, Igor's kale, the spider in the garden, the text about her; these were not things she reached out to and had deep thoughts about. They pushed in on her and told her who she was.

Igor said, "Lisa, do you wish me for be coach?"

"Yes!" Lisa shouted.

"OK. Maybe I show something. Let me play this position. Give father's cell number."

Ted wasn't her real father; her real dad had died in a car crash when she was an infant. But Lisa didn't tell Igor anything about that, and she gave him Ted's number. Her coach assumed a mild face. His voice lost its guttural harshness, becoming feminine and smooth. His English was suddenly nearly perfect. And a meeting was arranged for coffee at the Orinda Starbucks in one hour. "Wait here for moment," he said. "I walk you to train."

When he returned, Igor's bike shoes made an obnoxious *click click* upon the street. Dressed in tight green spandex, he was suddenly the splashy color in the neighborhood. And Lisa was embarrassed to be seen with him. He was trying to show her something, some kind of grandmaster move. But Lisa could not see what it was. Three features of the position kept coming back to her, startling her awareness:

a) Bike outfits scandalized Lisa. Once, in the SUV with Jan, they had pulled up at a stoplight alongside her therapist, Dr. Frohlich. A suit of yellow spandex gripped his body. Lisa saw the points of two little tits, the indentation of his ass crack, and the snug balls of her counselor. Jan had waved to him, politely, as if nothing was strange, as if he wasn't naked. Igor's lean health chastised the way she had wanted to play the position: in secret, lying.

b) But was he really naked? Igor's green spandex was as bright as Lisa's blue top had been on that first day. Now it was as if he were returning that oversaturated color to Jan's side of the mountain. He was wearing the uniform of her therapist and the professional men of Orinda. Jan probably wouldn't talk to Igor if he dressed as he normally did. The original color of his clothes was always lost, faded and lightly torn, as if by a thousand brambles. That beaten-up look fit the slope of watery wind, where Ruth found heathered fabrics in secondhand stores.

c) The mountain was too big. In Orinda, the fog would often crest the ridge and begin to descend, gripping the slope like icing glacially falling down the side of a cake. But the white blanket rarely came all the way down. The great barrier protected Orinda from the infestations and cold on the other side. It seemed superhuman to climb over it. But Lisa believed Igor would do it, and that he was doing it for her.

♟

Lisa met Igor outside the Berkeley Public Library. That was the arrangement. She again took the short shuttle from school to the train station. The other girls offered each other visions of summer: there were horses, European capitals and special schools. They went through the tunnel, to the other side of the mountain. Lisa went toward the water. A veteran of dangerous travel, Lisa now confidently stood upon the MacArthur Station platform. And she proceeded one stop past Ashby, to the stop at UC Berkeley, where Jan hoped she would attend school one day.

But Igor did not lead Lisa inside the Berkeley Public Library. He led her away, to a park across from Berkeley High. Public school kids, done with the day, smoked pot and giggled. They loitered. *Loitering with intent*, Lisa heard herself say in Ted's voice.

Igor laid himself out on top of a stubby ledge next to some homeless people and said, "Now a pleasure, you find in pack." The worn denim of Igor's bag was pliant but firm, like the belly of a pig Lisa had once petted at the children's zoo. She put her hands inside and pulled out a stack of photocopies. To her horror, she discovered the next two hundred and fifty mate-in-twos from the Polgar book. "I enjoy," Igor said. "Please tell where pieces are," and he closed his eyes.

Lisa looked past Igor. She saw that the ledge they sat on formed a circle around a dirty old fountain that hadn't pumped water since forever. Crumbling children's tiles covered the sides of the ledge like a crusty plaque, proclaiming things like: "God is Love" and "Wake up!" A sign said they were now resting on the Peace Wall. Older boys with tattoos shouted and did stunts with their skateboards at the far end of the park.

Lisa had wanted to learn about the conversation of the pieces. That was the flowing elation she wanted to know. She was like a beginning cyclist who just wanted to ride, and Igor kept making her dismount, to change her tire with rubber-blackened hands. Lisa stammered: "OK, so like, that one problem you did was real cool and all. But these problems are so dumb! What's the point of mating in two moves if you have so much extra material. I mean, just look at this problem: white has an extra queen and rook!"

"Grandmaster Julio Becerra," Igor announced, "told me one time his Cuban coach make this exercise with him. This trainer, he make blindfold training back when Che and Castro love Soviet Masters that come to play there, long before Judit's father make his book, long before Julio come to Miami. Igor long time no trainer have. Now, Lisa, tell where pieces are."

"You made these copies, for me?" Lisa wondered aloud.

"No," Igor said. "Your friend Ruth make these problems. She call me, she give. It is a pleasure." Igor pronounced Ruth's name 'Root,' and patiently waited in the sun for his problem. He enjoyed the hot early June days, before the fog got sucked over Berkeley in July, sealing everyone within a much smaller and colder place.

Reluctantly, Lisa let the pieces out of the box. This time she could tell that Igor wanted to fight. Hardly was the final piece stated when Igor shouted out the pieces as if he were slamming them onto the board: "Knight f4, if king e7 then queen e6, if x then y, if p then q, . . ." The variations ripped through the flowchart instantly, like storm water through a drain. *No way*, Lisa thought. She protested, "You had already looked at that one!"

"Please pick them for random!" Igor cried. He began to hoot like a child after each of his small victories, and he yelled things like, "Take zyat Meester Spyat! Nyext!"

Through Igor, Lisa let go. She let go of the set, the pieces and all the accoutrements that everyone said were necessary. Igor was like a dolphin who could dive for the truth on the dark ocean floor. He found answers in places that had never seen sunlight. Then he would again surface in the fresh air. And Lisa would throw another colored ring out into the expanse.

"Thank you for be trainer today, Lisa. Problems for me what scales are for musician: I always continue practice. Like pattern I have played so many times that I forget him, problem help remember, for kiss his clean beauty like play major chord . . . We meet twice a week, Monday and Thursday. For Thursday you do these two hundred fifty problem. Use paper. Wednesday you play Ruth, game one of big training match. Thursday we think about this game. Friday game two with Ruth; four-game match—will be rated. Each lesson you bring new two hundred fifty problem."

Game One

Next to each of Lisa's games at the Girls Championship there was a rectangular clock. Two windows, one for each player, showed an hour of time for the whole game. After her opponent made a move, she would tap a button on the clock and the seconds in Lisa's window would begin counting down. This drove all the girls crazy, as if the clock were a little boy shouting "MOVE!" The fear of using the whole hour and losing on time was tremendous. So everybody moved too fast, and only one of Lisa's games had passed the hour mark in that tournament, barely more than half of the total possible duration.

In Lisa's training match with Ruth, Igor stretched the game out to a time control of forty moves in two hours; after forty moves each player would receive another hour for the rest of the game. Each player would also automatically get an additional thirty seconds added for each move played. This meant that a game might last more than six hours. "Is proper chess," Igor said.

Lisa imagined stretching herself into thought to be as simple as letting the bathwater run. Soon, she would be covered and be able to see herself, reflected within it. But as the water ran in her first long game with Ruth, Lisa found herself unable to hold the weight of her thoughts. Variations dove under the suds and slipped around her ankles. They were unruly, and became more so as the water deepened. Finally underwater, Lisa saw only hopeful shimmers of light that flitted about on the surface above her. Prospects of her own gain, and truth, would come and then quickly vanish. Desperate to not have these apparitions disappear, Lisa's hand grabbed the pieces and played the moves before they could get away. They were her lifelines. She did not have the lung capacity to take them under with her, to examine them in her pool.

On Thursday, Igor again took Lisa to the park. He told Lisa that they would walk and talk at the same time. And that while they walked they would hold their arms outstretched to the sides, to help them consider the game she had lost to Ruth. But after only about a minute, Lisa cried in pain and put her arms down. Igor barked, "Keep arms up!" Lisa tried again, but didn't last much longer.

Lisa hated the attention they attracted. Young fingers pointed at them with laughter, older ones pointed at them with some kind of accusation, as if Igor were torturing her. The pain in her arms encouraged Lisa to complain. "This is so dumb!" she yelled.

But Igor laughed at her, and said, "Best part of exercise I did not for truth plan: chessplayer need for learn big suffering of insult without mind losing board. It is a pleasure."

It's like he's training me to be homeless, Lisa thought.

Igor continued, "I wish for hope Lisa understand that my arm also hurt, like Lisa hurt, but I not put them down. Your body and mind are react to first pain. Entire system say insupportable. But then we discover we can go beyond that pain. This suggest first impression false, is lie. Perhaps experience same thing with food. If stop eating, body shout like unruly child. But if suffer that first impression, pain not increase into big crescendo, it go away. Pain is false, illusion."

Lisa tried raising her arms for as long as she could, and then dropped them to rest. "But what does that have to do with chess?" Lisa asked.

"Pain we feel in arm, pain we feel when eat less, those pains easy for understand," Igor said. "We know where they come from. Not so easy for understand why body jump on mind like angry policeman on peaceful demonstrator during the chess. He shout, "MOVE!" Maybe you meet this man in last game. But it is clear: We shall not obey this man. He unhappy we make new way. But we not wish his old way. We must take his beatings until he tired and walk away. Now, for next game I wish for very simple something do: On scoresheet, write how much time the Lisa spend on each move. Stretch time, make longer. Think about this stupid arm exercise I make us do. Maybe hand remember pain when it reach to touch piece. Always look for new question in position."

Game Two

On Monday, Igor again met Lisa in front of the library. Lisa's body was carrying her to the library doors, but Igor stopped her. "Lisa, I wish for see scoresheet." Igor took the little piece of paper, and Lisa stared up at him while he entered a different world, somehow separate from the shoving traffic, examining her and the second game she had lost against Ruth.

Black to move

"I understand," Igor said finally. "We make for big walk." This time Igor went up the mountain, toward the Berkeley campus. As they waited at the first stoplight, Lisa complained that she had lost because she didn't know any openings. Igor laughed at Lisa, and said, "Tell me all logical opening move against first move Ruth play against you, 1. ♘d4, queen pawn."

Lisa wasn't sure what he meant, but she was proud to repeat the names of the openings she had picked up from Ruth, the internet and her old chess class: "Umm, there's the Queen's gambit, the Slav, the King's Indian, the Queen's Indian, the Nimzo Indian, the Benoni, the Dutch." Lisa was losing her breath with the names and the beginning of the hill when Igor cut her off.

"Nyet, Nyet, Nyet. Tell me all move that are logical."

"What the hell you mean, logical?"

"Logical move those that fight for center and strive for harmony."

"Zose zat fight for zenter and strive for harmony?" This guy has been living in this country forever, Lisa thought, *and he still can't talk right.*

Igor continued: "Both side begin game asleep behind pawn, like life before education. Before battle begin not clear what harmony of pieces is, their cooperation only understood against opponent thought and intention. But your pieces born with knowledge that center important is. Any piece not fight for center lazy, and in discord with friends. Now, tell all first move that are logical against queen pawn."

The hill steepened, and Lisa huffed out a list: "Knight f6, pawn d5, pawn g6, ..."

Then Igor said, "Now, I want you for see that all these moves same ones that have names. They not good moves because have names, not because grandmaster play them and make big thought. They good moves because they fight for center and strive for harmony. And, for most important, Lisa—rated 1495—find all of them using own judgment, without big help. Lisa know opening."

"Well, that's obviously not true," Lisa grumbled to herself. Drops of sweat rolled off her brow into her eyes. She tried to wipe her eyes dry, but her fingers carried the black grime of MacArthur

Station and it felt like a wasp was sticking its stinger through her left retina. Sharp sunlight bounced off the lenses of her glasses.

"Keep up!" the ruthless ogre demanded from above.

"Fuck this!" Lisa gave her solemn oath. Igor began descending the hill toward her. She shouted, "What the hell does this death march have to do with chess?"

From above her, spoken with the even breaths of someone taking a stroll out in their garden, Lisa heard the monster say, "Long time ago, in Soviet time, old coach like for say: Boys, if you not sweat now you either not try hard enough or you haven't reached the puberty!" Igor thought this was real funny, some bright little jewel that was going to make everybody feel just fine.

Lisa thought: *Jan takes me to the doctor so that he can tell me—again— that I'm going straight to hell if I don't lose twenty-five pounds. Dr. Frohlich also makes little comments. Jan probably makes them say something. Igor should be the one to understand that I don't want to change, that I don't want to be like other people.*

I've seen girls start talking about boys. They leave themselves to worry about their split ends and what they're going to wear. I don't want to become stupid! Can't you understand, Igor, of all people? Being fat makes me invisible. They don't see me and I don't see them. But how would Igor ever be able to understand the horror of girls playing with their split ends? He probably doesn't even know what a split end is.

He's definitely on a mission to change my body. Did he make a deal with my mom? Is that why I'm allowed to study chess? It was a horrible thought, a conspiracy.

The chessplayers stood in silence for a time on the steep slope. Then Igor quietly asked, "How did you know how to control center when I ask you for say logical opening moves?" Lisa was proud that she had done something right, but did not know how she had done it. Igor pressed her: "Why important for control center?" Lisa had no answer. She had heard that the center was important. That natural assumption had somehow slipped past the bouncer of her mind and was now dancing with the other truths up in her club. Igor set a mild pace, julienning his stride into tiny sections.

"Lisa, I wish for discuss your move ten in game with Ruth, knight h5, tell me your thoughts."

Lisa quickly fell into the rationalized darkness of autismal variations. It sounded like this: 'Well, I was threatening x, but I didn't see that she could do y and then z. If p then q; missed r . . .' Lisa's myopia marched her up the hill.

By the time they reached the Berkeley Rose Garden, Lisa had become even more convinced that 10...♘h5 was wrong because she hadn't foreseen 14. ♗c4 a couple moves down the road. Igor called out to a group of six boys who had been abandoned to a ball as their mothers moved among the rosebushes to talk as adults. Except for one small boy, they were all ruddy, outside creatures.

Igor called to them: "Hey! Can we play with you? I know game, is a very nice." A stern pregame discussion of the regulations was quickly underway.

Lisa hated sports. Just like this, the rules for some stupid game like kickball or dodgeball would be hastily explained. Lisa would not understand. And she would soon find herself in the wrong place, getting run over by a boy, hit with the ball, laughed at. Every time she threw a ball, the thing would just plop down in front of her, as if it didn't want to play either. These memories paralyzed Lisa, and she directed her silent anger at Igor: *What the fuck? I hate ballgame. What happened to our freakin' chess lesson? I don't want a life coach, I want a chess coach!*

Igor took Lisa and the smallest boy onto his team. It would be a fat girl, the little guy and an old man versus five sturdy boys. The rules were that Igor stood in the middle and had Lisa and the little one on opposite sides of him, forming the diameter of the circle. The five boys were assigned posts on the perimeter. No one was allowed to move from their spots in the circle. Igor gave them the ball and told them that they would get a point if they could move the ball to the other side of the circle. And if a side lost control of the ball or moved from their assigned position then the other team would gain possession.

The boys couldn't get through the center. Igor's big hands intercepted their passes like crude thoughts trying to cross his chessboard. Igor got the ball and passed to Lisa, the ball rolled sadly back to Igor, Igor passed it to the little guy. Point!—that's all each team had to do: move the ball from one side of the circle to the other. Igor then gave the ball back to the five boys.

The boys loved it. They tried to strategize ways to get the ball past Igor in the center. Lisa was alone in her rage. Igor smiled at her and asked, "Lisa, what we doing?" She shrugged and thought, *Fuck off.* The game continued, and the boys did score a couple points, but they were losing badly. Lisa found insufficient reward in the voluble frustration of the five brutes. "Lisa," Igor said. "What we doing?"

"I dunno, playing a stupid game?"

Igor thanked the sweaty boys for the game and began to head back down the hill with Lisa. "I tell you for big truth, Lisa," Igor said, "when I run or ride bike I think world flat. Ho! Of course, I have long ago agreed to make big believe that world round. But whenever in motion with big sweat I forget. Ha! Same thing maybe for you and center. You have agreed that important is. But when big Ruth hunt you, and you run like scared rabbit, you forget. You think only about evasive maneuver. You must pull back, reflect, see that center of board powerful; like heavy star, light bend around center squares. You must feel this truth, not enough for make believe it."

Lisa imagined light bending around herself. She was the center; all life was suddenly a stream and she a boulder in it.

"Now we talk to pieces," Igor said.

Lisa smiled. She had wanted precisely this: to learn the conversation of the pieces. Yet when Igor said "talk to pieces," she couldn't help hearing it through the ears of others, and he sounded crazy.

"How does knight on h5 feel?"

"She's a disappointment," Lisa answered. "Her family needed her to concentrate on all the important squares in the center. But she left them, to go off and do her own thing on the side of the board."

"Good. Good. Talk to pieces, ask if go up hill or down. Today we learn how difference feel. And next time you ask knight for go to h5, he tell you: NO WAY LADY, I not gonna do it. I will not decentralize."

Game Three

Lisa ditched her last couple classes on Thursday. They were pointless anyway. The shuttle wasn't there to take her, but it was easy to walk the four blocks to the train—even though they always told the kids it was so dangerous. No one tried to stop her; she was invisible and free.

Lisa had lost to Ruth the day before, once again brutally. And she dreaded her punishment. *He's probably going to make me do something like Bikram yoga*, Lisa thought. *He'll turn me into a puddle of sweat.*

Lisa wanted to be admitted into the temple, to be accepted and enjoy a warm and carpeted conversation. But Ruth would always squish her. And Igor would never let her in. So she would take her revenge. She would sneak into the Berkeley Public Library without permission.

The outside walls of the building looked like a boy had poured his green Gatorade all over it twenty years ago and no one had ever bothered to clean up the sticky mess. The fungi and bacteria of the street had eaten the brightness away, leaving a matte puke color. But underneath all of that there were outlines of athletic women wrapped in tight cloth, climbing staircases up into the emptiness. The images were faint; the fineness of their lines had been lost.

Inside, hairy men with enormous black trash bags casually dragged their life's belongings across broad granite floors. The old socks of homelessness pinched Lisa's nose as she watched a man play blitz chess on one of the public internet portals. This library wasn't a temple. It was just another adult scam, like the way they used chess to trick kids into concentrating.

Lisa left the library at 3:30, a half hour before she was supposed to meet with Igor. She was sneaky like that; Igor would never know that she had gone in without his permission. Fooling adults was easy. To kill time, she laid herself out on the Peace Wall as Igor had and did chess problems, using the photocopies Ruth had made for her. Then she walked back to the library, as if she hadn't already been there, to wait for her teacher.

Igor took the record of her game into his big hands and looked down at her with a questioning smile, as if asking, "Have you failed again?" Lisa knew that Ruth had emailed him and described the game. But he needed to see the moves. Lisa had carefully noted on her scoresheet how much time she and Ruth used on each move. She had tried to follow his principles. In his own world, the Russian softly spoke, "tak, tak, tak," quickly reconstructing the game in his mind to a metronome beat. Then he looked up at the mountain, his big stone, his personal gym. "We go inside," he said.

Igor led Lisa up to the third floor of the Berkeley Public Library, the children's floor. He said they would take advantage of Lisa's age and use the ample space there. From behind a bookshelf of Dr. Seuss and *Where the Wild Things Are*, Igor pulled out a magnificent wooden set that he had hidden. Until then, Lisa had never played on anything but plastic. Igor told her the history, how he had the set made after he became a grandmaster, to commemorate his passage. He said it was his one item of physical beauty, of decadence.

For his black pieces and squares, Igor had found a block of Indian rosewood, called *sheesham*, while playing a tournament in Punjab. Dark swirls wound their way through the wood, like a slowly moving mist that covers a distant light. For his white wood, Igor went back to Cuba. He told Lisa about his fateful tournament there, the Capablanca Memorial, and about his escape in Gander. He told her about the need to go back, to play well. There he had acquired a piece of boxwood, as if it were a trophy. To Lisa, its pure and unchanging light suggested truth.

Igor said that he had packed these two tropical treasures into a deep suitcase, neglecting his clothes, and brought them to the Estonian master carver Kalju Muutnik. Kalju's hands had only ever known the hearty woods of the coldest north, forests reaching back to the time of Neanderthal spears. There in Estonia, Kalju gave the exotic southern woods an Eastern European modesty and grace.

Igor then told Lisa, laughingly, how he had strapped the board to his back on the day of their first lesson at the library, and how he thought the police might even pull him and his bicycle to the side of the road for a safety violation. But then Igor became suddenly silent, grave. And Lisa was again all alone, left outside of his contemplation.

Finally, he said, "On bicycle, people don't see squares, I only show other side, piece of wood."

"Because Jan doesn't get it?"

"Father not understand. My chess become personal, like board turned inward."

Lisa imagined herself at Igor's side; they would march the willing into chess. Those that stayed behind would have nothing. They would not share their board with them.

Igor set up Lisa's position out of the opening: "You have played well, pieces fight for center and try for sing like choir. I think you this critical position. You white, it your move, what for play?" Lisa contemplated the position. Igor wanted her to see something here, but she didn't know what it was.

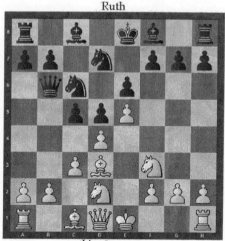

Ruth

Lisa to move

Softly, as if he were slipping his thought underneath hers, Igor began, "Yes, now need physical board. Not blind; mind travel down many trail that forget where they start. Many mistake. Need for come back to board for breath and big look. Board like mirror, correct false presumption.

"Lisa materialist. She win games by taking, always taking—take, take, take—never give. Zen Lisa trade off pieces of opponent, until king frightened and lonely. This truth of game Lisa understand without Igor's help. In Russia we call this method 'Gang Fight': If you find self on streets of Moscow with fifty angry men who make fight with forty-five other, it in best interest if mutual bludgeon happen, if fighters trade themselves away. If twenty-five from each side go, ratio go from initial ten-to-nine to five-to-four. Trade fifteen more comrade and force ratio of two-to-one become crushing.

"This Lisa's method, like capitalist she steal your stuff and then charge interest on losses. Nobody happy. Yes, all chessplayer must first learn to hold onto their stuff before they can let it go. In life same, we must know how for use things—how to make basic survive—before we can ask if anything else is." Lisa continued to stare into the position without finding a way into it.

"The chess, Lisa," Igor said, "happen in three dimension. First easy for understand, you know well: material, stuff. Second seem easy, but in fact very complicated: time. Not time on clock, is time on board—tempo. It seem easy for understand because we know that we must use our time for *économique*, for bring pieces into game. But in fact not so simple, we will see that it require we answer question: 'time for do what?' We will see that time more valuable in some circumstance than other. We will see that time speed and slow. Sometime we don't wish for move at all. Third dimension most difficult. And require big artist for use: quality of position. One quality already see: center. But other qualities need for understand, like space."

Lisa looked upon the game that had frustrated her so deeply, suddenly seen through Igor's dimensions and wooden pieces. Her coach continued, "I wish you for feel pain when lose time, same kind of pain when someone take your stuff. You need to feel awkward piece like cramp in leg, loss of central square like toothache. Now, let us look at position in front of us, you had advantage of white pieces and it is your move:

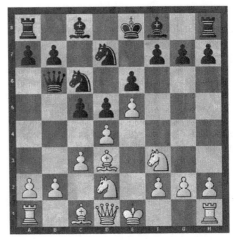

What is material balance?"

"Even."

"Yes. Who ahead in time?"

"Umm, well we each have three pieces out so it's even."

"Nyet, it is your move, so you up one tempo."

"OK."

"Who has more central control?"

"Maybe Ruth does? She has three pawns that fight for the four center squares. I only have two. My e5 pawn occupies the center, but it fights for squares that are beyond it."

"Good. Who has more space?"

"I do."

"Yes. Good for see, center and space different question. E5 pawn grab position, try to push black pieces back into box, look at king. Now we talk to pieces, which piece feel most unhappy about the life?"

"My knight on d2 is a disaster. She's blocking my bishop on c1 from coming out to protect my pawn on d4. She's stumbling over the knight on f3, and she can't even go to b3 because Ruth could then play pawn c4, and give my bishop and knight the fork, the double-attack, the wham-bam."

"Good, what about black pieces, which uncomfortable?"

"Well, I guess the bishop on c8 is kinda stuck. But black doesn't have to do anything like defend a freakin' center pawn so it doesn't really make a difference. Look at my pawn on d4! Black's already clearly better."

"Perhaps. Do you feel like any of your moves up to this point illogical?"

"Uh, how should I know? I don't know any openings and I don't know any theory."

"I mean logic of control center and pieces strive for harmony. Did you offend these principles?"

"Umm, no—but look where that got me, my position is a mess!"

"It seem you keep advantage in time that you start with as white, you have advantage in space, and communication problem are mirrored in opponent. You should be better."

"But my pawn!"

"Listen: You have to make mistake before opponent can punish."

"Well, I'm worse here so I must have done something wrong earlier."

"Let us see if we find something here, in this position. In game you play pawn takes c5. And after Ruth take back on c5 with bishop she suddenly ahead

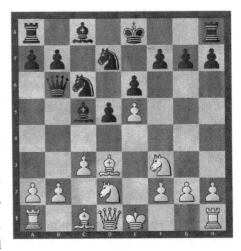

in development and your e5 pawn weak. So must unfortunate be."

"Yes, it was."

Igor became silent for a moment. As Lisa was thinking, tending her cows on the plain, his voice came in like a gentle wind over her activity, not intruding. He whispered: "I once had bicycle stolen when I your age, communist times. It hurt very much, I walk all over neighborhood for week, trying to find. I think it hurt so much because I identify self with it. When neighborhood kids come together, we compare bike, trying to make big car talk we see in parent. We see selves in stuff we show each other. But thief not only take away identity, he use my identity to make himself bigger."

Lisa's thoughts broke in on Igor's quiet soliloquy: "I guess I have to castle." Black would win a pawn, and Lisa felt her position tumbling forward into uncertainty, like an inexperienced skier on her first black diamond run: 8. castles ♗xd4 9. ♗xd4 ♘xd4 10. ♘xd4 ♛xd4 11. ♘f3.

"Good. What have you gained for pawn?"

"Well, at least now my d2 knight won't need therapy."

"Ha! Is for truth. Knight had issues, he take only bathroom in six person house at eight in morning. Everybody yell at him. What else you see?"

Ruth to move

"Ruth's bishop on c8 is still stuck. And I've won some time."

"How much time you won?"

"Well, I have two more pieces out than black. But since Ruth will now have to move her queen I will gain another move. So I will have three tempi."

"Good. One rough measure of the material is for say that pawn worth three tempi."

"Why does it have to be a rough measure?"

"Because value of time change."

"How can time change? A tempo is a tempo and an hour is an hour."

"You watch maybe sport on television? Ballgame?

"No!"

"Always same clock make same countdown. Make peoples think that time only one rhythm must have. Is maybe nice world, if you zombie. Clock time not real time! Look for see: Before Ruth steal precious pawn on d4, position closed and pieces feel like Lisa staring at clock with nothing to do. But after she take, then they are pushed out of house. Things begin for move. What ideas now awake in position?"

"Well, my dark-square bishop is now free to come out, even if she can't threaten anything directly."

"Good. Whose fate tied to bishop?"

"Umm, well if my bishop comes out, then my rook on a1 can come to the c-file and talk to the awkward bishop on c8."

"Good. Who else might have thoughts?"

"Well, depending on where the black queen goes my queen could go to c2 and touch h7 and the c-file. Maybe she could also go to a4, pin the d7 knight, and think about sliding over to g4."

"Good. And what about the black?"

"Ruth needs to think about her own king more than before. And it's not clear that she will be entirely safe even if she can castle."

"Good. Pawn structure like social contract that bind. Careers of pieces determined by opportunities they discover in structure. It is when structure open that they can really move. That is when value of time go up. That when revolution happen."

"But black can play so many different moves. It's not like I can calculate out what I got for my pawn!"

"But you gain time, knight out of therapy, and opponent with discord?"

"Yes."

"Good. Learn for trust quality and time as much as you trust in calculation and pawn. Learn for feel them. And when you talk to queen she maybe tell you that she now smell black king blood at thirty part per million, like shark."

Game Four

From Jan's SUV, Lisa saw Igor. He sat on one of the oversized concrete blocks in front of the Berkeley Public Library. From his grayed shorts that had once been jeans dangled two legs so thickly knotted with hair that they looked like braids. Worn sandals stood in a careless clump beneath his bare feet. A knight and a bishop merrily danced on his faded T-shirt. *Knoxville Open 1988*, it still said. Monday afternoon hurried past Lisa's teacher as he hunched forward, talking to himself, waiting for Lisa to show up.

The rolled-up windows muted the drone of a beggar woman: "Miisterr, can you spare some change??" The university Jan wanted her to attend was close, just a couple blocks away, but this was not it. Lisa got out of the car. She had just made a bargain with Jan, for this.

♟

Lisa had entered her game with Ruth the previous Friday as a seeker. She would be like a nineteenth-century physicist who suddenly begins to see space/time bending around the smallest kernels of sand. Her pieces would be supple gymnasts gracefully bounding off the structures that rose about them.

Lisa made a contract with her pieces. They agreed that they were bound to the space/time fluctuation that rippled through the board on every move. They were not separate from the board they wandered over, even if their identities did seem so wooden and fixed. They agreed to give themselves, to sacrifice themselves to alter the flow of energy, when their time came. In return, Lisa would take leave of all the bothersome assumptions of the phony world. Her own failings and petty challenges would forget themselves. Together, they would strive for pure thought.

Against Ruth's queen pawn, 1. ♙d4, Lisa played 1...♘c6. It seemed odd and unconventional, but it followed Igor's principles— so it had to be good. Ruth's pawn could come forward to d5 and shove her knight. Ruth would gain space, but her pawn would no longer fight for the four center squares. That d5 pawn could either become a syringe, dripping poison into Lisa's position, or the advanced troop could become overextended, without a supply line.

50

Ruth was circumspect and played 2. ♗c4. And now Lisa played 2...♟e5, demand-ing that Ruth advance her pawn. Ruth obliged, and Lisa understood that it was time to reflect. She thought for twenty minutes, until she found her plan: her knight would first go to e7, blocking her dark-square bishop—making a temporary mess of things. But the knight's path was clear, he would

Ruth

Lisa to move

go to g6. Then her other knight would come to f6; her dark square bishop would come out, to c5 or b4, depending on how Ruth played, then she would play d6, freeing her light-square bishop. This was the direction her pieces would follow.

Ruth's thought met Lisa's, and they reached the following posi-tion:[2]

Lisa began to regret the plan she had felt so proud of. Ruth's space advantage in the center and on the queenside felt like a four-hundred-pound sumo wrestler, thick folds of skin suffocating her, pushing her off the mat.

---

[2]This position arose after: 1. ♙d4 ♞c6 2. ♙c4 ♟e5 3. ♙d5 ♞e7 4. ♙e4 ♞f6 5. ♞c3 ♞g6 6. ♙a3 ♝c5 7. ♝e2 ♙d6 8. ♞f3 castles 9. ♙b4 ♝b6 10. castles

Each side was equally developed, but it was her move. One little tempo was all she had, in return, in compensation, for her lack of space. Yet time was receding; the position's freeways were crowded, and movement was slowing to a long gaseous halt. Lisa felt the solidity of Ruth's position all around her, constricting her pieces into breathless silence. *Yes, Ruth had foreseen this position,* Lisa thought. *Ruth saw that time would disappear in the thick grasping hands of her spatial advantage. And now she is going to push me off the board.*

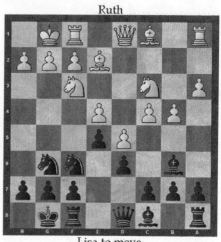

Ruth

Lisa to move

Sensing it would be better to wait for death in a state of contemplation than to hurry it along with moves, Lisa decided to gaze upon the center squares, as a mystic. Maybe she would be able to feel the weight of the squares and the bending of the light.

The center said very little to Lisa. It was locked, as dreary and stubborn as a long school day. But Lisa waited still, she waited for the pieces to speak.

The center began to whisper that it was pointed, that it had direction. Ruth's two center pawns pointed toward the queenside; Lisa's pointed to the kingside. Lisa followed this motion to f4, a dark square. An omen: the dark squares were hers. *Yes, the dark squares will be the base of my operations. Upon those squares I will slam my siege ladders up against Ruth's kingside fortress.*

Fifty minutes after Ruth played 10. castles, Lisa readied herself to play 10...♘h5, aiming to plant her knight on the f4 square, supported by her other knight on g6.

But the knight did not want to go there. "No way, lady," he said. "I will not leave the center."

Lisa tried to tell him about the dark squares and the pointing.

He responded: "You treated me so badly last time, and now this! It's even the same square. Can't you see how embarrassing this is? Just imagine what Igor will say!"

Lisa apologized to the knight. "You are right, the last time you were sent to h5 was a real scandal." Then she sang him a song: "Mistreated knight, think of h5 as a place to jump off from, just a little stop on the way to a much better life. You will be proud on the f4 outpost." With great reluctance, the knight trusted Lisa and overcame the trauma of his past.

Ruth had several options now. She played to dominate Lisa's pieces with 11. ♟g3; that pawn controlled the square Lisa's knight wanted to jump into, and told him that he had no value on that side of the board. And it was true. But in return, Ruth had given Lisa a weakness, in front of the king. And this weakness allowed Lisa to win a tempo by attacking Ruth's rook with 11...♝h3. The bishop thanked the knight on h5. After the obligatory 12. ♖e1, Lisa returned the knight to where it

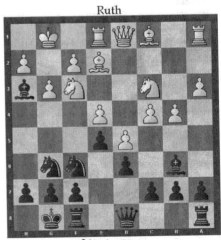

Ruth

Lisa to move

had been on f6. But it was not an admission of failure. Now that the rook no longer defended f2, Lisa's knight now made a threat of going to g4 to attack the weak dark square on f2. This had not been foreseen, but the f2 square's dark color had been prophesied. And all of Lisa's pieces were tickled by this geometric initiative.

One hour later, as Lisa's pieces were surrounding Ruth's king with thirsty daggers, Ruth whispered, "Lisa, I offer you a draw." Lisa's eyes rose up to look at Ruth's humble apartment as if for the first time. Afghan carpets covered hardwood floors. A framed poster from the Marcel Duchamp exhibit *The Art of Chess* hung between two bookshelves. Everything here was creased with experience. Quiet comfort and elevation, with a cat's fur to stroke. Next to Lisa, on top of the same paisley-covered table that Ruth had directed the Girls Championship tournament from, was a signed copy of a book called *Chess Bitch*. Ruth was giving it to her. The woman on the cover of the book wore a pink wig. She was mysterious, and hot. She had won the US Women's Championship. Ruth knew her.

Lisa thought about Ruth's title, WIM. She thought about the score of the match—zero-to-three—and how a draw meant that she would have something. She looked at the clock; she now only had five minutes to make the time control at move forty, ten moves away. Ruth's cat, Alehkine, had a little bell on its neck. *Why did it have to tinkle like that?* Five minutes to make ten moves. She imagined shaking Ruth's hand, and being welcomed onto Ruth's rung of the sisterhood.

Lisa's clock continued to tick. Her pieces reminded her of the contract. They had fulfilled their end of the bargain. "What?" they asked Lisa. "Do you think you are going to find meaning in the sloppy congratulations of that world?" But Lisa did want a place in that world. Five minutes to make ten moves. She wanted to be Ruth's friend.

Her pieces decided to continue. But Lisa was divided, and could not retain control. Fish were escaping from her net of variations. Play progressed for a couple moves, then Lisa's teeth began to chatter, and she began to slobber, as if she were going to have an epileptic fit. Ruth had to stop the game.

Lisa couldn't remember any of that stuff; that was just the story that Jan had demanded of Ruth. Lisa remembered being woken by Jan on Ruth's old velvet couch, covered with a crocheted blanket and Alekhine's orange hairs.

The next day, Saturday, Jan woke Lisa early. She said she couldn't leave her alone with her chess. She said she was worried, and that helping out at the store would be good for her.

There, at Domestique, Lisa caused a scene. She wasn't trying to. But she couldn't stop thinking about the game, about how she was going to finish Ruth off when they resumed. She walked through the store with her arms outstretched, as Igor had taught her. The pain helped her focus; the pain was negating the weakness in her body and whatever it was that had made her even consider breaking the contract she had made with her pieces. It wasn't like that much stuff fell from the shelves, and nothing really valuable broke. But Stephanie and Britt, Jan's employees, did begin to follow her.

They must have told Jan, who was working in the inventory room. And Lisa knew she was in for it; Jan hated to be interrupted. She marched Lisa back to the boxes and crates. Why did she have to squeeze her hand so hard, pushing it down below her waist, making her hobble and feel like she was about eight years old?

Surrounded by her wares, Jan yelled, "Stop it, just stop it!" Lisa didn't say anything. She just stood there like a mute who didn't understand what Jan was so excited about. "I need you to behave, Lisa. OK? I need you to be decent, OK? Lisa, are you listening to me?" But Lisa didn't say anything. Jan raised her eyes to the high ceiling of her inventory room and yelled, "Oh God! I wish I had never taken you to chess class! Why did I ever let that disgusting man teach you?" Then she stared at Lisa and shouted, "Say something, damnit!"

As if she were the adult, Lisa calmly said, "Pieces are thinking, please don't disturb them."

That evening, Jan scheduled an emergency session with Dr. Frohlich. He would mediate their fight. "You agree to do whatever he says, OK?" Jan demanded.

"Fine. Whatever," Lisa said. "Pieces don't give a damn."

♟

"Resume game?" Igor asked. He had sat down next to Lisa amongst the beanbags in the storytelling corner of the children's floor, saying something about reflection and a well-thought-out move, even if the board of life is never fully disclosed. Lisa rehearsed her map of variations: 36 . . . ♘d3! If x then y, if p then q. That's how the game would continue when it was resumed.

Igor wanted to know things, to lay everything out: the notation to the game, the loss of control, the stopping of the clocks, what her father said about it all.

"Look," Lisa said, "you don't need to worry about it, OK? Everything is under control. I made a bargain with Jan."

"You make bargain?"

"It's not a big deal, OK? I have to go to Dr. Frohlich. But I can keep playing chess."

"Who Dr. Frohlich?"

"He's a psychiatrist, maybe a psychologist. I don't know. Jan made me talk to him a couple of times before. But I'm not sick, OK?"

"What he say?"

"Oh, Frohlich doesn't know anything about chess. He gave me the usual questions about when I first started playing chess, what my favorite piece is, you know, that's the kind of thing they like to ask you. So I talked to him forever and I have to talk to him again." It was true that Frohlich was among the chessless. But chess wasn't his favorite subject. He wanted to know why Lisa cut her arms. But she never had an answer that he liked. And if Igor never asked her about her scars, then why did they have to be such a big deal?

"Maybe not so bad," Igor said. "Sometime non–chessplayer interesting thing say."

Lisa then added, as if it were an afterthought of the bargain, "And I have to take some pills."

"What pill?"

From an internal pouch of her unicorn backpack, Lisa brought out a ziploc bag of bright blue pills. "I have to take two a day." Igor took some out of the bag, and stroked the little beads like a Paleolithic hunter-gatherer fondling the mystery of seeds. Lisa said, "I've been taking them since Sunday morning. They don't really do anything."

A tiny label on each pill read EQUINOX. Together, Lisa and Igor went to the computer center and read on *Wikipedia*: "Equinox is designed specifically for children diagnosed on the Asperger spectrum. While there is no cure for Asperger Syndrome, Equinox alleviates some of its symptoms, notably episodes of self-absorbed depression and extreme anxiety. A child on Equinox will not feel highs and lows as strongly as before. This dulling of the emotions has been clinically proven to promote the acculturation process of the child."

It sounded like the big words Jan and her teachers used when they talked about fixing Lisa's bad grades. They talked behind her back. Like now, no one had ever told her. But now she knew: She was Aspergers. And they had to fix it. Lisa stared at the active chemical in Equinox on the screen. It looked like a beehive.

Igor knew what the chemical abbreviations meant. He knew how to read the formula like her scoresheet. And he wanted to tell her about some Russian guy named Mendeleev and the wonder of chemistry. He could be such a pest about things like that. But he couldn't tell her what the drug was doing right now, inside her. He could only point the way back to the beanbags, up on the children's floor.

Lisa tried to see herself from the outside, like the words did: She was self-absorbed in Jan's store and anxious in her game with Ruth. True. But those were her best moments! She had striven to a higher view, to purge the uncleanliness from her mind. She had wanted to be pure, like Igor's boxwood pieces.

The adult world said that her thought was chemical. Recombinant beehives joined hands in predictable patterns and made her think stuff. For people like her, who lived in the Asperger building, the corridors led to patterns of self-absorption and anxiety. But she didn't know any Asperger kids. And she couldn't see the building. She couldn't see the scientists either. They said her thought was bound, and they knew how to bind it.

Lisa hated thinking of the world like that. If it were true then everything would be like the poster of the surface of Mars she had seen: lifeless, scarred and empty. Lisa sat with her teacher for a long while, contemplating that world of dust and rock. Then she asked the oversized man whose long naked legs grew like shoots of thorny blackberry from the crunchy beanbag: "Will the pill stop me from feeling my pieces?"

Igor hovered over his next thought like Lisa had seen him do before a move. To her, that ritual meant that he was assuming a deep moral responsibility for the coming move. "Will dull connection," he finally said.

"But why?" Lisa asked. "Why would they do that to me?"

Igor looked away, first out the window, then to a group of toddlers falling over one another, laughing. Sweeping this scene before him with a round motion of his arm he said, "In life not possible meaning find. Not like chess. Life chaos. Drug hope soften this loss. I know this moment."

"But why won't they let me play chess? My mom, Frohlich, Equinox. All of them want me to be part of their stupid adult world." Igor didn't say anything.

In Igor's silence, Lisa caught herself thinking like Jan: The flat rectangular cushions on Frohlich's couch were inelegant. They were covered in a coarse cloth that looked like a yard sale and scratched like bedbugs. Like the thin walls of his office in downtown Orinda, everything about Frohlich was undistinguished. He reminded her of her stepfather, Ted.

Pieces hadn't really cared. They weren't paying attention to Frohlich. Pieces were free, uninhibited by their physical surroundings. They hadn't thought about the tissues that Frohlich had nudged in Lisa's direction. Maybe she was supposed to have cried. Maybe she was Aspergers because she hadn't, because she'd been so oblivious to all his n00b questions about her relationship to chess.

"Listen," Lisa announced. "I know you think I should play the position straight with my mom. That everything should be out in the open, the way it is in chess. But spandex prophylaxis isn't going to save this position."

"What you mean? You wish for play position in disguise?"

"I'm not going to take the pills," Lisa said. "It's not that hard, other kids do all kinds of stuff with their pills. Adults think they're so clever. But we are the ones who have to stick Mendeleev in our mouths. I just won't take the pills. It's easy to pretend I did."

"Lisa," Igor slowly began, "many now say Igor criminal. They say he not father. He cruel. He—once big drunk—feel the right to take away nice drug from another."

"What are you talking about?" Lisa said. "You're not doing anything. I'm the one who won't take the pills!"

Igor told Lisa, "Not for excuse but for explain, I wish for tell you why I push your pieces. I one time play tournament in Grand Manan, is island in Canada. Was nice November night, and I decide to go for swim in Atlantic. It was a pleasure. I come back to hotel and everybody scream. They say: 'you must be hypothermic! Was goat trail down cliff to water, you could have died! Thorns cut your legs, you bleed!' Like thousand old lady they jump around me.

"Was always same. My chess comrades are warriors, we go past this world of small expectation. No one understand our trail to water. With other chess fighters we make big laugh at these little mens. They can say nothing to us. Water we find is vodka.

"We travel Greyhound. Each weekend, tournament in different place. Americans are for us like roadside attraction. We say hi, keep going. Maybe see you next year. But tournament bar is same: Alexander Ivanov, Dmitri Gurevich, Sergey Kudrin, Jaan Ehlvest, Alexander Yermolinsky, Alexander Shabalov and good friend Aleksander Wojtkiewicz. These friend know Russian language, language of chess.

"During week, maybe not see each other. Is quiet time of three-dollar vodka. At tournament we drink expensive, time for celebrate and shout. You know saying? 'One Russian make lonely man. Two make chess game. Three make political conspiracy.' We become big Russian men.

"Was hard for understand that our chess like fine blade. We must cut many, many weak American mens. Must become like bread knife, always cut. Vodka and fat help Igor and friends become this tool.

"Long time for understand that we sick. Of course, many American tell us before. They say we must count calorie and run treadmill, like scared rabbit. They say vodka bad. We laugh at them.

"Then Aleksander Wojtkiewicz begin for die. No one understand disease, no one help, no health insurance. I like delivery horse: Same way he have rounds around city, I go around country. Cannot stop, always make same. I leave friend. I play in tournaments without him. Because Aleksander not there, I one time share hotel cabinet with American chessplayer, Eric. Whole life he drink Pepsi, not vodka, but is same. He already lose one leg. Middle of night, middle of tournament, he begin his moan. He say diabetes is come to fingers. He cannot feel.

"I still hear this moan. Was like call of friend from other side. Aleksander call me. You understand? Medical man come to room. He can do nothing. Two month later Eric lose arm and Aleksander dead.

"Please understand: fat and vodka like Equinox—stop us from feeling pieces, is big escape."

Lisa couldn't understand why Igor was giving such a long speech. She suspected that he was hiding something from her, as if he were holding a cloth over her board while he moved her pieces. Had he made an arrangement with Jan that day he rode his bike over the mountain? Like: He's allowed to teach her if she loses weight?

It's shit like this, Lisa thought, *that makes the journal so useless. In real life, I can never see all the pieces or who's moving them; thick fog rolling in on everyone from some far place in the deep Pacific, making Ruth's clothes brown.*

Like Jan: From somewhere on the other side of the wall she is lobbing stones at me. But what does she want? Igor at least knows how to leave that world. I can see his path, going down to the water to be cleansed.

Lisa pushed herself up out of the beanbag, thrust out her arms to her sides, and said, "I can take a lot more pain now." Igor smiled, and joined her. Together they buzzed around the children's floor like airplanes, like idiots.

When they sat back down, Igor said: "There is something else need for discuss: You need for call Ruth and resign game."

"What!?" Lisa screamed. All the kids in the room stopped what they were doing and stared at them. Parents looked over at Igor, as if he might be a child molester.

"Is proper chess culture, Lisa," Igor said. "Game can never be stopped. Resume not possible."

"That's so unfair!" Lisa said. "It's my game. I played those moves!"

"Chess bigger," Igor said. "Your game with Ruth not exist only in head. It also game of opponent. The chess not belong to you. Tradition spread and shared all over world. You expected for resign in France and China."

"Why'd she stop the game then? Because she pitied me? Would she have stopped the game if I were a boy? Why is everyone trying to stop me from playing chess? And what was going on with her draw offer? I was crushing her!"

Igor laughed at Lisa: "She offer draw in lost position? Ho, ho, ho, she give you wet rag to face? Ha, ha, maybe you awake now. Ruth still great fighter. Give everything to struggle. Like night Odysseus cross enemy line to kill men in sleep. She want to crush Lisa so bad she give her big lesson. Ha!"

Igor demanded that she mime the rest of her game. She and Ruth would play the rest of the game out, but only for practice. They had decided that Lisa had already lost the game, and the match too—four games to zero. Her rating would fall off a cliff. Everyone was against her.

THE CITY

Boxwood light smoothed every corner of the long hallway into gentle curves. Only rosewood door handles poked out into the empty quiet. The handles attached to thick doors that led outward, to some trial, and Lisa was asked to open one. She wanted the warm and pure light to fill her. But she didn't feel worthy, and made her choice in haste.

They entered a narrow antechamber whose carpeted walls muted a distant violin. Igor made them wait there, saying something about music culture, until they heard silence. Lisa complained that she wasn't ready. Igor said that she wouldn't be an awkward piece, that she would fit.

Quiet came. And Lisa soon found herself on the balcony of a music hall. A wiry old man was already on the stage behind a dinky piano. He looked like one of Lisa's teachers, in a button-down shirt with beige slacks and brown dress shoes with brown shoelaces. Lisa remembered her own glasses as the man strained his eyes to see the notes right in front of him. His were so thick they seemed to have become part of his body, like a respirator for his eyes.

Then a young man bounded onto the stage with his great cello. His T-shirt said *Bayreuther Osterfestival 2006*. Lisa had to laugh when she saw looping leather sandals on top of scratchy black wool socks barely hidden underneath his brown corduroy pants. Jan had taught her that black and brown must never be mixed, and that pants must always cover the ankles—no matter what.

63

The old man began the song on his dinky piano. His notes were off. Like a miscast chess problem, they were just wrong. And he kept on being wrong. He droned. And—as if there was nothing left to be angry or sad about—his piano never raised or lowered its voice.

Why am I even here? Igor had met Lisa on Post Street, in front of the San Francisco Mechanics Chess Club. That's where Jan had agreed to let her go, to play in the Tuesday Night Marathon Tournament. But Igor had wanted to take her somewhere else first. He said they would have enough time and that her father would never know. But Lisa knew it was going to be a long march as they turned to walk into the cold summer wind of Market Street.

Blinking lights offered pizza and ice cream. Homeless people crouched in the crevices and doorways of tall buildings. Igor told Lisa some things. But she couldn't understand anything; the wind took his words and hurled them down the wide boulevard behind them. Finally they came to two great glass doors. Igor entered and gave a woman in a smart black suit some kind of secret hand gesture. But Lisa couldn't see what it was. And the woman pointed them into the boxwood hallway.

Just then, the young man's instrument began to sing. His cello rose high, in joy, far above the old man's river of murky sludge. It could play louder too. And there was a moment when Lisa didn't really have to hear the dinky piano. The cellist, with his untrimmed beard and long hair, had overcome him. And the song became consonant.

But then the young cellist began to lament. His instrument became quieter as the twangy awfulness of the cheap piano surrounded him. It was like he began to accept his fate, as if the old man was right, there was nothing that could be done.

No. Please don't.

The song ended. The teacher nodded curtly and walked off stage, showing no signs of approval or disapproval. The student shined with a broad smile. Alone on stage, he opened his frame with his bow and gathered the wild applause of his friends and family in the audience. Igor said they had to go. She still had a game to play.

On the way back to the Mechanics Chess Club, Igor told Lisa about the Baroque, Vivaldi and b-flat minor. He told her about the treble, the bass and the pianoforte. He called the cheap piano a harpsichord, and said that it couldn't raise or lower its voice. He said that the student's cello was also an old instrument, that it squeaked. It didn't have the expansiveness of its modern equivalent. Igor laughed at them: "This conservatory believe in genuine connection, like chef who use dull knife to recreate feast of eighteenth century."

Igor said no, the student was not talented, not talented enough. Were he a chessplayer he might reach 2100. He would be a reasonable player, but he would never have the chance to play with the greatest talents of his generation.

"Yes, Lisa," he said, "is possible for feel music. Is advantage of music over chess: Fan not need any special understanding. We also see big disadvantage: Young man hear applause. He doesn't know how good he is. He has no measure, no way for see hisself."

♟

From framed photographs, serious men guarded the quiet foyer of the Mechanics Chess Club. They wore dark suits and sober expressions. *They are the Mechanics*, Lisa thought, *who built the bridges and played maneuvering chess*. Igor pointed Lisa to some of his favorite photos: Jose Raul Capablanca in his visit to the club in 1916; Vassily Smyslov playing a simultaneous exhibition at the club in 1976. Aloud, Lisa realized, "It's the same room, through all that time, it's the same room they are all playing in."

"Yes, Lisa," Igor responded. "Open door. Many world champion have played in room you about to play in."

Lisa opened the milky glass door and the violent noise whipped her. Pieces slammed the boards and unsuited men yelled stuff like, "Bow down, bitch. Show this wizard respect!"

Tattered old Russians clapped Igor on the back. They called him Igor Vasilyevich, and pulled her teacher away from her. Their yellow teeth mouthed dirty jokes in Russian, and Igor laughed with them.

Lisa was shoved to the perimeter of the big hall by the pretournament bustle. No one knew her. Alone, she was left to the photographs of old masters that circled the room. Underneath the picture of a really old guy, Lisa read, "Chess, like music and love, has the power to make men happy." She saw Bobby. *He couldn't have been insane. He looks so breezy and free.* She saw Karpov and Kasparov. She saw an old picture of Igor; he was laughing, with a red Santa face. Ruth wasn't there.

How come I'm not on the wall? Lisa wondered. *I'm the Girls Champion! I'm Igor's student!* Then Lisa remembered her zero-four loss to Ruth. That defeat had demoted her to the low elevation of 1402. Lisa felt that her chess study had been like one of those rough sponges Jan sold at her store, to scour the skin into perfection. But instead of immaculate exfoliation, her face had slipped off like rice paper.

There were about forty-five men in the big room, no women; Lisa looked down onto the wooden chess table where she would soon sit down against one of them. There was a built-in rectangular leather pouch for the dead pieces to the board's side. Lisa touched the soft wood. Small dents and nicks revealed themselves to her fingertips. Lisa listened to the pieces falling onto the soft wood, rolling over the withered wood like thunderstorms, trying to engrave their memory. Those battles had left scars, like the ones on Igor's face and arms.

Lisa was paired against Vladislav Andreivich Tyomkin, one of Igor's friends. In the moments before the game officially began, Vlad was cordial with Lisa, though he did not know she was Igor's student. He encouraged her chess, and told her how he had attended a lecture by Mikhail Botvinnik when he was her age, at the Pioneer Palace. *He's only 1620,* Lisa thought. *I'm so much better than that. He's old and weak. He's going to miss stuff. I will just wait. Then I will punish him. I will take away his points and add them to my own. Then I will beat somebody else.*

Vlad outplayed Lisa out of the opening and began the squeeze. Lisa had been too cautious, playing as if she were the parent, waiting for the child to fall on its face. There was a vise upon her bicep, being tightened into inevitable explosion. A little rope held her big toe, holding her down. Desperate, Lisa remembered Ruth's trick. Thinking Vlad would only understand her if she talked to him in Igor's voice, she said in her deepest, most masculine tone: "I offer draw."

Vlad was offended. "Look at position," he said. "Do you feel equal?"

Lisa began making gestures of despair, as if she were about to resign: deep sighs with a palm to a downcast face. These motions did reflect how she felt, but they were also calculated exaggerations. Assuming victory, Vlad slipped. He was ready to shake her hand, and congratulate himself, when a variation escaped his net like a loose fish.

The free toe freed Lisa's arm, and her pieces knew the anger of liberated repression: All of the squares that Vlad didn't need to control when his opponent was subjugated were now open wounds into which Lisa's pieces drove salted blades of sarcasm. She sat on her feet, driving her preadolescent bosom over the board, and cruelly slammed her pieces into the weakened territory of the old Russian's position.

"Pizda," Vlad muttered. Lisa wanted his disappointment. She wanted him to writhe. "Manda," he breathed. Lisa felt the humid spittle of Vlad's curses coat her knight that was already deep in his position. An old friend arose from the darkness to hand Lisa a pattern from the mate-in-twos. She grabbed the wet knight with her entire palm, and pushed Vlad's warm saliva into the soil of ten thousand hands. The knight sounded like a whip when it landed, like it might break the old board.

A crowd came to look upon the beautiful mate and the disgraced Russian. Some of the younger Americans crowned Vlad with "Ahh SNAP!" and "Ohhh DAMN!" Vlad looked Lisa in the eye, not shaking her hand, and said, "You think we play Nintendo? You will never beat me again, never!"

THE TALK

Walgreens was one of Jan's enemies. Cheap, cheap, cheap; the checkout girl passed Lisa her new black notebook as if it were just another thing. It cost $4.37 with tax. A superfluous flap read "College Ruled" and had a picture of a fifteen-year-old boy playing an electric guitar. Lisa could have used one of the journals from Domestique, but those were all unlined—and Lisa had come to think of their milky blankness as deceitful. She needed lines, to write out the variations.

Lisa wanted a written record of the special meeting Igor had arranged "to tell ze chess." His words would give her notebook meaning, like the way Jan used to put colorful postcards on the front covers of her childhood journals. But this book would be free of life's cloudiness, it would only be for chess.

Just as Igor had pointed her to the three dimensions, he would now hint at what chess really was. Lisa knew that she wouldn't understand all the words of her initiation; it would probably be like the secret hand gesture—the one Igor had given the attendant in the black suit at the music school. So she went in as a scribe, prepared to copy everything faithfully and to only think about it later.

But the talk was a disaster. It began with an unfairness. Igor said that she had disrespected chess in her game with Vlad: the way she had offered a draw; the way she pretended that she was about to resign (Igor saw everything!); the way she hunched over the board; and especially the way she had slammed the pieces, trying to humiliate her opponent.

"But did I break any rules?" Lisa demanded.

Igor said that wasn't the point. He said something about "sacred ceremony of game." And that today he would talk about "chess culture," whatever the hell that was supposed to mean. He was clearly taking Vlad's side, just like when he took Ruth's side when he forced her to resign her game. At least she had kicked Vlad's ass and taken his rating points. She had moved up the hierarchy, one step closer to being on the wall of the Mechanics—that was chess culture.

♟

On the paisley-covered table, now without a chessboard on it, Ruth put tea in Lisa's cup of hot water and told her to watch the leaves open. The tea box said 洞庭碧螺春, Ruth called it Green Snail Tea. Alehkine was allowed to sit in Lisa's lap. And Ruth's tiny apartment suddenly seemed to Lisa like what Domestique was trying to sell: the orange tint of the tablecloth close to the ground where Alehkine rubbed himself; the slightly lighter path in the dark wood of the entryway where her shoeless feet had also walked; the lacy throw over the back of the sofa where Lisa had once slept. But Ruth said the apartment was not hers, she did not own it.

This wasn't how Lisa had imagined meeting Ruth again. She had wanted to return to Ruth's apartment as the victor, so high above her level that she wouldn't need to fret during the game, as if she would be dispensing wisdom from an overabundant orb of shining light. But now she needed Ruth's help, to help her understand what chess was about. And it hurt Lisa to ask. Ringing Ruth's doorbell felt like one of Igor's exercises, self-inflicted and full of pain.

But what exactly did she want to ask Ruth? Lisa realized too late that she didn't really know. She kinda just wanted to ask, "What is chess?" But that sounded dumb. So Lisa asked Ruth, "What did your mom say when you started taking chess seriously?"

"Oh, I started too late," she said. "I was already in college, and I never had to tell her about it."

"Well, umm, why is it important to measure yourself in chess?"

"What does Igor say?"

It was so dumb. Why couldn't Ruth just tell her what *she* thought? To draw her out, Lisa asked her the hot question that got everybody excited: "Why are all the top players men?"

But Ruth solemnly answered, "What does Igor say?"

"I dunno!" Lisa shouted. "He's been in this country so long, and he still talks funny, having a *momient* with his *opponient*."

"Please listen, Lisa," Ruth said. "I didn't have a chess coach. And most everybody you play with here—they didn't have a coach either. They didn't have somebody for whom chess was part of their soul. For us, chess is a magical world that we can look into—but not a place we can live in. That's why you need to follow Igor."

To refute Ruth, Lisa quoted Igor directly. She knew Ruth would think what he said was disgusting—even criminal. Then she would be on her side. And when she read his words from her chess notebook she did it in his accent. She was really good at imitating him:

"Please understand Vlad, Lisa, man you play at Mechanics. We both learn chess at Pioneer Palace. Chess our fadder. He teach to be man. Chess is man's strength. Chess is one man breaking anozer, fucking hym."

But Ruth didn't condemn Igor. She instead thought for a long time, nodding, with a wise smile on her face. And then said: "I was cruel to you in our match, Lisa. I wanted to scrub you clean, to leave you with the best of my chess, and see my chess reflected in yours."

But chess couldn't be just a cruel boxing match between men! Lisa had felt something so much deeper. Trying to get Ruth on her side, to give her some other way of looking at chess, Lisa said, "OK, OK, what about this: American men like womenz, zey tsink chess pastime. Zhey only know outside, same way girl tsink about clothes, never know own power."

Ruth was silent. It seemed to Lisa that they were both among the chessless—along with Jan and Ted, and that they always had been.

"What else did he say?" Ruth asked.

"Ugh. He talked to me forever about Fischer. But it had nothing to do with me."

"Read it to me, Lisa."

"Bobby go alone into game. Boards set up through apartment, he play many games against self. Bobby go out to Walden Pond, is American tradition. But Bobby went much further zan zis Pondboy. Pondboy, I find, only go tsree mile from Cambridge, Massachussets. Googlemap show, big disappointment."

Ruth told Lisa about trees, flowers and some guy Lisa had never heard of named Thoreau. But all that seemed pretty pointless. And if Igor thought the guy was a n00b then it's not like she was going to care about what he said.

Lisa had told Igor that she wanted to learn the Russian tradition, that she hated Americans. But Igor wouldn't let her forget that she was, in fact, an American. He said he felt horror when he thought about chess from Lisa's perspective. There were no predetermined crevices in the rock to use as footholds, just a smooth blank nothingness, as if the skin of someone's face had grown over their mouth, nose and eyes, leaving a slippery pearl.

"Igor is teaching me in the Russian tradition, Ruth. So whatever all that means, it's not my problem." But Ruth made her keep reading.

"Already, I see zis Pondboy, zis Bobby Fischer, in you, Lisa. Bobby say Russians cheat hym. Bobby say CIA follow hym, make mind gyame wit hym. Fellow American not believe, zey say he crazy. When he win, zen zey like hym. Single man march against big Soviet. He make same sweet song of isolation Americans feel in career and marriage. Zey heroes wid hym. Until Bobby try to come home, after long time at pond and battlefield. Wounded, no longer able to fight, you understyand? He is loud, he make tsreats, he become homeless. Americans not help. History show Russians cheat (of course we cheat, what u tsink?). History show CIA file so big you need wheelbarrow for carry. Who is crazy? I ask you."

"This has nothing to do with me!" Lisa yelled at Ruth.

Ruth turned her face away and confessed, "It's true, I also didn't do anything to help Bobby." Then Ruth turned back to Lisa, and brought her moist, hazel eyes close to her face. "I think Igor is trying to say that you will be alone," she said, "that you will have to make your own way."

"But Bobby went crazy. What does all this have to do with me?"

"Listen, Lisa: We tell our kids that they should learn, that they should go to school. We tell them that thinking, reading and art are the highest achievements. And we construct palaces for them to pursue these things—a thought palace with the noblest marble floors, wood paneling and vaulted ceilings. But then we say that the palace is not real, we say that it's only a training ground for the real world. We tell our children not to pursue music in earnest, or painting, or chess. We say they will not be able to earn a living with it. We tell them that they will not be able to become professionals with these arts.

"It's the biggest regret of my life, Lisa, that I believed them. Because if you ask the same people: What is important? What gives your life meaning? What gives you joy? You always get a fumbling toward the beautiful. A song. An insight. A harmony that not only explained their self to the world, but elevated them, for a timeless moment, beyond all the stuff around us that points to death."

Lisa began to cry, for this was the truth she was looking for. This was chess.

♟

Lisa told Ruth about her new training regimen with Igor: No more two times a week; they would study every weekday. Igor said they would need all their energy to play through the games from the 1960 World Championship match between Mikhail Tal and Mikhail Botvinnik, played at the Pushkin Theatre in Moscow. Lisa and Igor would give themselves as much time as the combatants. They would try to guess their moves. They would see not only if they were right, but they would compare the amount of time used on each decision to the time that had been noted by the Soviet scorekeepers. The time they spent would be a measure of the urgency and possibility they saw in the position. They would do this in one sitting, usually four to five hours, replicating the intellectual time control of 1960 which gave each player two and a half hours for the first forty moves.

They would discuss their decisions the following day, measuring their justifications and reasoning against the notes Tal gives in his book on the match. They would learn how the contestants felt about their pieces, how they felt about each other. They would learn the situations they sought. As well as those they feared. They would participate in their failings. They would see that the best players make mistakes, a lot of mistakes. And they would learn to analyze those mistakes, to reconstruct their genealogies.

But Lisa held back a big part of her training from Ruth. Because it made her feel like a cheat, and she didn't want to be anything less than perfect in Ruth's eyes. Lisa had struck a deal with Igor, and she was pretty sure she couldn't fulfill her end of the bargain. In exchange for his teaching her the Russian tradition she would teach him the tradition of the journal. But the journal was private! That was the whole point. Her only hope would be finding grandma Lena's journals. Maybe Lisa would be able to discover some kind of example in them.

TAL AND BOTVINNIK

Ted said that the mountain was too big, and that Lisa would never make it. "I've looked it up, it's seven hundred and fifty feet of elevation gain. I couldn't even do that." But Jan's bike fit Lisa. "And it's way too dangerous, all those drunks going up to Inspiration Point, cutting corners way too fast. And you have such a steep descent." But the helmet fit too. "Look, I'll drive you over there." *No.* "Let me at least follow you from behind." *No. I'm going alone.*

It was the same mountain in between Orinda and Berkeley that Igor had climbed over to meet her parents. Lisa still didn't fully understand how Igor had got Jan to let her study with him. It had been a grandmaster move, the kind of strategic thinking that she would have to practice herself if she were to ever understand it.

Lisa began on the side of the mountain where she had grown up, in Orinda. The birds sang in the still stickiness of the burning sun, and a humid breeze came off the nearby reservoirs, pushing the smells of the big leaf maple and the sticky monkey flower up her nose. Lisa imagined the dimensions of material, time and quality of position flowing all about her like cords and ropes. She could feel their electricity. And when she really concentrated she could see them, curving around her thoughts and whipping the future infinity she could not yet see. One clever move could arrange their paths and show that they were not separate things. They were one. Lisa's ascent up the mountain would integrate all her variables into one robust motion: she would overwhelm the servility of the treadmills Jan wanted her to run; she would free her mind for the fourth hour of play; and she would now be able to go wherever she wanted, on her own.

Lisa gave herself four hours for the eleven miles to Berkeley and seven hundred and fifty feet of elevation gain. A gentler way for her to get to her first Russian chess lesson after Jan said she wouldn't even take her to the train would have been to ride Jan's bike three miles to the Orinda station along some flat roads. But Igor had said that her moves needed to be "for économique." He said that the moves of average players have only one idea behind them. Like a dog chasing after a ball, their chess is full of just one greedy intention.

Lisa had to get off the bike and walk up the steep parts. But she didn't give up. After her experience with Igor's stupid arm exercise, Lisa expected a higher perspective on the other side of pain.

At last, Lisa came to the top. The noon sun was high and her vision vast: the Golden Gate Bridge, the skyscrapers of San Francisco, the Berkeley Pier, the Berkeley Public Library. Igor's garden was down there somewhere. The cold wind and fog of the other side of the mountain, of the vast Pacific Ocean in front of her, penetrated her sweat-soaked clothes

Lisa was drawn to a metallic dome that sunned itself like a heavy breast on a concrete podium. She pressed one of the oversized buttons, and water splashed against her forehead. Lisa drank deeply from the bosom-like fountain and began to feel her weak legs refreshed, her mind cleansed from all the torment that followed her. Surely, Igor had also drank from this same source.

In her spongy wet, Lisa briefly experienced the claim that we are in fact watery beings. She had pushed it all out, to begin again. The cold wind felt like an open refrigerator door and began to blow Lisa's fluid state dry. Pressed into the straps of her unicorn backpack Lisa could see the salty outline of her thick shoulders emerging.

Jan's damn pool story kept coming back to Lisa. She had heard it so many times already. When Jan was Lisa's age, she would spend every summer day at her rich friend's house. Boys were drawn to the clear blue water of Jennifer's pool. There were brightly colored rings to be fetched, beach balls and poolside games, way down there in the smoggy warmth of the South Bay. Jennifer's mom, Patsy, brought them iced tea. Jan had always wanted a pool then, and she thought it was just such a waste that Lisa never invited anyone over to their backyard pool.

Climbing over the mountain was a way to completely overwhelm Jan's weight loss agenda. Until now, Lisa had shared Jan's view of cyclists. From the high windshield of their SUV, she and Jan looked down on the fragile and naked bodies whose flesh Jan could rip open with a momentary lapse of concentration. Ted had bought Jan the bike as part of a long series of cruel fitness experiments: Bikram yoga, Boot Camp, Insanity. But Jan had never ridden her beautiful Colnago road bike. And now Lisa would ride out into Jan's view of danger.

♟

Ruth had prepared the games of the Tal-Botvinnik 1960 match as a series of flash cards for Lisa and Igor. They would only be able to see the move played and how much time each player used, but not the entire sequence of the game. Igor and Lisa both kept a separate scoresheet on which they would record their guess as to how Tal and Botvinnik would play each position and how much time they spent thinking about it.

Igor chose the first moves of game one quickly, as if he already knew what they were.[3] Lisa chastened his haste; with a grave look of

---

[3] Tal-Botvinnik, Game One: 1. ♟e4 ♟e6 2. ♟d4 ♟d5 3. ♞c3 ♝b4 4. ♟e5 ♟c5 5. ♟a3 ♝xc3 6. ♟xc3 ♛c7 7. ♛g4 ♟f5 8. ♛g3 ♞e7 9. ♛xg7

professional disapproval she said, "C'mon Igor, this is serious!" Ruth's light blue and pink flash cards seemed to blush in Igor's big and callused hands, her feminine cursive right up against his scars and hair—but Igor said nothing, and the white knight and black bishop that had already been removed from the game clicked around in his big hands like a carousel.

Lisa predicted almost all of game one incorrectly and suffered from muttering dissatisfaction. On move seven, Lisa wanted to play ♘f3. Tal played ♕g4, disregarding the most parochial rule dramatized in her new favorite movie, *Searching for Bobby Fischer*. Lisa got angry during the following day's reflective session, and she shouted a line from that movie at Igor: "Did you bring your queen

Botvinnik

Tal to move

out early, Josh, even though Bruce warned you time and again about that?"

Igor said, "Knight f3 bourgeois move."

But Lisa didn't know what the hell that was supposed to mean.

Igor read from Tal's notes: "After Knight f3, the game is sufficiently complicated, but insufficiently sharp."

♖g8 10. ♕xh7 ♗xd4 11. ♔d1 ♗d7 12. ♕h5+ ♘g6 13. ♘e2 ♗d3 14. ♗xd3 ♗a4+ 15. ♔e1 ♕xe5 16. ♗g5 ♘c6 17. ♗d4 ♕c7 18. ♗h4 ♗e5 19. ♖h3 ♕f7 20. ♗xe5 ♘cxe5 21. ♖e3 ♔d7 22. ♖b1 ♗b6 23. ♘f4 ♖ae8 24. ♖b4 ♗c6 25. ♕d1 ♘xf4 26. ♖xf4 ♘g6 27. ♖d4 ♖xe3+ 28. ♗xe3 ♔c7 29. ♗c4 ♗xc4 30. ♗xc4 ♕g7 31. ♗xg8 ♕xg8 32. ♗h5 black resigns

"Lisa," Igor explained, "this man Tal for truth Soviet, but not Russian. Was Latvian, small country, much proud anger. Russia call him Dionysus."

Then they came to the injustice of 11.♔d1. Tal's pieces were still trying to get out of bed, the position's dykes were beginning to break, and he moves his king—not even to the side of the board— but to where his queen had just stood.

Lisa said, "They played so badly fifty years ago, I would've beaten Tal in that game." And, "At least he was a strong enough player to put a question mark after 11. King d1."

Igor read from Tal's notes: "11.♔d1? Twenty years ago, a chess commentator would cringe in horror at such a move.

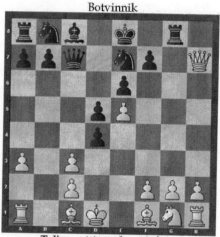

Botvinnik

Tal's position after 10.♔d1

At the very beginning of the game, the white king starts out on a journey! ... White prefers to mask his development plans for the white knight for the moment, keeping the possibility of either going to e2 or f3, and leaving the f1–a6 diagonal open. Losing the right to castle essentially had no meaning since, first of all, his opponent has not developed his pieces sufficiently and, second of all, black's own king was uncomfortable on e8."

"Whaat!?" Lisa cried. She wanted to throw the board, to hurt the pieces.

"Maybe Dionysus big joke make with question mark," Igor said.

"But it's Such a BAD move!"

"OK," Igor said. "We make for refute."

Lisa and Igor then conducted war with Tal. Lisa was so committed to punishing him that she allowed Igor to sacrifice a whole piece for only very distant-looking compensation.[4] They didn't even get a pawn for the knight who gave himself to explode white's central pawns. They only got Tal's king scrambling around in a permanent purgatory.

The analysis session was supposed to last only one day. But game one had too many questions, and Lisa needed to whip the river of Tal's criminality. She wanted proof, a clear variation that ended with Tal hung from a tree limb. Igor let her use his big hands to punish Tal, and to follow the rivulets to the capillaries of Tal's unjust thought.

Finally, when they had exhausted themselves upon game one, after four days, Igor walked Lisa down the stairs of Berkeley Public, to the midsummer light of her long ride home, and said, "I think you interesting that Tal make question mark after King d1. I think you he try for something difficult say. Maybe only possible in joke."

Lisa shouted back, "So he's contradicting himself?! Why would he say a move is bad by giving it a question mark and then defend it? And, if it's a joke, what's so funny about it?"

Igor smiled. "For truth, never given big thought about it. But I think you Dionysus wish for laugh at tradition of question mark. He wish for laugh at truth."

Chess was the only place Lisa had ever known truth, when she solved a problem or felt the harmony of her pieces. She certainly hadn't found truth in her journal or in life. Laughing at the truth of chess was bullshit, as wrong as Tal's moves were unjust. It was a goddamn heresy.

---

[4] This study arose after: 14... ♘c6 15. ♗f4 castles queenside 16. ♔e1 ♗d4 17. ♗c4 ♘ge5 18. ♗xe5 ♘ce5 19. ♘xd4 ♘g4.

Igor continued: "Game for big Dionysus aesthetic ideal. He break rule in opponent mind. First bring queen out, then king go to square queen was on. Next developing move is for put knight on e2—precise commitment Dionysus try for avoid when he play king d1. King then return to home square. What next? Amateur development of rooks from wing. For final, after black try for whole game evict white queen from king side, Tal volunteer for queen move back to starting position. Big laugh that undeveloped light-square bishop finish game."

"That's crazy talk," Lisa said. "Frohlich would give him Equinox."

♟

It upset Lisa that Tal took the bishop with the pawn in game three. His position would have been so whole and normal if he would have just taken the bishop with his queen.

Lisa's mind wandered, and she imagined what Igor's life as a drunk must have been. There were Greyhound

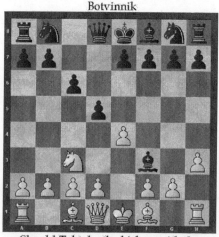

Should Tal take the bishop with the queen or the pawn?

stations, loud semitrucks and it was always dusk. He would hurt himself. The next morning he would have to tape his glasses back together. And she could hear him ask, "Uh, excuse, what city is?"

Lisa thought about the many times she had cut her arms with a razor. She also hurt herself. The dark blood would pulse out of her.

And she would feel better afterward, relieved, as if her grief had found a way out.

Lisa sat some time in silence with Igor, pondering the public pain of Tal's decision. Then she said, "Please kill me, I don't care anymore. That's what Tal is saying when he takes the bishop with the pawn. Botvinnik gets angry. The rules get angry. And the shark comes. That's how the bloody mess starts. Pretty soon no one knows who they are anymore."[5]

♙

A decision came in game twelve that Igor made very quickly. With a laughing smile he hid his sloppy Cyrillic handwriting behind his hairy hand. Lisa wanted to scream at him, "You can't know! There are too many plans that Tal can choose from!"

But the silence of their practice forced her inward. Lisa tried to imagine how

Botvinnik

What would Tal play?

---

[5]Tal-Botvinnik, Game Three: 1. ♙e4 ♙c6 2. ♘c3 ♙d5 3. ♘f3 ♗g4 4. ♙h3 ♗xf3 5. ♙xf3 ♙e6 6. ♙d4 ♘d7 7. ♗f4 ♗b4 8. ♙h4 ♘gf6 9. ♙e5 ♘h5 10. ♗g5 ♕a5 11. ♗d2 ♕b6 12. ♙a3 ♗e7 13. ♗e3 ♙g6 14. ♘a4 ♕d8 15. ♕d2 ♘g7 16. ♗g5 ♙h6 17. ♗xh6 ♘f5 18. ♗f4 ♖xh4 19. ♖xh4 ♘xh4 20. Castles queenside ♗b5 21. ♘c5 ♘xc5 22. ♙xc5 ♗xc5 23. ♗e2 ♗e7 24. ♔b1 ♕c7 25 ♖h1 castles queenside 26. ♗g3 ♘f5 27. ♖h7 ♖f8 28. ♗f4 ♕d8 29. ♗d3 ♖h8 30. ♖xh8 ♕xh8 31. ♕a5 ♕h1+ 32. ♘a2 ♕xf3 33. ♕a6+ ♔b8 34. ♕xc6 ♕xf4 35. ♗xb5 ♕xe5 36. ♕e8+ ♔b7 37. ♕c6+ ♔b8 draw agreed

she would play the position. But she had no idea. Then she tried to see the board as Tal might. She saw his bishops, how they were pointing at the white king's future home. Then she felt what she later read in Tal's notes: "The bishops smile at the white king."

Lisa saw that all of black's pieces could attack the king—except the rook on a8. She could not share in the bishops' gaze. In a flash, Lisa saw the kind of madness that happens when we are frank about our intentions. She saw what Tal and Igor had seen. The knight would decentralize and take the pawn, 13...♘xa5. The knight knew full well that the side of the board was not her proper place. She was getting out of the way of the queenside rook—she wanted to go to a6 and then swing all the way over to the other side of the board, to h6 or g6, to stare at the white king. The f6 knight would also have to get out of the way.

Thing was, even if the queenside rook did complete her journey to the kingside, she wouldn't really threaten anything concretely. The bully rook would simply look at the white king. She would share in the purpose of her friends. The path of murder is honest, Lisa thought. But you won't be able to live as your mom and school want you to. They will hurt you, for breaking their rules. And Botvinnik made Tal pay.[6] The discoordination of Tal's rooks was when the

---

[6]Botvinnik-Tal, game twelve: 1. ♗c4 ♘f6 2. ♗d4 ♗e6 3. ♘f3 ♗d5 4. ♘c3 ♗c5. 5. ♗e3 ♘c6 6. ♗a3 ♗d6 7. ♗xc5 ♗xc5 8. ♗b4 ♗d6 9. ♗b2 castles 10. ♗xd5 ♗xd5 11. ♘b5 ♗b8 12. ♗e2 ♗a5 13. ♗xa5 ♘xa5 14. Castles ♖a6 15. ♗e5 ♗xe5 16. ♘xe5 ♖e8 17. ♘d3 ♘e4 18. ♘f4 ♖e5 19. ♖c1 ♖h6 20. ♘d4 ♘c6 21. ♗g3 ♗g5 22. ♘d3 ♖e8 23. ♗g4 ♗xg4 24. ♕xg4 ♘xd4 25. ♗xd4 ♕f6 26. ♘e5 ♘d2. 27. ♖fd1 ♖xe5 28. ♖xd2 ♖e4 29. ♕c8+ ♔g7 30. ♕xb7 ♕e6 31. ♖f1 ♖e1 32. ♕b5 ♕h3 33. ♗f3 ♕e6 34. ♖df2 ♖f6 35. ♖xe1 ♕xe1+ 36. ♔g2 ♗g4 37. ♕d3 ♗h5 38. ♖f1 ♕e6 39. ♗xg4 ♖xf1 40. ♔xf1 ♗xg4 41. ♗a4 ♕b6 42. ♔f2 ♕b4 43. ♔e3 ♕xa4 44. ♔f4 ♕a2 45. ♕e3 ♕xh2 46. ♕e5+ ♔f8 47. ♕d6+ ♔g7 48. ♕xd5 ♕f2+ 49. ♔xg4 ♗f5+ 50. ♔g5 ♕xg3 51. ♔xf5 ♕g6+ 52. ♔f4 ♕f6+ 53. ♔e3 ♔f8 54. ♔d3 ♕f1+ 55. ♔e4 ♕g2+ 56. ♔e5 ♕g5+ 57. ♔e6 ♕e7+ 58. ♔f5 ♕c7 59. ♕a8+ ♔e7

boys shouted and wouldn't let her speak; the weakness of Tal's back rank was her fear of getting depantsed in public; the busted shell of pawns around his king was when school had stopped making sense.

Igor called Botvinnik the headmaster of the Soviet School. To Lisa, he was like the kids who always did what they were supposed to. They didn't think for themselves. They were phonies, because they grabbed at what other people wanted them to be. And they called their earnest never-give-up bullshit "character." Strive, be all somebody else wants you to be. Lisa knew that they would always have the advantage, closed and protected in the warm garments of success. To them, Lisa and the few other people who weren't phonies would always be the wounded, raving about something that the people with character would soon declare illegal.

♟

Lisa found the hustlers at Turk and Market. Every Tuesday night, after her game at the Mechanics, she would go to them. She would stay there as long as she could. Then she would lie to Jan, telling her when she arrived home on the last train that her game at the Mechanics had gone the distance. Lisa played blitz chess with the hustlers. Each player got three minutes for the whole game.

Lanh owned the equipment. From his heavily laden shopping cart the slender Vietnamese man would first unpack and set up his foldout tables, then he would wait for the hustlers to rent his chipped plastic pieces, along with his thin placemat boards and his ancient analog clocks. Igor's friend, Vlad, sometimes made a couple dollars there.

---

60. ♕e4+ ♚d8 61. ♕h4+ ♚c8 62. ♕h8+ ♚b7 63. ♕e5 ♕f7+ 64. ♚e4 ♕g6+ 65. ♕f5 ♕d6 66. ♕f7+ ♚c8 67. ♕f5+ ♚d8 68. ♕a5+ ♚e8 69. ♙d5 ♚e7 70. ♕a7+ ♚d8 71. ♕a8+ ♚d7 72. ♚f5 ♚e7 draw agreed

"You want me little Lisa, you want me?" The hustlers called to her. "Well, you gonna have to get me, ooh, now you let me in, gave me the penetration. NO! I'm not going anywhere, sugar, now, oh, I'm feeling it. Take That, You Little BITCH!" Lisa liked being called "bitch." She liked saying it too: "bitch, bitch, bitch." The queen was a fucking bitch. She'd fuck your shit up.

Like young boys who disappear into video games, clean-shaven men in suits would enter Lanh's world. The n00bs in suits rightly saw—as spectators—that many atrocities of logic were committed in Lanh's encampment. And they wanted to punish these mistakes. But when the red blood began to flow they were never able to escape the hustle. The demons of street life surrounded the peaceful equanimity of these successful men: The pieces inhaled the diseases of Market street, scratched their balls and banged out four-letter words on hungry metal pots. Bad mojo flowed into these men who took the elevators up into the tall buildings of the financial district, and a couple dollars trickled back down.

With much practice, Lisa learned to only hear the percussion of the clock being slapped and the scraping sound that the unfelted bottoms of Lanh's pieces made against his thin paper boards. And she made some money, lots of money.

Lanh built his fortress every night. Up against a massive wind-blocking building, he leaned two of his plastic tables. The third wall would be formed by his shopping cart. Because he was a careful man (who had enemies—many of the hustlers didn't like the way he did business, thought he charged too much), he would always tie himself to his shopping cart with a rope so it wouldn't get stolen.

Leo, who said he had a rating of 2200, was the man at the top. His pewter face was like one of Lanh's knights, broken by several falls to the pavement and then smoothed over by many eager fingers. The few times Lisa beat Leo she felt his waning life force flow into her. She took the chess from the veteran soldier's legless body, packed into his small wheelchair like an old finger into a wedding ring. Lisa cherished the grimace Leo made as he passed her his worn dollar over Lanh's table.

Lisa was the only person the hustlers didn't mind giving their money to. Lanh even let Lisa play for free. The men said that times were slow when she wasn't there. The foot traffic needed to be drawn in. They liked it when Lisa talked smack and won. The crowd that gathered would always bring more people, especially the suckers who needed to escape from whatever world they were coming from.

All of the experienced chessplayers, especially Ruth, disapproved of Lisa playing with the hustlers. They called the play of Lanh's clients cheap, and artificial, without any kind of depth. They said their minds would coarsen Lisa's. They worried over her, and threatened to call Jan. But Lisa had seen Josh play against the Washington Square Park hustlers in her favorite movie; that's where Bobby had also played. And Ruth had lent Lisa her autographed copy of *Chess Bitch*; that book was all about women who played chess with dirty men.

♟

But Tuesday was just one day in the week. Lisa wanted to raise her rating, she wanted to rise in the hierarchy. To prove herself, Lisa played in all the weekend tournaments. For a tournament in Palo Alto Lisa took the train to Fremont and then biked across the Dumbarton Bridge. For a tournament at a McDonalds in Vallejo she followed an industrial road past a refinery to cross the Carquinez Bridge. In late July, when the only tournament happened to be way up north in Sebastopol, Lisa took a bus to Santa Rosa and then biked the seven and a half miles to the tournament site.

Lisa found the Ethiopian men who played rated games at Colonial Donut in Oakland. She would follow their example, and slowly sip on a small cup of coffee for hours. After she kicked their asses, she would listen to tales of the old country and learn about the food their wives cooked for them. Sometimes she would buy a maple syrup donut from the Chinese lady who was always there; it dripped a little, but it sounded healthy.

Lisa was not alone. Ruth always knew where she was. And the men she played against wanted to help her. With broad smiles of American benevolence, the weekend warriors told Lisa that they wanted to support women's chess. They gave her free rides and meals. They shared their stories with her: *the fish that got away, the time I played Seirawan at the Last Exit when we were both thirteen in Seattle, Bobby Fischer's whores in Budapest.* There were rarely any women at the tournaments. The ones that did show up weren't any good. Ruth had stopped playing competitively, and Lisa never saw any of the girls from the Northern California Championship at the tournaments.

People sometimes made nasty comments, about her and Igor, as if they were lovers or something. But only dumb Americans said that kind of stuff. They didn't know anything about the Russian tradition or pure thought.

By the end of July, Lisa had over two hundred Facebook friends; nearly all of them were chessplayers—Lisa counted. Later in the summer, when Lisa was trying to find a ride and accommodation for the Central California Open in Fresno, she simply posted "Fresno?" as her Facebook status and more than twenty people posted to her wall with encouragement and offers of help.

FRESNO

Jan said that men were going to come to the house and take everything away. Jan would lose Domestique and the house. Ted would lose his TV and his collection of old Mercedes cars. Lisa would lose Jan's bicycle. They were going to have to move, and Lisa would have to go to a public school. Jan was sorry. The economy was bad and the big-box stores were taking over.

Lisa should have seen it coming. Ted never shouted at the race-cars anymore. He just watched them go around and around on his big TV. And it was too good to be true that Jan had let her play so much chess over the summer. Lisa had wanted to believe that Jan finally saw how amazing chess was, but was still too proud to admit it.

Jan said she would have to start public school in a month, and that next week they would move to a place called Emeryville. All of this was to be expected of people on the other side of the wall. The chessless would always mumble and fumble. You couldn't really blame them for who they were.

The person Lisa did blame was Igor. The National Girls Championship in Lubbock was approaching. And he wouldn't play with her at the big warm-up tournament in Fresno.

Without him, chess often felt lonely. At her weekend tournaments and at Turk and Market, her games were against boys or men who played chess as if it were a video game, panting toward a momentary oblivion. Like one of Jan's friends on a treadmill, everything could became pointless there. And Lisa's pieces sometimes refused to speak. If he would only come with her, just once. With its struggles and hardships, the tournament in Fresno would be like a pilgrimage.

She asked him, "Hey, so did the tournament organizers give you a hotel room in Fresno?"

Igor told Lisa, again, that he wasn't going to play in Fresno.

"What?! Everyone is gonna be there. You have to play. It's the Central California Championship. Easy money, eighteen hundred for first."

Igor declined. But he couldn't give Lisa a good enough excuse. He could only offer a mumbling kind of no, the kind that old people give kids when they don't want to be pinned down by their own arguments. Igor said he knew what Fresno would be like: He would neither eat nor sleep well, he would have to play two games a day for each of the three days of the tournament. That meant he could play up to twelve hours a day. And he would have to play against several players much weaker than himself. This was American chess culture, he said: nasty, brutish and long.

But while Igor excused himself from the Central California Championship, he told Lisa that she had to play in it. The traditional American chess tournament, smaller versions of which she had played in all summer, was a kind of purgatory that she had to go through. Bobby, and every other American player, had been processed through the violence of the weekend tournament.

Igor told Lisa of the malnourished exhaustion that clings to the players like mold on a towel in a damp bathroom. Lisa would have to somehow enter into these minds and not become infected with their premature attacks and superficial tactics. Like chickens, desperate to survive, they would run from her. She would have to chase them and cut them down, thousands of them. "Butcher have special coat. Easy for him clean blood, intestine and screams from self. You not have this coat—not yet."

Igor said that only after Lisa had mastered the American tournament and improved her rating would she be able to play in nobler events where chess was properly worshipped. Being a girl would enable that opportunity. It was to these events, one round a day, with closely matched opposition, that Lisa's chess aspired.

"Aww, maaan!" Lisa shouted. "I don't get it. Yer gonna let some chump take our money? Or one of those travelling Russian clowns? That's our money. Have some pride."

Lisa would not accept that Igor didn't want to play. She would not accept his explanation that what was necessary for her chess was very much not so for his. Nor would she accept that the extraordinary prize was not that much money. It was the biggest prize of all the tournaments Lisa had played in that summer.

Two days later, Lisa told Igor that Jan wouldn't let her play unless Igor came with her. It was a lie. But it was what should have been. And it would help Igor do what was right. Lisa had already forgotten the time before the chaos of the bankruptcy, when Jan would have never let her go—especially with Igor. Now she could do pretty much anything.

But Igor refused.

At their next lesson, Lisa arranged to get a call from Robert Rasmussen, the president of the Fresno chess club. He really wanted her to play in his tournament, and had posted an invitation on her Facebook wall. Now, Lisa knew that Igor would kill her if her phone rang during their study of Tal and Botvinnik. So Robert's call came precisely two minutes before the lesson officially began. She handed her phone to Igor and said, "It's for you!" Then she stood next to her coach and eavesdropped:

"Grandmaster!" Mr. Rasmussen said. "We would really like to have you play in our tournament. What can we do to make it happen?"

Igor was silent.

"One of our members has a great big house you can stay in. He even has a lake, with a landscaped island, it's like Robinson Crusoe out there!

"He has a room for Lisa too, and a daughter just a little older than her.

"Sir, will you play with us?"

Igor made a bleating noise; maybe it was Russian.

"Wonderful, that's truly wonderful. Sir, I will pick you and Lisa up from the train at eleven thirty-four. The first round starts at twelve. You can't miss me—I'm five-four, three hundred pounds and I walk with a cane."

Igor said nothing. The time of the lesson had arrived, and Igor's soul naturally turned toward Tal and Botvinnik, like a bird who is roused from its nest by the first red fingers of early dawn.

Lisa's heart also flew. She had steered him to what was right. She had made him a better person. Lisa felt her chess as she did her new bicycling tummy: Her hardship promised powerful muscles, and her quick progress hinted at a beautiful steel just beneath her layer of flab. And she decided it was time.

After the lesson, Lisa announced: "I'm gonna play in the Open section." Anyone could play in the Open Section. But just about everyone in the Open was at least 2000. And Lisa's progress over the summer had only lifted her to 1872. She wanted to play with noble minds, closer to Tal and Botvinnik.

"Ho, Ho!" Igor laughed. "You favorite for win under 2000 section. Twelve hundred dollars! Twelve hundred dollars, Lisa. You rich. Easy money." With a gaping mouth, Igor awkwardly spelled out, "O-M-G." Lisa laughed, and he continued: "Lisa, that only six hundred less than first place in Open. Organizer know that weakies no pay big entry fee for play people like me. They like sheep in own corral where wolf cannot come for kill. That where they fight each other, over some dollars." Then he imitated Lisa's voice: "Aww, maaan! I don't get it. You gonna let some local chump take our money?"

Lisa gave Igor a devious smile and they laughed together. Money really hadn't been the point. Lisa felt they were laughing at all the false pretexts the chessless use to hide the real reasons for the stuff they do. They laughed at themselves for pretending to be part of that lower world.

♟

Lisa and Igor got off the train in Fresno to one hundred degrees of sticky wet. Lisa shouted, "How can it be so hot here? It was so cold when we left this morning! We didn't come that far."

"Cold wind of Pacific," Igor said. "He like unsatisfied lover. He know about heat in valley. All summer he blow, he punish us, trying to find his woman."

Robert was there with an SUV to drive them the short distance to the tournament. He opened the sliding back door for Igor and said, "I'm so happy you could join us, Grandmaster Ivanov!" Then he opened the passenger door for Lisa. "Have you beat him yet?" he asked with a wink.

The playing hall was a great windowless cave with many torches. It could have been a Marriot, or a Hilton. Once again, Lisa found herself to be the only woman amongst the 230 players. There was an older woman in the under-1000 section. But she was not a real chessplayer to Lisa. She hadn't done the Polgar problems. She didn't know anything about the Russian tradition. And she probably never had to lie to her mother so that she could play chess.

After her first round loss, Lisa slouched up to Igor, the man who had broken the will of generations of American chess talent. Without words, she spoke to him. *He was a 2300, a master. I'm only a 1872. It's not so bad that I lost. Look at all the people in this room I would crush.* The beating helped put Lisa in her place; it gave her a class to belong to. The violence from above stung Lisa, and she now needed someone beneath her to stick it into.

The pairings for round two's evening game were soon posted. And Lisa was again expected to lose. "Aww, maaan," she whined. "I gotta play Davidson with white. He plays the Najdorf. He's got the whole thing mapped out. He knows everything. He showed me some lines at the Mechanics. It would be better to be black." This question about openings had been a fight between them from the very start, and Igor said nothing.

When Lisa told the men she met at tournaments that she was studying with Igor, they would nod knowingly, wisely. They said that Igor would teach her the finer points of the Queen's Indian and the sharpness of the Sicilian. But when she said that Igor wouldn't teach her openings, they condemned him. So Lisa began to tell a little lie. She told the men that they were studying the most ambitious king's pawn variations for white and the King's Indian Defense for black. This met with great approval, and these were in fact the openings that Lisa was playing. They were also the ones Tal used in his match against Botvinnik.

The men talked about their repertoires as if they were a fancy piece of sports equipment that would not only give them a competitive edge, but would somehow allow them to experience the full power of the game. On an expensive surfboard, they would ride the thoughts of past masters. With their professional tennis racket, they would use spin and torque.

Now, feeling small and humiliated after her first-round loss, Lisa wanted this power. She wanted to sense the power of Igor's big hands in her moves; the way she had used them to pursue Tal's injustice in game one. Like a horrible child who whines for candy or death, she kept after Igor. "Why can't I ever learn any openings? Everyone says I need to learn theory."

Igor took Lisa for a short walk to the travelling bookstore. Opening books dominated the selection like women's clothing at a department store. All the latest fashions were showcased. Lisa saw a prostrate black king; he was weary of life, and dripped shiny red blood. *Crushing the Caro-Kann*, the book's title read. Another promised to destroy her pet opening, the King's Indian Defense. "Kill K.I.D.," it said in big Russian Army letters. They were a little like the Dungeons and Dragons modules she had seen boys play with: *The Dark Dungeon of Death*, and *The Lair of the Pale Bard*.

"Lisa, look under table."

Lisa obeyed Igor and crawled into a landscape of worn boxes. From the secrets of an ancient time, Lisa pulled out *Trends in the Bogo-Indian*, from 1986, fifty cents. She showed the pamphlet to Igor, as if asking him if she had discovered a treasure.

Igor answered with "Pa, pa, paaa," which he found very funny. "Keep looking!" he commanded, and continued with his inane "Pa, pa, paaa."

"Is that from a horror movie or something?" Lisa asked.

"Nyet! Keep looking. Pa, pa, paaa."

Lisa found a 507-page tome on the King's Gambit, in German, from 1887. "Oh! Very nice, we smell," Igor said, and he jumped down to the floor like a five-year-old. Together, they took in the ancient vanilla lignin of the vintage work. "Pa, pa, paaa," he sang.

"OK, Igor, that's really annoying!"

Igor closed his eyes for a brief moment, as he often did before he played a move. He then stood tall and sang out to the low ceiling of the bookstore. Three vulgar notes—*Pa, pa,* and *paaa*—began running over creeks and fields, along narrow cobblestone roads.

Each was a traveler with its own mask and path, but bound to the common caravan. The chessplayers in the bookstore gathered around Igor's baritone. Like Lisa, they did not know the song, but they recognized the struggle. And they yearned for consonance.

Igor blushed, so happy to see that his unprofessional voice could bring such pleasure to others. "Lisa," Igor said, "I wish for say that first notes not important. Art seen in development of first moves. Please understand Russian view: endgame foundation of house. Opening like paint, can be changed."

They walked away from the bookstore, and Igor said: "You know, music is a pleasure. Everyone understand music. I sing personal variations of Beethoven Third Symphony. No one recognize, but not important, they still enjoy. Chess take big study for appreciate. Also, in music, is possible for follow master to resolution of theme. You can play his music. In chess opening, only possible to follow a little way, then you on your own."

"That's what I want," Lisa said. "I want to try to play the theme to the resolution, just once. Like . . . like the time I played "Chopsticks" on the piano. I didn't know what I was doing. Everything just flowed out of me."

Igor laughed and said, "This man. Davidson. He always play same thing?"

"Yes, it's horrible!" Lisa said.

"Big weakness," Igor laughed. "Remember how Ruth crawl inside mind with draw offer?"

"That was so mean!" Lisa recalled.

"For truth. Now maybe climb around Davidson mind. We do some opening, yes?"

Lisa was shocked that Igor was giving her what she wanted. But it seemed way too late, the round was about to start.

"We gonna call the Panda. Panda on boat in New Hampshire, but always have computer. I turn up volume, you hear his tricks."

And soon he was on the phone, "Hey Panda, need favor. Student have white pieces against some guy who always play same move. Name Renard Davidson."

The Panda laughed. "You've got a student!? Are you teaching him bougie chess?"

"Nyet! We study Tal. Student play king pawn."

"Oh damn, a'ight. I'll call you back in ten."

Lisa didn't understand a thing. The round was in fifteen minutes, how could she learn to face one of black's main weapons in just five minutes? And what was bougie chess?

The voice of the mysterious man on the other side of the continent again spoke through Igor's phone. "Your student's right, the guy always plays the same thing." The Panda spoke a sequence rapidly through the phone, in Russian. Lisa understood only some *slon*s and *kon*s to which Igor said *tak*.

Lisa and Igor found a private spot on the side of a sweaty Fresno street and Igor transliterated the moves onto the chessboard. It was a little involved on the surface—the variation went all the way into the twentieth move—but Igor said it was actually quite simple: the guy would repeat his moves because he thought them objectively best. And this belief in the truth of his moves would be so strong that he wouldn't deviate from his customary path, even if he smelled something foul.

Lisa played her moves tentatively against Davidson, as if she didn't know what she was doing. She pretended to study the board. But her eyes fixed themselves just beyond the pieces, on the upper curve of Renard's bowling-ball belly. It was like Ted's. And as her opponent followed the habitual path that the Panda had prophesied, Lisa imagined the racecars going around and around.

On move twenty, Lisa played the Panda's idea: one of her pieces gave herself to alter the flows of time and quality of position. Davidson's king was now very awkwardly placed. But he wasn't going to get mated any time soon. His main problem felt at first very intangible to Lisa: his pieces were having difficulty talking to one another. The only seemingly safe chance of communication was by carrier pigeon, a wishful process that required the help of the elements. Lisa's pieces all had the iPhone5. Both players now sank into reflection, and Lisa realized that she needed to channel the thoughts of this mysterious man on the other side of the continent.

Lisa suddenly realized that her opponent needed to see that placing his hopes in carrier pigeons was delusional, especially since her iPhones were all equipped with an avian GPS monitoring app. He too would need to give up a piece. His only chance would be for his knight to light himself on fire and gallop into Lisa's camp. Yes, he would die. But he would give his fellows enough time to find themselves as Lisa surrounded and killed the kamikaze knight.

Davidson didn't lose any of his material by sending the carrier pigeon up. And it was not even clear how he could lose anything tangible in the next couple moves. But he had lost a tempo. And with that tempo Lisa moved on top of him, completely. *Fuck you, Ted.* She sealed off his structure. He might have felt safe, he still wasn't going to lose any of his stuff immediately, but the walls were now slowly moving in. He would be forced to choose a prison wall to climb. That's when she would catch him and plant her boot on the criminal's neck.

Rows of spectators began to assemble behind Lisa's board, and the mate-in-twos began to whine and yelp like hungry hunting dogs. They saw Ted's head bob up on the courtyard wall, trying to find a way out. Lisa had only used twenty minutes to fake thinking about the Panda's first twenty moves, so she had plenty of quiet time to patiently plan every detail of the execution.

Lisa was elated when her opponent resigned. In a matter-of-fact tone, Lisa asked if he would like to look at the game. That was the custom, both players would briefly pretend to be objective in the post-mortem. But Renard said no, and slumped away. *Fuck you, Ted,* Lisa thought. *You got what you deserved, clinging to all your stuff like a baby.*

For that game Lisa won the best game prize and the upset prize for the tournament, $100. Everyone was astonished that a girl had beaten someone rated so much higher with such a reputation in the Najdorf so quickly. They said that Lisa's novelty was of the highest theoretical importance to the Sicilian Najdorf. But Lisa was confused, and she told Igor, "I always thought that my first win against a master would feel more special. I thought I would have to do something brilliant. I mean, many of the Panda's moves I didn't understand. I have no idea what I would of done if Davidson had played something else."

Igor smiled. "Opponent part of game. Opponent always have weakness. In this game your opponent like politician who always say same thing, who think he special because of opening truth he think he know. Easy for predict rigid thought. When he see you making powerful moves, big red light should have turn on. Like three notes I sing today, he could make variation. But he was convinced of his truth. Chess cruel. You search for weakness in opponent thought. Use weakness for push pieces into the emptiness. What chance for Mr. Davidson! Now he can think about the truth and the life. Like when Ruth offer you draw in losing position, you give opponent chance for think."

"It wasn't like cheating, what we did?" Lisa asked.

"What you mean? You take Panda's theme and play to resolution!"

♟

Lisa sat up front with their host, Asa Silber, on the long ride out to his lake house. Igor said he wanted to sit in back. He had won both of his games, but he was tired, and needed a moment to close his eyes. Asa and Lisa were quickly off on a romp through Lisa's now-famous game. And they began to eagerly follow the many paths of possibility that the game contained after her piece sacrifice. Asa shook his head violently at many of these variations, like a horse unhappy with his feed, and protested: "But you're down a piece!"

Lisa, struggling to explain herself, said: "C'mon, it's just like game nine of the Tal-Botvinnik match." As everyone knows a misty rainbow in the afternoon sun, Lisa thought all chessplayers knew this game. And she imitated Igor: "OK, structure different, but is same for way black not make for coordinate." Asa thought it was hilarious, the way she talked like Igor. And it

Botvinnik, to move

Tal's fantasy, from game 9

was in that happiness that Lisa understood that the position from Tal's game had been inside her, swimming around, helping her channel the Panda. In her analysis of game nine with Igor, she had also repeatedly said "But I'm down a piece!" Somehow the idea of the position had given her direction. And she was able to summon the three chords of material, time and quality of position to flow through her like Igor's ridiculous "pa, pa, paaa."

"Me and Igor ain't playin' no bougie chess!" Lisa yelled.

"Ha ha! And what does that mean?" Asa asked.

"It means I play like a badass," Lisa answered.

Asa smiled at Igor in his rearview mirror. After a time that seemed like forever, the tired man in the back seat said, "Bourgeois move is when don't think for self, only follow safe expectation of others."

Enjoying the ease of her new friendship with Asa, Lisa did not notice what a long commute it was. But as they entered the house, Lisa had no conversation or social graces for Asa's family. Time slowed for her. Eyes downcast, Lisa mumbled rehearsed answers to their well-meaning questions as to her favorite piece and when she had learned to play. They were shut out from chess. And the moment the conversation stopped addressing her directly she disappeared.

Igor later gave Lisa a big old speech about Asa's family. He said that Asa had grown up in a Jewish community in Detroit, and it was there that he learned to play chess. But the lox bagels Asa served them didn't seem so strange. Igor said that the name of Asa's eldest son was super Jewish. And that Elijah, now a senior in high school, had flawlessly adopted the Christian fervor of his mother and Fresno. Nor did his religious mother seem to feel any tension in marrying a Jew. But Lisa didn't understand what the big deal was supposed to be. Igor said that Asa knew his last name had been shortened from the original Zilberstein, but that he didn't know what it meant. Asa had no access to the playfulness of that German name's Jewish construction. "Don't you see, Lisa? We at end of history!"

But that was just one of Igor's speeches. Lisa didn't sense any history as she entered the house. She didn't think food or names were important. She couldn't have told you the difference between the old and new testaments. She didn't notice. She was a chess hunter. And in the same way she found the hustlers at Turk and Market, and the Ethiopian players at Colonial Donut in Oakland, she now found Dr. Silber's two giant trophy cases. She tried to hide there, in a corner of the living room.

Each case contained five levels, and on each level was a chess set. There was a Renaissance set, a *Star Trek* set, a *Star Wars* set, a space aliens set, and several ornately carved wooden sets. Lisa studied the collection intently. They were all she had in this foreign environment, non-regulation chess pieces offering her an oblique reflection of who she was.

From the kitchen, Dr. Silber tried to introduce his daughter, Laynee, to Lisa—just one year older than her—and his wife, Roxie. But they weren't chessplayers. *Why don't they just go away?* Lisa thought. *Like Jan and Frohlich with all their meaningless questions, they make me so tired.*

Lisa imagined Dr. Silber trying to seduce his children into the game with his space alien set—neon blue versus neon pink. But his children had not followed him, and now his weird sets were all that was left of his chess, like some kind of monument. *Every day, he passes his sets in his living room. The trophy cases are like an altar to chess, the true path he didn't follow. His chess set collection probably gets bigger and brighter every year, like the way Jan's shoe closet grows as she gets older.*

"Uuha, Stephanie says I can keep studying French cuz there's a tribe of Indians that speak it an' I can talk to them when we go down to Mexico." Like a little rubber ball, Laynee Silber bounced this and other text messages against the tired chessplayers.

Her father asked Igor, "Do you like wine? My good friend gave me this bottle. He had a great career as an architect, but wine is what he loves best. So he gave it all up for a vineyard in Sonoma." Silent, Igor turned the bottle. Dark shades wiggled from purple to black in his oversized pachyderm hands. And Lisa could tell he wanted to drink the whole bottle. He would bathe himself in the fancy wine words that Jan and Ted used, words like "terroir" and "mellowed tannic," to elevate the bruises and deprivations of his life into fantasies of rich complexity.

Laynee interrupted Igor's ancient desire, "Hey so, are you a nerd like my dad?" As Igor looked up, Lisa saw that the wine was just a little plaything. There was a deeper, more powerful foe caged in Igor's body. His name was vodka, and he grimaced like a naked wrestler next to the fancy California wine. Igor said, "I not know this word. Dad and me both chessplayer." Lisa looked through the glass panes of the trophy cases, across the wide living room, and fixed her eyes on the foreign Russian: *Really? You don't understand? The word "nerd," Igor, it's a little ball of shit that you have to yank from the hairs of your ass. How can you not see how she hates us?*

Igor would never be able to understand how much she suffered. Lisa leaned her forehead against Asa's trophy case. She had beaten her first master that day! It was something she had fantasized about. She had imagined that it would complete her. That win would make her special. Her achievement would be like a shield against all the ridicule and loneliness. But she felt empty.

Laynee was normal. Standing in the dining room with Igor and her dad, she was natural in her flirty dress with its splashy colors. Jan wanted Lisa to dance lightly through life the way Laynee did, with the ease of beauty. And Lisa had wanted to! She wanted to please Jan so badly. But she had been awkward and fat. A Laynee had always been inside Lisa, but she would never come out. She arose only in private, as her accuser. She always had flouncy blonde hair, and Lisa hated that bitch.

Lisa lightly banged her head against the glass pane of the trophy case, as if she were tapping out a telegraph. Asa crossed the room. He opened the case and took out his nicest wooden set. "Lisa," he said, "you were telling me, in the car, about a position from the Tal-Botvinnik match. I nodded my head as if I knew it. But I don't. Would you show it to me?"

As Lisa and Asa set up the pieces, Laynee laughed at her father playfully, and said, "It's the only religion my father has."

"For truth, they go now to temple," Igor said.

"I never really learned, didn't want to," Laynee said. "He was always so intense about it. But now I wish I could."

"Is possible for hear what they see," Igor said.

"What?"

"You have sound system, yes? Please find this piece on the YouTube." And Igor wrote down "RV 424; II Largo." It was the same Vivaldi piece Igor and Lisa had listened to at the beginning of the summer. Laynee couldn't find an interpretation with period instruments like they had heard at the conservatory. So Ofra Harnoy played a modern cello to an accompaniment of strings and what sounded like an organ. The modern cello was more robust; it lacked the fragile scratching, like turkey feathers on tin, that Lisa had heard from the scruffy boy's instrument.

During the analysis, Lisa playfully shouted things in Igor's voice, like, "Zhou mus' take opponient into deep dark forest where two plus two iz five." And, "Zhou know, me and wife, we like opposite-colored bishops. Communication not so good." Imitating her master was fun, and everyone loved it. But Laynee was mostly solemn. She stood close to the board and listened to the song several times. For Lisa, it was obvious how the song was like chess. But poor Laynee! She was among the chessless and would never get it.

♟

Lisa lost her game the following morning. And she unloaded her grief upon Igor as he marched her through Fresno's barren streets in search of food. "I mean, so I played queen takes b3 and I thought he had to play rook takes b3 when I then had rook a1 check! Bishop f1 rook takes f1 king takes f1 bishop h3 check king g1 rook a1 check and I have him, right, but he had the zwischenzug, knight f5 after bishop f1, and even then I could have survived . . ." Lisa assumed that everyone knew her subvariations. And the world—well, at least Igor—did not interrupt the myopic rhythm of her recounted moves. His head nodded "tak" to each of her moves. Lisa was describing a disease she was struggling to recover from with absurd sounding medical terms and Igor pretended that he knew what they meant.

Igor said he had to find them something to eat. They only had thirty minutes until the next round. Downtown Fresno looked like a bomb had gone off in 1959 and they were only now allowed back in. Cracked facades spoke to a vibrant time before the Tal-Botvinnik match. Fresno's old movie theatres now advertised "Iglesi a Victori osa, Domingo 9 a 11." An army of homeless people gathered in the city's main square in front of the courthouse. The jail had just spit them out, and they were trying to get back in. It was the only way out of the heat.

But Lisa didn't see any of that. She flagellated herself with the correct decisions that now seemed obvious. "I'm so retarded! How come I couldn't just play knight takes pawn?"

In ninety-six-degree heat, twenty minutes before the round, they entered a convenience store. The spent smell of stale crackers and month-old jelly beans greeted the players in a blast of forced air that pushed their sweaty clothes against them. The playing hall would also be cold. The sticky wet of their shorts and T-shirts would feel like Irkutsk by the end of the first hour.

Uncle Smirnoff saw Igor. Snickers saw Lisa. *'Member me, old friend? 'Member our firs' kiss? Your wittle baby teeth finding hidden nut in my warm chocolate?* Lisa held four bars and a Coke in an unstable clutch of chest and hands. Igor shouted "Nyet!" and started pulling the candy away. Two bars fell like small wooden planks onto the linoleum. Lisa screamed as he forcibly unpried her thumb for the last two. The injustice! *Honey. Don't leave me. He can't do that. You are free to love whomever you choose.* Lisa expected the adult behind the counter to help. But the Pakistani man did not look at her. He didn't care about the injustice she faced. "It's my money, Igor! And it is healthy. It has peanuts, look!"

Igor rudely dragged Lisa from the store, like Jan had once dragged her back to the inventory room. He cussed in Russian, and forced Lisa back to the hotel bar where he ordered two soups. White toast buttered into pliant submission came first. Lisa's tongue sucked the salt from the floppy sponge until the beep of a microwave in the back of the kitchen announced the soup. Brined potatoes stuck up like icebergs within a gelatinous cream. "Eat, Lisa, eat," he demanded. "The round is about to start." Lisa swallowed too fast. And a hard lump soon sat at the bottom of her gut like a corn cob or an avocado peel that won't compost in black earth.

The round was late in starting. Ready, set, no wait, sorry, we still have some stuff to figure out. The father of Lisa's next opponent politely guided Igor into a discussion of his son's chess. How could he help the boy improve? The two men stood before tiny ten-year-old Kash Patel. He too was playing in the Open Section. Lisa peeped from behind, still angry and confused by Igor's rough mistreatment of her. Kash's mom served her son warm *saag* from a silver tiffin, and the smells of spinach, garlic and turmeric ran through each other like colored threads in an embroidery.

Kash's father, Vinay, placed a special cylindrical cushion on his son's chair, giving Kash a whole extra foot so that he could properly reach his opponent's pieces. Vinay then overlaid the cushion with a patterned Brahmin cloth, as if it were a prayer blanket. Kash sat still, a gentle fulfillment in his posture. Lisa fidgeted on the other side of the board. She needed to touch everything around her, like an infant harvesting bacteria.

The first shivers of hotel cold reached Lisa's sweaty clothes as the game began. Her pieces marched underneath the looming canopy of high rainforest trees, and foreign birds chattered her mind into misdirection. Why wasn't Jan there, to give her a warm blanket and a hot soup?

Igor was fighting it out, on board one. So she would too. She would find strength on the other side of pain. Lisa began rocking back and forth. She would not move too fast. Her body began to daven, like an old Jew studying his Talmud, rhythmically squeezing out the salty fidgets and the damp of her clothes. Lisa won, and Vinay Patel applauded her victory. He invited Lisa to join them outside for a Brahmin picnic while doctor Silber and Igor finished playing their games.

♟

That evening, Laynee Silber came to sit with the exhausted chessplayers. Like cows whose feeding has been interrupted, they briefly looked up at the odd intruder, but then continued to speak in monosyllabic grunts and eat everything placed in front of them. The lush hair that tumbled down onto Laynee's face and pajamas in great unbrushed clumps made Lisa nervous. As Laynee began speaking, Lisa said to herself, *I can't take her seriously.*

"Hey, so I couldn't sleep last night, after we listened to the music. I had never really listened to classical music before. Anyways, I want to say I'm sorry for using the N-word. I had never really thought about it. All I could see was that whenever I thought of the word I thought of my brother. My brother's this straight-A student, see. He's always studying, always doing what he's supposed to. And he's always ahead of me, an' I can never be as good as him. Jus' about every class I have the teacher looks at me with big ol' eyes and says 'oh, so you're Elijah's sister,' all loud, so the whole class hears. And everyone thinks on that first day of class that I'm supposed to be this star student of somethin'. So, what I'm trying to say is that I feel that weight pushing down on me all the time, and the only way I can push it off me, to feel like somebody too, is to call him a nerd. And that's what everyone else calls him, so I hadn't really even thought about it much til las' night. An' I was thinkin' that maybe they call him a nerd because they also don' want him or the other nerds to hold anything over us, an' I thought that was kinda funny cuz my brother doesn't really hold anything over us. It's only the teachers that point to him, an' tell us that we should be like him. But see, then I thought that's kinda strange cuz the teachers aren't really nerds themselves. I mean it's not like they're really that interested in the things they're teaching, they're not studying every night themselves or anything. They're kinda like the rest of us, even if they do use my brother as someone to point to. An' as I was sitting with you guys last night listening to the music and watching you talk about chess I suddenly realized that studying has to be so much more. Like a thick tree trunk that rises up from the beginning of time, everyone can come up to touch it. You just have to realize that it's there. Last night I felt I could see past the teachers and my brother. And I realized that I was trapping myself by calling my brother and you guys the N-word. I don't know if I will play chess or anything, but I do know that I want to experience more. I wanna hear more music, and I wanna talk to you guys."

Lisa shook with anger. *But she hasn't made the sacrifices! She probably plays soccer. Her hair bounces off her back as she trots over to the bench, she screams in delight, and giggles with an orange peel as her smile. Boys fetch brightly colored rings from the bottom of her dad's pool while she and her friends laugh and drink iced tea.*

But everyone loved her little speech. Asa proudly said, "My daughter's a writer." And as they were going off to bed, Lisa had to overhear Igor ask Laynee, "You make journal?"

♟

Kayaks and paddleboats were moored to the Silbers' island clubhouse. To get there, Lisa and Igor passed by a cement swimming pool. A float that looked like a tiger had lost most of its air. The burnt animal fat of the poolside grill glistened in the cool morning sun. They began to shamble over the wobbly rope bridge, out to the other side, where trees and boulders formed nooks of secrecy and adventure.

But they only made it to the middle of the bridge. Lisa felt drawn to look into the lake, and Igor stood beside her. Yellows, greens and blacks flickered across the deep blue like quickly changing flowers. The bottomless quiet of that perfect dark blue would hush those deceits. Its warm bliss would cleanse her return. And she would again be whole and pure.

"Do you think Asa would mind if we went in?" Lisa asked her coach.

"No, he not mind, we go."

Lisa stumbled down the wobbly bridge to the shore and Igor was right behind her. But before they could get their shoes off, Asa honked the horn of his SUV and shouted, "Hey guys, we're gonna be late for the round!"

♟

It was the big game, the final round. Mr. Rasmussen, president of the Fresno Chess Club, proudly stood next to an old-fashioned demonstration board to play out the moves between Igor and his opponent, Enrico Guzman. A few fans had come to watch. Maybe they learned about the tournament from the newspaper article Mr. Rasmussen had maneuvered into the local paper. Maybe they heard the local talk show interview he had arranged for Igor. This battle would decide who won the tournament he had worked so hard to organize. Igor and his opponent were on the stage, with only Robert and his big board next to them. Everyone else was below.

From across the room, Lisa saw the two players shake hands and agree to a quick draw. While her own clock ticked, she walked onto the raised stage that Igor and his opponent had already abandoned. Like an unfinished meal, the position stood before her, the butter was beginning to congeal around the potatoes and the steak was stiffening like a corpse. Lisa saw some of the older players come by and shake their heads with sad but knowing smiles. Mr. Rasmussen looked down on her and said, "Oh, you know, grandmaster draw." *Does that mean they didn't want to fight?* Lisa wondered. She overheard one of the weakies say, "He was such a talent, gave it all to vodka, I guess."

Lisa fought. She won one game and lost the other that day and finished her tournament with a very respectable 50 percent score. That result pushed her all the way up to 1787, making her the country's highest rated girl in her under-fourteen age group. Like a seeker who has returned from the big mountain with delicious cuts and fulfilling bruises, Lisa asked Igor, "Why did you offer a draw?"

"Is tradition," he answered. "We share first place money."

"But what about the theme and the resolution?"

Igor pointed to the envelope in his shirt pocket, stuffed with a small percentage of the crumply bills amateurs had saved for their entry fees. "This resolution," he said.

"But, I mean, why would you agree to stop playing?" Lisa asked her coach. "Why would you want to leave the game?"

Igor didn't answer her question. He only said, "Tradition say Igor must now buy drink for friends." Apparently, the bearer of the envelope had to redistribute some of his dollars at the hotel bar. It was a communist thing. And Lisa was informed that it would be a while before they returned home. Igor had found them a ride with a player named Demetrius who had to first deal with some "women trouble" ("You not understand"). And Igor didn't know how long that would take.

Lisa could either join the men at the bar and have Igor treat her to a three-dollar bottle of water, or she could join the Patel family's post-tournament celebration of Brahmin treats and blitz chess. The Patels were staying overnight before driving back to the South Bay in the morning, and Lisa was about to go up to their hotel room. But Igor's old student, Jeffrey Phillips, came up and introduced himself. He said that he had really wanted to meet her, and had been watching her play.

Soon Lisa and the two men were lounging on the broad white couches next to the hotel bar. Eighty feet above them a pyramid skylight announced that it was already darkest night. Asa joined them, and several other players came for the drink Igor eagerly offered—to fulfill the obligation of the envelope. But Lisa only remembered what Igor and Jeffrey talked about.

Jeffrey never did say how he started playing chess. He didn't look like a chessplayer either: A gleaming dagger cut open four blood teardrops on his lean left forearm. He kept the tattoo hidden, like Lisa hid her scars, and it would occasionally poke out from underneath his long shirtsleeves.

Jeffrey had been unable to understand school. Even when he tried his best to do what they wanted, he would fail. "But Jeffrey, you're so smart," they would tell him. He began sitting at the back of the class. His ears dutifully heard his name at roll call, and his mouth would say "here" or "present." But then he would recede. The melancholy pot he smoked before class opened up into the enterprising geometry of *Korchnoi's 400 Best Games*. That was the book he always had with him. Through Korchnoi, while everyone else did what they were told, Jeffrey grabbed the centers of fierce Soviet opponents and played for domination.

Jeffrey made up his own stories as to why Korchnoi moved the way he did. With his pocket chess set at the back of the class, Jeffrey sat with a balcony view of the surgery room at a grand hospital. But he didn't have anyone to tell him the names of the surgeon's tools. Nor was he ever present when the surgeon practiced those tools with other men and invented new ones. He only had his own words. That private knowledge was good enough to win local tournaments and crown him as Utah's representative to the Denker Tournament of High School Champions, the genderless equivalent of the Polgar tournament Lisa had qualified to play in. And playing in that tournament had been his proudest moment.

But coming out of high school, Jeffrey had been unable to make it in the chess world. Russians beat him down every time he went to one of the bigger tournaments. To those men, Jeffrey's moves were like glib assertions. At the hotel bar they would laugh and say, "Da. Amerikanskiy make big shot into emptiness." It was at one of those big tournaments, in Reno, that he had first played Igor.

Jeffrey remembered staring up into the big oily thumbprints coating Igor's glasses, held together with an improvised machinery of scotch tape and safety pins. Then came an unflinching layer of alcoholic mucus. Jeffrey looked for something beyond that, some kind of life that could feel pain. But he only found silence.

Igor's big hand would forcefully grab a piece, his pudgy fingers easily enveloping the cheap plastic. Then he would push it so deeply inside Jeffrey's position that he knew he would never be strong enough. That was the adjective for chess skill Lisa had heard all summer; she had used it herself—not insightful or wise, but *strong*.

Jeffrey returned home to party. Like a saw with worn and rusty teeth, drugs and alcohol tried to cut chess from his soul. Little jobs found him in his small town, and gave him enough money to hurt himself. It was mostly booze and pot. But he discovered other drugs too, with names that sounded like chemicals.

Then one day, several years later, Igor found a comfortable bed and a piano while playing a little tournament in a small Utah town. It was a place to stop for a while, and he met Jeffrey at the local chess club—though Igor didn't remember having played him. His lessons with Igor began as friendly banter. And Jeffrey didn't think much of them at first. It was just cool to hang out with the guy, to get wildly drunk with him and see him throw down a crushing move on the board, yelling, "First big drink, then big fuck!" But slowly, little hints and gestures from Igor began pointing Jeffrey's chess to where it had wanted to go in high school. The hidden mysteries of his adolescent dreamworld began to rouse themselves, and his chess began to feel weighty, like a slight man whose frame suddenly explodes with powerful muscles.

He was in his mid-twenties. It wasn't too late! He got a night shift as a parking lot attendant and did all the tasks Igor gave him in the streetlight glare of his little hut: endgame studies, famous games and most of all the study of his own games. Igor gave him ways to approach various positions and the game. He was finally understanding all the things he couldn't by himself, in high school. He would make International Master! Maybe someday even GM.

But then Igor left, on one of his journeys, and Jeffrey's chess became lonesome. He missed Igor's grand view of the game, where chess stood at the center of everything. Girls wouldn't date him; they said he was a late-night parking lot attendant who played with little plastic figurines. Jeffrey's chess progress again halted, and he began to rewrap his old wound with more urgent acts of self-destruction. Then, as penance, as a way out, Jeffrey enlisted in the army. That was right before 9/11. But he refused to talk about any of that.

Jeffrey said that chess now calmed him. It was a way for him to remember. In brief moments, he could feel the magnificence of positions spreading outward, allowing him to perceive the splendor of everything. Jeffrey had won the under 2200 prize and proudly laid out some worn dollars on the table before his old master. *Let me fulfill the obligation of the envelope. Let me buy you a drink, Igor. Let us share a drunk.*

That's when their ride back to the Bay, Demetrius Jordan, finally came to meet Lisa and Igor on the soft couches next to the hotel bar. The big black man looked so depressed, like he had just been mated by an obnoxious eight-year-old boy. Igor ordered him a beer and a shot of whiskey.

He was so down that everyone else started to feel sad; even though no one knew what the miserable woman had done to him. "Fuck the womens," Igor said. "They not understand the chess." *It was true*, Lisa thought, *Jan never would get it.* Igor tried to cheer him up; he told of the old times, before computers, when grandmasters were giant men.

Lisa wasn't ready to be sad, the joy of her successful tournament filled her like the memory of Asa's deep blue lake. Lisa sprang out of her seat to stand in the middle of the men. Everyone's eyes were suddenly on the shy girl who hadn't said anything for at least the last hour. She had never been good at this kind of thing, being in front of people. It never went well. So she put so much energy into what she said that she yelled. "Hey! So the Panda gave me some of his opening prep and it felt like I was wearing a MASSIVE strap-on!" Lisa did some pelvic thrusts and shouted, "I WAS SO POWER-FUL!!" All the men broke down laughing. They laughed until they cried, Demetrius too. He shouted back: "Oh darlin', I need me a Panda! Ha ha. Where do I get one?"

But then Igor got real solemn. "Before go," he said. "I wish for tell Jeffrey story: For lesson, Jeffrey barter gifts. One was Bobby Fischer *Collected Game*. Was beautiful book, hardbind, notation of all games have, with some gloss photo of man in middle. Bobby picture look so clean, like he strong, invincible—so far from breakdown of later life.

"Jeffrey improve his chess; he inspire. When I leave Utah, for again make soldier march for win Church's Fried Chicken Grand Prix, I take this collection of Fischer. I play every game on little travel set, in café, on bus. Own chess was a shit, no prospect for beauty. Bobby try for universal, for truth outside tradition. Was hot summer on bus. Fat lady sit next to me, child on lap. He find my pawn, stick in face. He eat! Whole summer, friends say, 'Igor, you play without pawn?' You understand? Ha ha. Like for say, 'You have screw loose?' They think I crazy, all alone in big Fischer study.

"Jeffry, listen for big truth: games I study from Fischer book. Your book. They try for find clear blue water I see this morning in Dr. Silber lake. I understand now. I want swim in this water. But I never find." Igor then reached out and touched Jeffrey's arm. They beheld one another.

Trying to be helpful, Dr. Silber said, "Isn't that a beautiful color! It's called H2O blue. I took one gallon of the stuff on the canoe and spread it out this spring. And it's still there! It's that concentrated. It's a dye that creates a more opaque layer at the surface of the water, and that blocks the photosynthesis of the algae that I am constantly battling."

Lisa shouted, "What? The water's not real?"

Dr. Silber chuckled a little, and everyone fell silent. Finally, Igor said, "You know, Jeffrey, I remember now that Fischer book have stamp of Provo Public Library on inside cover." Jeffrey laughed and said, "I fucking liberated that book."

♟

Demetrius Jordan's jet-black convertible BMW was the kind of sports car where the back seat seems meant as more of a formality than a place for people to sit. The prestige of the leather front seats pushed itself back boldly, making the back seat look like a padded shelf. The seatbelt was too small for her, and Lisa secretly unclicked it before they even started. She figured the seatbelts weren't meant to be used by a person anyway. It was probably some law that you had to have them in the back seat.

Top down, they sped away, and everyone felt real cool with the hot summer wind swirling all around. Lisa poked her head between the two men and shouted into the less volatile air currents. She asked Demetrius about his tournament, what his rating was, who his teacher was.

"I've never been able to play against the queen pawn" he said. "I've tried everything, like a middle-aged man who's never been able to keep a relationship. I never say the right words. She's always looking at my bad skin and my bald head. Whole thing makes me tired. I never have any power, to finish." Both men laughed.

Lisa confidently announced, "Oh, King's Indian for sure. You can play it against the English and knight f3 too. First couple moves you don't even have to think. You just go ahead and build that death star."

Demetrius grinned. "Alright, alright, 'sac sac mate,' right?"

Lisa didn't know that Demetrius was quoting Fischer. But she loved the steaming vulgarity of that phrase's need to kill. And she screamed out to the quickly vanishing California farmland, "Oh, I'm definitely gonna get my sac on!" Lisa then rehearsed her own openings for Demetrius as if they were an elegant flowchart. She sounded professional, offering Tal's openings from 1960 as if they were her personal secrets.

After a time, the exhilarating breeze of the hot central valley at eighty-five miles per hour began to fray at the already tired chessplayers, and Demetrius pulled over to put the top up. The car now felt intimate, and Demetrius began confessing his woman troubles to the grandmaster. A pretense of their conversation seemed to be that Lisa was asleep in the back, not paying attention. But Lisa thought this was an adult sham, and that they were actually saying: *Please, Lisa, feel free to listen. We men always follow the same paths in these conversations. They are worn and familiar. It is maybe the closest we ever come to each other.*

Demetrius began his complaint by saying that he needed a girl-friend who played chess. At least one who understood something about chess. If she didn't, how would she understand and suffer his trips to places like Fresno? How would she know the pains and joys he suffered at the board? Igor didn't say much in reply. And Demetrius's hope for a chessplaying bride began to feel immodest after being spoken, as if that wish needed to put some clothes on: "I mean, I just want a woman who will tolerate my game, you know what I mean?"

Igor said, "Don't do it, man. Is disease, itch make worse."

Demetrius mentioned a woman way down in LA. She was 1800, he 1950. Together, they would study the classic games over their morning coffee. They would develop a whole vocabulary to talk about the game, with inside jokes that only they would understand. They would watch over each other's progress, and become incredibly strong. They would reach expert (2000), maybe even master (2200)! Then they would go on a tour together, travelling the world.

Igor laughed and said, "I think you wear chess goggles, yes?"

"You know her?"

"All Soviet player know. We share. We good communists."

"Well fuck, man. What am I supposed to do? Tell me what I'm supposed to do!"

"You must cut," Igor said.

Then, as if Igor were telling a secret dream that could only be spoken very softly, he said, "She sometime call to me. She in Eastern Europe, big chess culture. She say, 'Odysseus, come home. Tell me about your struggle.' But is fantasy, you understand? Lifetime take for cut."

Igor fell silent. And Demetrius began telling about his experiences dating black women; how they openly despised his chess, and actively worked against that part of his life.

Igor replied, "At least they honest. White American woman make underground system to stop the chess. Their anti-intellectualism always, how you say, 'passive-aggressive.' They never admit hatred to themselves."

Demetrius became thoughtful for a time, and then said, "The bitch of it is that black women hate chess because they associate it with white people."

"Such cruel misunderstanding," Igor said.

"They see a rich white man in a tailored suit. He holds his pinky finger out while he drinks his coffee from a little dainty cup."

"Ho!" Igor laughed. "Chessplayer poorest on planet!"

"Nah, man," Demetrius said. "It's deeper than that. They see the same whitey whose children their mother raised. Same whitey who cheated their grandfathers. Same whitey whose blood is inside their lighter-skinned cousins. He's always one move ahead, controlling everything—can't be beat."

"Such misdirected hatred."

"Amen, Igor, Amen."

"Women never understand us, Demetrius, sacrifices we make. We share this trouble, that why we brothers."

♟

At 3:20 A.M., Lisa wiggled out of the sports car into the soft Orinda night. She said her goodbyes to the two men and walked up a steep grassy lawn to a mansion that was not her own. But they didn't pull away. The black convertible continued to quietly hum on the curb and Lisa realized that Demetrius was doing that adult thing where they wait until you're inside the house. Her old house was two blocks away, with a foreclosed sign in front of it. There was no way she was going to admit this trouble to Igor and the world. If she ever told the truth everyone would make such a fuss, and they wouldn't let her spend this one last night in Orinda.

She rushed back down the slope to the car. "It's not dangerous here," she said. "I'll be fine."

Demetrius said, "Hey, Lisa, you're my friend, I just want to make sure you're safely inside."

"I always use the back door," Lisa lied. Then, after a pause in which Demetrius still didn't drive away, Lisa said, "Umm . . . see, it's just that I don't want Jan to see you here."

Insulted, the black man drove away with the Russian. Alone, Lisa looked up to the stern mountain she had climbed over on her bicycle. That bulge blocked the Pacific wind that rolled underneath the Golden Gate Bridge and bit into Berkeley and Oakland. The foothills to the east guarded against the wild heat of the Central Valley that Lisa had just experienced. She had been protected, in Orinda.

Lisa had often daydreamed about escaping out of her old window and climbing down the tree. In her mind, Lisa had practiced clambering down the branches of the great oak. She would be meeting her older friends; together they would do illegal things. She now laughed at herself and that memory. She never had any friends who broke things in the middle of the night. And she wouldn't have been able to climb back up the tree in the early morning; she had been too fat. Now she climbed like an orangutan. And she was right, they hadn't locked her old window.

All of her stuff was gone, all of Jan's stuff too. It seemed right that her domestic fantasies ended up looking like an empty warehouse. Lisa laid herself out on the bare wooden floor where her bed had been, and thought about her K-12 Northern California Girls Championship trophy. Four levels of marble elevated a golden queen all the way up to the height of her chin. That queen had hovered by Lisa's bed. Her rising brass spires replaced the slouching plush bear Jan had given Lisa as a child; and she had hummed the same prayer when Lisa closed her eyes as when she awoke to its loyal shine in the morning sun: *I am proof, Lisa, that you have a gift. When you study chess, and suffer, you are making sacrifices to me. I see your work, Lisa. And I will reward you. Together we will make a path.* That trophy had qualified Lisa to play in the Polgar Girls tournament, and had bestowed her summer study with an unambiguous vector. Lisa was now a pilgrim, and she would soon consult an oracle in Lubbock, Texas. That oracle would tell her if she belonged to the chess elite.

Jan said that there was no space for the trophy at their new apartment, and that the golden queen would have to go into storage. She had shoved her into a black plastic bag with a bunch of random stuff. Lisa saw the screws coming loose. Jan scratched the queen in her thoughtless haste, and Lisa saw the plastic underneath. Lisa imagined her golden queen suffering with other trophies in a shed. She would be pushed up against a tin sheet. Spiders would build their nests in her nooks and hollows.

But no. Jan had probably lied. She hadn't put the trophy into storage. She had thrown her trophy away, along with the rest of her lonely Orinda childhood.

LUBBOCK

Coming off the plane, Lisa thought she saw the word "chess" far down the terminal. She ran to it. All summer she had been like a metal detector, trying to find the game underneath what the Bay Area had thrown away. Now she read a glossy poster on a tripod: HERE AT TEXAS TECH WE PLAY CHESS! Behind the sign was a chess set whose pieces were the size of small children. Lisa jumped onto the oversized board where some non-chessplayers had assembled a nonsense position. She moved a bishop forcefully and shouted like Leo did at Turk and Market: "Check to the miserable king!" Lisa laughed heartily and began to right the pieces. "C'mon Igor," she called, "let's play a game." But Igor hadn't caught up to her.

Suddenly alone, Lisa remembered her night in Orinda. The life-sized queen was as big as the trophy Jan had put in the black plastic bag. Up close and large, the bishop really was unhappy; the knight's snarl was vicious. The pieces reproached Lisa: What are you doing on our board? You are like a little boy playing with ants when you move us. You think you are bigger, that you are in control. You interfere with our supply lines. You bring ants from a different nest to battle us.

"Wanna play?" A thin Indian girl with glasses timidly stepped onto a corner of the board. Lisa turned to her, surprised to find this quiet creature in her world. The young woman leaned her weight upon the bald head of a white pawn and introduced herself as Saheli.

Her dress had a modest elegance, with simple lines and cloth that looked handmade. "OK," Lisa said.

Saheli's father came up to the edge of the board and began to hover over his daughter's moves. He woggled his head as if he were speaking a language, conveying the muttering dissatisfaction he felt in his daughter's play. Then he scolded her, "तुम अपना घोड़ा बोर्ड के किनारे पर क्यों लेके जाते हो ? तुम्हे पता है ना की विशी कभी ऐसे नहीं खेलता."

More girls came up; they must have all been on the same connecting flight. They must also be playing in the Polgar tournament, each the best player from their state. Lisa found herself tumbling along with them, first through baggage claim and then onto the curb where they were loaded up into silvery vans. Lisa's vehicle soon became small in the darkness of many-laned highways circling the city. Distant neon signs flirted precut meat, of various slabs and sauciness. But Lisa didn't notice. She and Saheli exchanged ratings and specialized opening knowledge. They talked about specific positions, without a set. Saheli talked about the flaws in her game, and whom she feared the most. Lisa bragged, "Right now I'm ranked seventy-ninth of all the women in the country. But if you take away the Asian and Jewish last names I'm already number nine!"

Lisa discovered that Saheli was driven by pursuits that weren't chess. The fifteen-year-old from Georgia made sure to get an A in every class. Her father trained her for something called the Math Olympiad. And he was already taking her around the country to visit the top colleges and universities.

Lisa felt many emotions next to this striver. Her own deep remorse at having failed to achieve at school condemned Saheli: Why do you do what they tell you? Why wouldn't you give everything to chess? That's why your rating isn't as high as mine. But Lisa felt flattered that this accomplished young woman was a friend and peer. And she looked out to the other girls, seated across several tables at a restaurant called Ribs! They are the best, Lisa thought. And I am sitting with them.

Lisa didn't understand Saheli's math thing. But she got the impression from Saheli and her father that they thought math and chess were somehow bound together. Lisa wished Jan could see her chess as if it were math. If she did, maybe she would also bring her a special dish in a tiffin, like Saheli's father had for his daughter.

♟

Lisa's round-one opponent sat uncomfortably in the parched branches of a scraggly piñon tree's crown. She had scuttled her covered wagon with the intent of scrambling up this last sad bastion. The representative from South Carolina, rated 890, didn't know how to control her horses, how to use her reins. Far away from her lush homeland, Lisa stood in front of Ashley Rosedale's tree, not with a rusty ax, but with flamethrowers and missiles.

I hate you, Ashley, with your flouncy blond hair and fancy clothes. You haven't made the sacrifices. You don't even have enough chess culture to resign this position. You are an insult to chess. I'm going to push my pawns all the way into you and then turn them into knights. With five knights, I'm going to give you the Rodeo Mate.

♟

At the lunch buffet, Lisa saw two Asian girls giggle at the wiggliness of their food. Lisa quickly flensed a rectangular section of mac 'n' cheese and shouted, "Hey! Look at this." Lisa thudded her food down onto her plate. As she had hoped, the structure of her casserole wobbled like a tall building in an earthquake. Everyone saw Lisa's trick, and everyone laughed. Triumphant, Lisa repeated her marvel with a square of green jello whose fruit pieces floated like little bricks without enough comrades. Holding the two artistic achievements high, Lisa danced them back to her table of new friends.

The sugar and white carbs shot through the young throng, and the girls convulsed into silliness. They gave each other names; Lisa became *The Wrangler*, Saheli *Deep Blue*. They soiled and spilled upon the tablecloth. Dr. Pepper was snorted through nostrils. Eyelids were turned back to reveal the animal they all shared.

♟

The representative from Maryland, rated 1050, struggled with the strong waves of the Pacific Ocean. Lisa had a K-9 unit that wouldn't let her come ashore and the Alaskan current gripped her. But Tracy Zuo wouldn't resign, and Lisa patiently waited for her to die of hypothermia. Lisa was friendly to Tracy after the game, and her advice was startlingly simple: "Don't gimme your toys!" Lisa knew this phase of chess from her own experience. And she muted her own three-dimensional view of the game for Tracy. She knew that Tracy had to first appreciate the value of material objects, to know how to effectively manipulate them, before she could reevaluate the clinginess she felt toward them.

That evening, a pizza party was held at a place called the Main Event. Jan had brought Lisa to many playhouses like this one, to parties with other kids. Lisa remembered bearing the heavy bowling ball to the dumb black line and shrugging it off, like an unwanted child into life. "Gutterball!" the boys would always shout. *Fine*, Lisa would scowl to herself. *That's who I am then. I don't care about your stupid pins anyway.*

But that evening, at the Main Event, the girls loaded the air hockey puck with a wad of gum at the rim, hoping for an ecstatic spin. They gave stories to the pool balls, finding secret alliances among the anonymous spheres. They enchanted the bowling ball with a spell before pushing it down the lane with their socked feet. And they made fun of the boys who took their video games so seriously.

Cheese and bread burned into one another, and the black smell bit into the hairless nostrils of the young girls like nicotine. They shot high above themselves, eating more and more of the divine pizza. Too powerful to imagine sleep when they returned to the hotel lobby, they sent Igor and the other adults up to their rooms. *Go to your drowsy books and TV screens.* Once free, Lisa said, "Hey guys, let's get some Cokes!" Lisa wanted to subvert Igor, that domineering bastard. And she wanted a Coke.

The Asian girls for whom a Coke would have been a rebellion did not get one. Instead, they ate Sang Lee's dark chocolate. They said it was the good stuff.

"Hey Saheli, Let me buy you a Coke, c'mon." Lisa wanted her friends to share in the terrible guilt and accusation Igor had put upon her. She could agree to exercise. She felt that in her body. She could feel her body being molded, and punished into a better form. But it was obvious that Igor was being a jerk about the Cokes and food. I mean, it's just a Coke, right? And she wanted to get lit with her friends, sharing this truth.

Saheli politely said no. But Lisa kept pressing. "It's not pure," Saheli finally said. Lisa and the four North Asian girls found this both fascinating and silly, while the two other Indian girls, Eesha and Bodda, woggled their heads. "What's that thing you guys do with your head?" the North Asian girls and Lisa asked. The Indian girls told their new friends about the head woggle. Lisa asked many questions about their Brahmin ways. She wanted to be pure, and belong to an intellectual people who distanced themselves from the muddle of the everyday world.

Lisa said, "It's like you guys have a tradition. I don't have one. That's why Igor is giving me the Russian tradition." The girls became silent.

Bodda asked, "Is he like a master of something? All the coaches ask him questions, as if he has some kind of power."

Lisa said that Igor was the strongest player ever. And that he was teaching her his secrets. The girls all wanted to know more about her teacher, and gathered around her. But Lisa was shy, and said that she couldn't tell them the whole truth at one time; she wasn't strong enough yet. She had to tell them in pieces.

Trying to impress, Lisa told them how Igor could play blindfold, without a set, and that he was helping her carve her own inner board. She told them about Tal and the mysticism of Dionysus. Lisa felt like somebody, with the undivided attention of her gifted friends.

But Lisa wanted more. She wanted to be their equal. She said, "Igor taught me how the central squares are heavier, and how the wavelengths of chess bend around them, the way light from a distant galaxy bends around the sun. It's mathematical."

"Wow," Sang Lee said. "Like the field equations? Mass tells space/time how to curve and curved space/time tells mass how to move?"

"Precisely so," Lisa answered. Desperately hoping her shameful ignorance would not be discovered, Lisa began telling her new friends about her deepest and most vulnerable experience. She said that she felt the pieces as parts of her soul. And that she talked to them.

Saheli, usually quiet, became excited: "Chaturanga!" she shouted. Everyone stared at her in disbelief as she got down on the floor and did something like a pushup. "It means the four supports in Sanskrit, you know, Old-Indian."

But the girls, led by Lisa, said, "Umm, no, that's a pushup."

Saheli responded, "No, no, it's not a pushup. It's a position of the yoga where you feel your four limbs and their stretch through the body. You feel and strengthen yourself." Her audience didn't understand what she was trying to say. "Chaturanga is the original name for chess," she continued, "named after the four supports of the army: infantry, cavalry, elephants and chariots."

The group shouted, "But there are no elephants in chess!"

"But there are," Saheli said. "The infantry became the pawns, the cavalry the knights, the elephants the bishops, and the chariots the rooks."

"What about the queen, she's the most powerful piece!" the group shouted.

"But the queen was not the queen, she was the raja's adviser. And the adviser could only move one square." After a silence, Saheli continued quietly, "Your teacher is very wise, Lisa, he knows the secrets of the ancient Indian tradition; he knows that chaturanga is yoga for the soul. Yoga isn't just about improving your body, and chess is not just an exercise for your brain."

"That's so Hogwarts!" Michelle Quan said. "And so long ago, maybe like two hundred years."

"More like two thousand!" Saheli answered. "And now chaturanga has come back to India, and Anand is World Champion."

"Hogwarts is a school," Lisa said. "And school sucks. Chess is much deeper and more beautiful than school."

Lisa felt she had said too much, and blushed. Now she was the outsider, sitting next to the strivers.

Saheli looked into Lisa's eyes and quietly said: "School can be pretty dumb. Right? I mean it doesn't really seem like the teachers are interested in what they're teaching. It's always about some test. Most of the other kids are hopeless. And the boys are always so dumb."

After a pause, Lisa asked: "So why do you do it then?"

"It's only for a little while," Saheli said. The other girls nodded. "Then we'll go to the best colleges in the world. 'Til then we'll prove ourselves at the Math Olympiad, on the violin, in the spelling bee and at chess."

Lisa was overwhelmed, and she shouted, "You play the violin too?!"

"Not so well, but Christine wins all the competitions."

Lisa looked over to Christine Chen—she had been sitting right beside her the entire time, peering quietly. "That's Hogwarts!" Lisa sighed. She had wanted to pull up her long sleeves, so sticky and wet in the warm Texas night, and show her new friends the scars on her arms. But she kept them covered, kind of like how Jeffrey hid his war tattoos. She wanted to tell them that she sucked at school. But she admired them so much that she couldn't. And she resolved to try again, at her new school, starting next week.

♟

The alarm clock between her bed and Igor's said 2:25 A.M. It was the middle of the night, and there was no way she could get enough rest for the critical games the next day.

He was still awake. Lisa could tell; when he slept the thick hairs that dangled from his nose like ropes made his breath sound like an air purification system. "Igor," Lisa whispered. "I fucked up again. I never do the right thing. It's so late . . ."

Igor cut her off and said, "I hope you make nice time with new friends, Lisa." Lisa needed that. To her, if felt like she had yet to rise far enough in the theocratic hierarchy to have a papal line of communication with chess. Igor had to absolve her, because somewhere in a black garbage bag, a queen on top of a trophy was accusing Lisa of sinning against her. That austere bitch was saying

128

that Lisa had failed, by not getting enough sleep, by not properly respecting her.

♟

Lisa faced Christine Chen in round three the next morning. At 1600, she was stronger than Lisa's first two opponents. Chen employed a turtle-like defensive structure which Lisa had to carefully turn over by hopping around the vulnerable spots like a fox, forcing Christine to switch her center of gravity, all the while taking care that a vicious counterbite didn't grab a paw. And Lisa eventually did turn Christine. She showed patience.

Winning, Lisa felt her chess as a thousand cords of threaded rebar, binding upper decks of freely flowing tactical fancy and speculation to an unshakable deep earth of positional understanding. Lisa had ripped out her inner muddle of hatred and estrangement; in its place she now beheld a transparent orb of vision and power. She had overcome herself and realized the fantasy that her journal had failed: she could understand the interrelationships around her, and guide them into an ideal vision of herself. The other girls could be clever. But they had never suffered enough to excavate their own view. They followed the expectations of others.

♟

By winning three games in a row, the pairing for round four was unavoidable. Lisa would have to play the number one seed, Zarra Mikhalevskaya. Igor said that the chess world is small, and that he was good friends with Zarra's grandfather, Big Mikh. He said that Lisa would one day have a chance to stay with a Brooklyn family like Zarra's—to taste the dark Russian bread that doesn't know it is poor, to sleep on Zarra's rollaway bed in the makeshift living room; to witness a family for whom chess and literature are not foreign

pursuits which require tournaments and schools to give them
direction and a measure of success.

Lisa's chess felt transparent to Zarra's thought from the very
first moves. Because the intentions of her pieces were so trivial, so
small, Zarra could see through her. Lisa could predict none of
Zarra's moves. After each one, staring at it, Lisa had the sensation
of an otherworldly grasping that crowded her pieces. But she could
never see or understand how Zarra moved through her. *But I've done
nothing wrong!* Lisa complained, as if to Igor. She recalled Zarra's
lineage: Her grandfather, Big Mikh, had learned the Soviet tradition
in Belarus before moving to Israel. And she heard Igor say, "Zarra
know this tournament not real chess. She study with father and
grandfather."

Two and a half hours into the game, Lisa's face involuntarily
met Igor's. He was at a distance where he could see Lisa's face, but
not the board, as if he didn't want to get too close to her execution.
Lisa was held underneath a thick and muddy water. Her head
slammed against unknown slabs, and her intestines were cut open
by unseen metallic poles. And even when she occasionally did
come to the surface of the water, desperately groping for something to hold on to, she could not see that it was the debris of her
own fallen rebar structure that she was impaling herself against.

Like an old domesticated pet who hides under the stairs to
experience the lonely bestiality of death, Lisa stumbled away from
the board in solitude. She didn't want to talk to Igor. She didn't
want to talk to anybody.

♟

Igor encouraged Lisa to seek out the midnight social gathering that
takes place on the final night of every chess tournament. There she
might be find comfort in some blitz chess and have a few laughs.

Igor said that it is in such meetings that Russian chess talents are initiated into the superhuman drinking rituals of their elders. "Is like night before battle," he said. "Time for say truth. Tell friend you love him." But Lisa's bedside queen would not allow it. She pointed out, correctly, that if Lisa did well the next day she might still earn a prize. And so she must sleep.

But Lisa couldn't sleep. Igor put away the board and turned out the lights, but the moves continued in her mind. Positions from her game against Zarra grabbed her and demanded to be played out. She whispered "damn" and "fuck." She twisted in the sheets, tossing the blanket on and off her. She went in the bathroom and mindlessly flipped the light switch. She forced all of this noisy despair onto her coach, as if he could do something about it, as if he was responsible.

Then she remembered what Igor had said about the cold water in the bay. "It reboot, like computer." Lisa got underneath the shower and she begged its coldest waters to numb her mind, to make her forget. Then she put on her headphones and listened to "RV 424; II Largo." Ofra Harnoy's cello called forth the boxwood pieces: "Speak!" But Ofra couldn't do it. Asa's blue lake was false. Like the sandaled student at the music school, Lisa felt the constant of death appear in her equations. It had always been there. All paths led to it. And there was no consolation for this sorrow.

♟

The alarm clock sounded and Lisa saw Igor examining the games of her next opponent, Sang Lee, in the half light of a curtained morning. He said it was his obligation to drag Lisa down to the breakfast buffet. Stoned, Lisa stared into the depths of the loud TV man as her sugarpuffs resignedly disassembled themselves and sought each other's company in a silty pile at the bottom of her bowl. Lisa wasn't able to understand what the TV man was saying—she only knew that he was angry. She couldn't play. It wasn't simply that she had lost her physical and emotional reserves in a night of torment. She had yet to medicate her loss.

Igor dragged Lisa away from the unhelpful breakfast buffet. Lisa thought he was going to give her some kind of heavy speech about being a fighter and all, and before he even said anything she took the very firm stance that she would not play. She would drop out of the tournament. She would not play.

Igor listened to her, then said, "I understand play not possible. Listen for truth: next opponent, Sang Lee, always play same opening move. Now, you have white pieces, and only have for make couple moves. I show. Move fifteen you stand little better. Ruth also like this position. She send us email. Sang feel like hunted lion. Running away, she will not see that hunter not ready for blood. That when you offer draw. If she not accept, then you can resign."

Lisa was so surprised that Igor wasn't going to make her be a fighter that she overlooked how he was teaching her to draw, to compromise, like he had done in his final round in Lubbock. But right then, fifteen thoughtless moves didn't seem like all that much to Lisa. She would make them for Igor, and for Ruth.

Round five happened as Igor foresaw. His robotic ritual was accomplished. She now had a full six hours to rest before round six. Lisa slept. And she won round six; but not with the free and breezy confidence of some shining orb. Lisa only had the sad determination that gets out of bed and follows the worn paths of existence.

Sang also won her final round, and so she and Lisa shared second and third place, behind Zarra. The adults applauded her and gave her another trophy. Some of the girls chanted, "Wrangler! Wrangler!" But she felt dirty. This draw thing that Igor had done to her, it was a degrading pantomime of her deepest spiritual experience. Her hands had then moved mechanically over her final-round opponent. She cut her and watched her bleed. She was becoming a butcher, like Igor had, staring into her opponent's inner life with cold eyes, detaching it from its intentions. And, for the first time, she had a sense of what vodka might be about.

EMERY HIGH

The flimsy orange flap of the children's chair cried out as Igor settled into it. His massive legs twined into a yogic ball underneath the chaturanga of its four silvery legs. Relentless silence arose as he straightened his back and gripped Lisa with his chess eyes.

There was no board between them. Lisa stared down, into the cartoon characters that ran through the soiled carpet of the Berkeley Public Library's children's room. Igor had said that you have to do something wrong before your opponent can punish you. She didn't know what she had done to bring the hardship of the last two weeks upon herself. But she knew that she had to close down her summer's hopes, like empty churches in a city that has lost its religion.

Jan said it was only right that she, Lisa and Ted wound up in Emeryville, trapped between Berkeley, Oakland and the shore of the Bay. She told Lisa that an ancient Indian civilization had once lived there. She said that the tribe would keep the remains of everything that had given them life. What they had eaten, what passed through them, the bodies of their pets and loved ones—all of this they piled in a heap. And they worshipped this heap, for it contained their past and was the fertilizer of their future.

By the time the white people came, the heap was immeasurably long and reached sixty feet high in some places. The white people named it a shellmound, because—since shells don't compost easily—that's what they saw the most of. Then the white people got rid of the mound and its people. Japanese workers came in big ships.

Warehouses and factories arose. Asphalt squished everything underneath its coarse pavement. Black workers filled the empty space left by the Japanese who had to go to jail during some war. A few cherry trees remember. Then the condominiums went up, where Lisa now lived. In the last fifteen years, several big stores like IKEA had moved in, on top of the shellmound. That was the store Jan blamed for putting her out of business.

Lisa's new room was a narrow rectangle that was originally intended as a closet. There was only space for a cot. Lisa's new trophy from the Polgar tournament had to be put into a black plastic bag, then "storage," along with her trophy from the Northern California Girls Championship.

Jan said she didn't have the energy to shop and cook, so Lisa was allowed to eat Ted's takeout food. For lunch, Lisa bit into the white meat of the breaded spicy chicken. For dinner, her teeth slid through the soft vesicles of his fried pork dumplings. She ate more and more, following Ted out into the wild oblivion of his culinary adventure. Breakfast was always the same: Golden Grahams with some raspberry jam from Trader Joe's.

Scabbery came to Lisa's face. Bacteria gnawed on her, just beneath the surface. As they multiplied they created an overwhelming pressure. And they would gratify Lisa with a wonderfully messy explosion on the mirror of the little bathroom that she shared with Jan and Ted. They helped distract Lisa from her main regret, that she was again failing school. She had not wanted to. She wanted to be like her new friends, Saheli, Christine Chen and Sang Lee. Those girls didn't have the overflowing flab that again came to her belly and made her drowsy.

Like when Lisa assumed that Igor knew all the subtleties of a game she had just played, she now assumed that the serene master who sat before her could see through the misery of her last two weeks. They had not studied in that time. It was a Russian thing.

Allow the bruises from the tournament time to heal. Let the exhausted nerves become sensitive again. Give the muscles space to grow back bigger and stronger.

Underneath Igor's chess eyes, Lisa felt compelled to come to what she saw as the most prominent feature of the position, what her coach often called the "first question," and said, "The kids at my new school call me a closet Asian. They all think I'm supposed to be some kinda math whiz or somethin'. But I'm already failing that class. Mr. Reese gets up at the chalkboard and shows us some monkey task, and then he says we gotta do his stupid problems; the same thing over and over. He cuts points from you if you start talking, and tells us we won't graduate if we don't do his problems. If we don't graduate we won't get a job. If we don't get a job we'll be homeless."

Lisa looked up into her teacher's silence. This was a man who had slept outside, on the street. The weakies said that people had spit on him, and that he had eaten other people's leftovers. He could laugh at Mr. Reese's cruel threat of homelessness.

When she was with Igor everything seemed so clear. She didn't have to tell him how cheap her life had become after the bankruptcy, or how she had snuck back into her old house for one final night— none of that mattered. Wealth. When she was with Igor it was so obvious: it didn't matter how much money you had or what your clothes looked like; wealth was the beauty you found and created—in every instant of your short life.

Igor leaned into Lisa's face. Slowly and clearly he whispered that he had seen the calculus arise within Book X of Euclid's *Elements*. He had witnessed the elegance of Kepler's third law. He had felt the power of the theoretical prediction of the bend in space/time before it had been measured. And now he saw a deforming wound beginning to bind Lisa, like a young sapling whose trunk will continue to display its early misdirection hundreds of years later.

"Lisa, we go outside," Igor said. "I wish for call my friend Arun. He big mathemathiker. Also chessplayer, big talent as child. For truth, I wish long time for call. I need him for tell the beauty of the mathematíque."

Outside, Lisa shouted, "Igor, you don't understand! I don't need beauty. I need Mr. Reese to give me an A. It's like a chess rating. It's the only way I can come to Saheli's level."

But Igor wasn't really listening to her. He was on the phone arranging their meeting. And he again took Lisa on a march. But this time, when they reached the entrance to the UC Berkeley campus, Lisa firmly refused. The old stone buildings covered in vines, the dark redwood groves—to all of that Jan had sacrificed 35,000 dollars a year. That's how much her old school, Mens Conscia Recti, had cost. Ted let Lisa know that little fact after the bankruptcy; Lisa was also to blame for their disaster. She had never done what the teachers at Mens had told her. And now she had completely failed Jan's hopes. To the university's upward sloping lawn that reminded Lisa of the mansion that wasn't hers, Lisa balled her fist and yelled, "Fuck you!"

As if she were a disobedient child, Igor grabbed her wrist and yanked her over the threshold. He said the mathematician was expecting them. The Russian ogre forced her to raise her eyes when they arrived at the math building. Everyone had dark skin, like Saheli, Christine and Sang—except they were all men. With smooth discipline they flowed in and out of the immense square block.

Cables, tubes and wires followed the warren-like corridors of Arun's building. Black grime glued scattered scabs of linoleum to the concrete floor. Igor found Arun at the end of an unlit hallway. His office was a cold rectangle, like the closet Lisa now lived in. A slight but fit Chinese man sat at the end of the room. He and Arun looked like inmates of a low-security prison cell. But they were not inmates, they were colleagues. Igor said that thousands of mathematicians across the world were industriously fighting for a desk in this very room.

Everyone told Lisa that she couldn't play chess for a living because you couldn't make any money with it. The men at the tournaments said she should study math. They said she was good at it, because she was a chessplayer. They made her imagine the warm air of the South Bay. There was a swimming pool and iced tea. Life was easy and everyone was happy. But these mathematicians didn't look rich.

Igor and Lisa walked with Arun, out into the dry fade of Berkeley fall. Arun remembered every move of every game that he had played with Igor. At various small tournaments across Indiana, where Arun had grown up, Igor crushed Arun twenty-three times. There were drop kicks, head butts, strangle holds and something to do with a crane.

But Igor couldn't remember any of those battles. He interrupted Arun's autistic recollection. And, like a foreign monk who travels to a distant abbey and asks to see their most beautiful illuminated manuscript, Igor asked Arun for mathematical beauty.

But Arun didn't understand Igor's question. "What do you mean by beauty?" he said.

Igor started poking around Arun's math. Big mistake. Like a million kernels of grain suddenly tumbling out of a silo, Igor and Lisa were quickly covered over by a subfield of number theory. In the same way Lisa assumed Igor knew her games, Arun assumed that Igor and Lisa knew his subject. But they were drowning after only a few sentences.

A sad silence followed. Igor knew some math, he was probably even a 2100, but he couldn't understand whatever special math Arun was talking about. Lisa tried to imagine Arun beholding an incredibly delicate flower. He and a number of men around the world had crafted its precise leaves, pistil and stem. Only they understood its secrets. Only they could see it. They would push deeper into that flower's truths, and then maybe create a new one.

Arun was like the crazy lady on the train platform, waiting for someone to recognize her special language and the deeper truth it pointed to. *At least in chess*, Lisa thought, *we have a common language. Everyone can play—after you're initiated.*

Lisa hadn't thought about crazy people all summer. She saw them all the time, at Turk and Market, in the halls of her new school, and there were always one or two of them at the weekend tournaments she went to. But she had stopped thinking about them. She didn't really even hear them anymore. But in listening to Arun, Lisa suddenly saw what chess was to Jan: inarticulate crazy talk. To her, Lisa was the wild woman on the train platform.

Channeling Jan's view of math, Lisa said, "So I guess you're real good at solving problems, calculating." Were Arun a real native Brahmin like Saheli, he could have done the head woggle, instead of just being awkward and silent. But he had been born in the States, like Lisa. She continued, "You know, doing math in your head, building bridges."

Arun laughed. "I've never built any bridges. That would most certainly be a bad idea, and calculating stuff, well, that's not real math, at least that's what my dad would say."

"What's real math then?" Lisa asked.

"Well," Arun said, "you try to prove new things, like I'm trying to count the number of permutations of integers which are inherently sequence-free."

Lisa's mind desperately tried to climb up onto the strange words, but she slid right back down. Saheli would know where the footholds were. They were probably written in Old Indian. "What is that good for?" she complained. "How can you use that?"

"You can't, at least not usually," Arun said.

Lisa flogged Arun with her math anxiety. "Well, why do we have to learn it then, what's the point?"

Arun answered Lisa calmly. "You don't have to learn it. I've never used math in my daily life, not any kind of advanced math anyway. I guess we do it for the same reasons we play chess. There's just something about it, I don't know. And maybe it is a little like a conspiracy that people have to take it in school, when they don't really need it. Mathematicians like me have always wanted to just do math, the way you want to play chess. So we convinced universities and rich people, a long long time ago, that kids needed to learn math in order to think logically. That might be a lie, I don't know, but we needed teaching jobs. And then people started being able to use some of the math we did in the sciences. And, well, we've had some jobs ever since. But they don't really like us, or understand what we do. They always want us to do something useful. But we just want to do math."

Arun had a lazy eye which seemed to wander far away from Igor and Lisa, lost in its own investigation. Igor remained disappointed, upset that his solemn question had not found an earnest answer. For her coach, Lisa demanded, "Listen, Arun, we need to know why math is beautiful. How is it like chess?"

Arun's body crumpled a little under the question. It was too abstract. But the man sank into himself and sought something to offer his friends. In that silence, Lisa felt Arun's generous spirit trying to lift her up out of the shortsighted selfishness of her entrenched battlefield.

"In math and chess we study interrelationships," Arun finally said. "We find truths. The rest of the world asks us for our truths; they want their everyday lives to have mathematical precision. But we can't put our world into their language. That's why your question is so hard." Arun paused for a time, then said, "Let's look for beauty in an example. What are you studying at school?"

All the time, all anyone ever wanted to know about was her damn math class, as if that's who she was. Some people, like Igor and Saheli, encouraged her to believe that something as beautiful as chess could somehow be found there. Others, like Jan and Mr. Reese, wanted her to pass through it and somehow find money, respectability and adulthood on the other side. Ashamed of her failure, Lisa whispered, "Do you know the ninety-degree triangle theorem?"

Arun said, "No, what's that?"

Lisa persecuted the man's ignorance: "How can you not know that? I thought you were a professor?"

Arun's face was calm and blank. He said, "No, really, I don't know it. What is it?"

Lisa pulled her math textbook out of her backpack. She had tried to study it several times in the last two weeks. There was no desk in her new room, so she would lie in bed with it. There, the problems would demean her. They stood in long lists, like the unexplained expectations Jan had, both infinite and catalogued. The book made Lisa sleepy. But she always kept it with her. The extra weight in her backpack made her remember who she wanted to be.

Arun looked upon the page Lisa took them to and read: "The ninety-degree triangle theorem. Find the unknown quantity." There was a picture of a mustachioed smiling triangle whose ruler pointed to a whole page of problems like $16+9=c^2$.

"I guess I usually thought of that as the Pythagorean Theorem," he said.

"Whatever," Lisa shrugged. She felt the eyes of the two men on her and her inadequacy. She thought both men were wondering why she couldn't do math. "C'mon Lisa, you're a chessplayer," they seemed to say. "This should be easy for you." *That's what they told Jeffrey*, Lisa remembered.

Arun asked: "Do you know why the theorem is true?"

"Look," Lisa said. "It doesn't matter if I prove the thing or not, OK? I just have to get all the answers right."

Arun closed his eyes, and in that silence Lisa's mathematical failures briefly left her. The shaded undergrowth of the Redwood grove they were in had a thick smell of grubs and slow decay. From out in the open fields, where the Pacific wind scraped all the old air away, Lisa could hear the yelps of smart boys playing ultimate Frisbee.

"Let me show you," Arun calmly said. He was ready to celebrate the rebirth of an ancient companion who was always the same, like an old friend who never changes his clothes. But Lisa wasn't. She knew she would never get it.

"Let's begin by drawing a right triangle on a piece of paper," he said. "Make it any way you like." Lisa again complained that this wasn't what the teacher wanted. It wouldn't help her pass the test. And she tried to make the whole situation impossible by creating the following oblong thing:

Arun continued: "Good, now we'll call the bottom line the rank, the side the file, and the diagonal the bishop. Now,  let's build a square out of each of those lines." Arun got down on his knees with the little black ants and began tearing out notebook paper. Everything was inexact. "You make the square out of the bishop's line, and I'll make the squares for the rank and the file." Three squares soon stood in front of them; smudged thumbprints and incautious tears did not seem to promise truth.

Lisa attacked the dubious edifice: "What do these hokey squares have to do with the problems I'm supposed to do? These are squares. My problems have numbers."

Arun calmly replied, "Well, when we say a number is squared this is what we're talking about."

Lisa didn't like this thought much at all. Where were the numbers? They hadn't talked about math this way at her school, and the distance

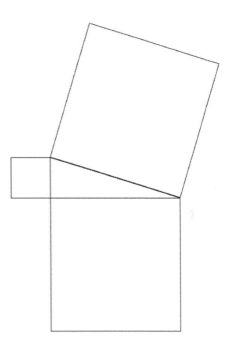

between the crude shapes before them and $9+16=25$ seemed tremendous.

Arun continued, "We want to say that if we add the area of the file square to the rank square we will get the bishop's square. So, let's begin by looking at what the equation would look like in our case." Arun then took the squares and rearranged them like this:

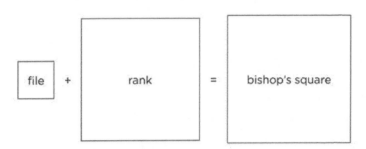

"That's so ridiculous," Lisa said. "How are you going to smoosh that little square into the bigger one?"

"Well, let's try." Arun said. "First, let's create a square whose sides are all the length of the bishop diagonal, sometimes called the hypotenuse. We'll need three new triangles the same size as our first one. Lisa and Arun made these triangles and then Arun arranged them like this on top of the matted pine needles:

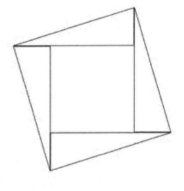

"So, Lisa," he said. "This has to be the same square we built out of the bishop's diagonal, right?"

Lisa stared at it for a moment, trying to not be deceived. But there it was; all four sides were the length of the bishop diagonal. Lisa thought it a neat trick that she could overlay their bishop square they had made on top of this one, but she was still certain that

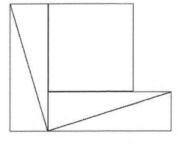

the little file square could not be squished into the rank square. Arun then began rearranging the triangles around the new square, the inside square, that they had outlined on the ground:

"Now, let's see if we can find the rank and file squares in this shape. If they are in there then they are equal to the square we built out of the bishop's diagonal. Which is what we wanted to prove, right?" "Right." Lisa answered. She stared triumphantly at the construction. It was clearly not going to work.

Then Arun overlaid the two squares they had created from the sides of the triangle, named the rank and the file squares. It was amazing. But Lisa didn't want to admit it. "These shapes aren't exact." Lisa cried. "There's no way they could ever be."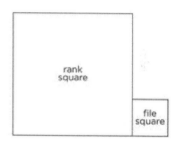

"Good, Lisa," Arun said. "You are right. The theorem is only correct for the perfect shapes in your head. Out here they can never be true."

♟

Lisa arrived at her next lesson at the Berkeley Public Library armed with a speech: "When all the information was gathered," she slowly recited, "it became clear that black's moves were good, but his position was bad. It was quite obvious that to obtain counterplay, it was necessary to play more actively."

"You speak like Tal?" Igor asked. "Note to move five of game ten?"

"Right. So look, I have a favor to ask. I want you to give me some more chess problems. I'm gonna find a seat in the back of my classes and do those while I pretend to be doing whatever it is they want me to do."

"Look, Lisa, I understand. America no intellectual culture have. This Mr. Reese, he weak mathematiker, rating maybe only eleven hundred, but . . ."

Lisa cut her teacher off. She spoke with so much force that she spat, like Igor did when he explained something fundamental about a position, and like the way she imagined he had once yelled, "First big drink, then big fuck!" with Jeffrey Phillips. "They only teach you how to play with the knobs, Igor! They never show you how the machine actually works!"

"But Lisa, what about triangles and religion of Arun's fathers? Maybe shit now, in class with player rated six hundred. But you improve, later come to higher level."

"I'm done with later," Lisa said. "The main thing they want is attendance. They want you to show up and be quiet; that's how they make their money. I'm gonna dress up like a bag lady, you know, real floppy clothes. I will become invisible. No one will bother me."

Igor looked down at his helpless overlarge hands. Math, music, chess—they were the wonder he had known in the world.

"Listen, Igor," Lisa said. "Don't be like my mom. She expects me to go to that place. But she doesn't know. She's never been there."

♟

Igor came to Lisa's school the next morning. He must have walked through the double doors, past the fat lady behind the thick pane of glass at reception. He had survived her slow eyes. No one asked the tall and lean man with the aristocratic posture what he was doing there. For Lisa, Igor had purchased slacks and a button-down shirt from Goodwill. He looked like a supreme bureaucrat from Sacramento, come for a surprise inspection.

LISA

In the halls and in the yard, Igor had seen the races self-segregate into herds: blacks, Hispanics, southeast Asians, whites. They shouted "nigger," "whitey," and "spic" at themselves. Igor had seen the pants drawn low over the naked ass cracks of overweight American children.

On a school map, Igor found Mr. Reese's classroom. From the hallway door, he watched Lisa's class. He saw the teacher's jeans, tattoos and piercings. He saw the mustachioed triangle struggle to marshal the class. He saw Reese dock points from misbehaving students, documenting their names and their point loss on the blackboard. But he didn't see Lisa.

Lisa imagined Igor meeting Janelle outside; she was late. Tight denim lollipopped her tits. High heels sprang her ass. Igor asked her, "Uh, Excuse. Is Lisa in this class?" Janelle's look insulted Lisa's teacher: *Who are you to say anything to me, old fool? Do you have any power here?* Then she said: "Lil' white fatty?" Igor assumed that's who Lisa must be, and he nodded. "Oh, that girl couldn't keep her trap shut. Reese sent her on down to Project Darkness." Igor wanted to ask her more, where Project Darkness was, but Janelle slipped through the door to the hooting satisfaction of her peers. Mr. Reese docked her 70 points. But she had also stopped caring.

Igor couldn't find Project Darkness on the school map, so he went back to the glass wall he had passed near the main entrance. "Uh, excuse," Igor asked the secretary. "I look for Lisa Schmied in Project Darkness."

Sitting behind her bulletproof glass wall, the lady with the slow eyes said, "There is no Project Darkness here, sir. But we do have a Project Light. Are you her parent or guardian?" Igor supposed he was. And he even got a visitor's pass to prove it.

Igor came to find Lisa in Project Light, a square cement block which the school map knew as Building I. He stood in the entrance while he waited for his eyes to adjust to the scant murmur of light.

Black craft paper covered the windows and cut the sun's broad spectrum to reveal the floating world that you can only see in murky half light. The other adults always called the levitating dancers that filled the room "dust." But Igor knew from his days of desperate alcoholism that yeast is everywhere. Thousands of spores were landing in his mouth and nostrils with their spades, eagerly digging for death. The misty cloudburst of a kid's sneeze didn't just fall to the ground. A diverse multitude of viruses would ride the moist particulate. Airborne bacterial colonies were hungry. If they did not eat soon, they would die. To retrieve Lisa, Igor had come to this hole—so incongruent, and hateful, to the clean mathematical architecture of his mind.

"Can I help you, sir?" A tiny voice spoke from behind Igor's thigh. Igor had not seen the woman in the darkness. But she was right beside him, guarding the door. Lisa's gray hoodie was slowly emerging from the darkness. There were about a dozen kids with her. Most were practicing the same pose as Lisa: Hands in pockets, the body crumples over to find a forehead post on the laminate particle board in front of it. The main difficulty is keeping the pose as still as possible, relaxing into it. The contact point of skin and laminate will become moist, and this creates a balance problem which can slide the head out from its peaceful slumber. From the mouths of Lisa's most experienced comrades hung the delicious drool which proved that they really could sleep through it all.

In his best English Igor said, "I need to speak to Lisa for couple minute. Outside. Is important." Lisa awoke to Igor's voice and proudly wiped the viscous stream of spittle onto her cotton forearm. Leaving class with Igor promised freedom, and she shouted, "Later, bitches!" to those who had to stay behind as she marched into the September sunshine with Igor.

Outside, Igor solemnly said: "Is big shit. You have right."

Finally, the adult world saw the injustice she faced. They would now set her free.

Igor continued, "For this purpose, I give you problems, Lisa. You obvious dissident. You can't, how you say, keep trap shut? Like Siberia here, Project Cold." Igor gave Lisa a hard stare, as if he were wearing a heavy coat in a gulag prison yard, come to share a bit of precious and stolen cheese rind with his best friend. "We work from Armenian grandmaster Kasparyan's book *Domination in 2545 Endgame Study*. Is favorite. Written for truth in Russian, but chess universal language."

Igor smiled at Lisa. "Not make sense to give book. They take away. I make photocopy, but not bind. Pages small enough for put inside whatever book they wish you for look." With his hairy hand, Igor pointed back at Project Darkness. "We then look solutions before each lesson."

Lisa shouted: "Whaddaya mean? YOU'RE SENDING ME BACK IN THERE??"

Her mentor looked up. His eyes passed beyond the chain-link fence that surrounded her new school, over the high clocktower of the Berkeley campus, and out to the mountain Lisa had climbed on her bike. "Not so easy for leave, Lisa."

"Whaddaya mean? You got the pass. Let's get out of here!"

Igor paused, and then said very quietly: "I had friend, was famous grandmaster, was student of Tal. Russians also put him in prison as young soul. He not wish for speak much about it. But sometime he say: Test of man is for be free in mind, wherever he is."

Lisa could not befriend this Eastern European vision of imprisoned freedom. Like Tal had said: She had done nothing wrong, she didn't deserve to be where she was, and she needed some fucking counterplay.

Igor continued: "Many time, we talk to pieces. I teach you how. It is a pleasure. These problems I give are for another. They know only mathematical labyrinthos underneath position. Must open mind. Be prepared to go deep. Sometime more than thirty move. But length not hard part. For truth, you will be numb with new way pieces wish for move. You will be blind, tapping in their emptiness. You sit hour, day, sometime week. Go aggressive into dark tunnel. Eventual you feel rope in dirt. Follow him."

CHALKIDIKI

With her good news, Lisa sprang up the wide granite steps of the Berkeley Public Library's tall staircase chamber. Noisy and potent, her footsteps slapped the quarried stone. She burst out of the noble stairwell onto the third floor, the children's floor, where Igor waited with his ornate wooden set.

"I had to *sign* for *this* LETTER!" Lisa shouted. Her teacher took the stack of official documents into his oversized hands and read: "The United States Chess Federation would like to congratulate you on being selected to play for the United States Chess Delegation to the World Youth Championships in Chalkidiki, Greece this December." And: "Your November rating of 1923 is the highest in the country for girls aged 12–14." Igor skimmed down the page, and then read so loudly that everyone on their floor could hear, "All travel expenses will be covered!"

Lisa shouted: "I can't believe I was chosen for the US Chess Team!"

"Ho-ho-ho!" Igor laughed. "You not chosen. No committee make for big sit and say: 'We like way Lisa look. We give her spot.' Not way it was. You make own way in the chess."

Lisa smiled and said, "Well, with your help."

Igor answered, "Maybe that why committee choose Igor for be coach on American team! Ha, I come too, Lisa!"

Her mentor beheld her, in the same intimate and thoughtful way she remembered him regarding Jeffrey Phillips in Fresno. Igor would take her away. The letter plainly stated that there was a higher order that she belonged to, and that her school must release her.

"Lisa!" Igor shouted. "I show you now big Russian tradition. We make Chess Dance. For celebratzk." Igor sat back on his heels into an imaginary chair. He clasped his arms in front of his torso to make a table. Then he started kicking his legs out, faster and faster. He shouted salutations in Russian. The librarian told him to be quiet. But he wouldn't, not until his dance was over. All the while he grinned, like a mischievous boy and a wild drunk.

Lisa thought she understood why it was Igor's chess dance. The pain of a thousand lunges would be embraced until it liberated him. He needed to smile through the torture he inflicted on himself. But Lisa disapproved. It wasn't personal enough, he was following some kind of Russian dance. It wasn't his. And she thought the gay frivolity of Igor's broad smile inconsonant with the prayer she hoped her chess dance would be.

Lisa began her dance with a reserved face, thoughtful. As if that expression held too much weight, her body folded in on itself and she collapsed into an unstructured ball, limp. She then unfurled upward slowly, blooming anew into her thoughtful pose. Lisa collapsed a second time. Then her body became suddenly muscular, tense, and an explosion went off. Lisa sprang viciously toward Igor, and the heat of warrior qi flowed out of her. Her eyes pushed so far out that Igor had to see the little red veins that reached back into an impolite dissection of catalogued bones and unnamed soft tissues. Lisa's tongue and palms stretched out toward Igor as if she were hitting him as hard as she could. Big Igor jumped back. Then she retreated back into her thoughtful pose, and repeated the cycle, several times around the room.

The librarian tried to shush Lisa too. But that only gave her dance more power; it made her think about how Christine, Saheli and Sang would crush in Reese's class. They would keep their traps shut. They would do what they were supposed to. And they would score like a zillion on the SAT. That's how they would be exceptional. But Lisa couldn't follow their example. And the lousy math textbook she carried around was too heavy.

The argument Lisa was going to have with Jan festered: *Look Jan, she would say. I can do a mate-in-five in my head. It's true the same way math is true. But there's a difference. The interesting positions in chess aren't about truth. They are at war with each other. And that's what life is, right, a war?* Lisa had given this speech to Jan several times as she watched time pass in the big black and white clock that hung over Reese's class.

In this imagined argument, Lisa was always smug, convinced by her overwhelming victory. But then Jan would answer: *Damnit Lisa, it's a war if you don't learn math. Look at my life. I had nothing to fall back on after the store fell apart. The kids who learned math are all down in Silicon Valley, just laughing it up. They have so much money that they work for fun.* Lisa didn't have a great comeback. So she waited to start this argument, and the heavy book continued to wear her down. She hoped that Greece would show her something beyond math, beyond Christine, Saheli and Sang. And she would show that special thing to Jan.

"Lisa," Igor said. "I like dance very much. We celebrate with something beautiful. Remember game one of Tal-Botvinnik match? That game Tal ideal: move Kd1 make people think about the chess and the life. Everyone think they can refute Tal unorthodox play. They see unconventional pieces developed, coming together in center. They laugh, make big face. But then previous discord and confusion resolve into major key. They must ask themselves big question. I now wish for show my chess ideal. Game is Paul Morphy versus Evil Duke. Not know if duke evil for truth, that only what they say."[7]

The two sat down to the ancient game from 1858. They gently reassured Igor's magnificent pieces, stroking them to the center of their squares. Lisa's face no longer wore the exaggerated pursed expression that Americans commonly make when they imagine themselves concentrating, the face of someone about to get punched. Lisa's face was open, prepared to attune itself to the choir of the conversation. Her hands passed playfully amongst the pieces as they moved into the game and began to feel the harmony of Morphy's thought. Her fingers knew to caress the derivative notes, and drive the dominant theme like a screw into Igor's hand-carved wooden board. Lisa felt the Duke's sorrow, and heard him crying at the mouth of his kingside cave, begging his pieces to get out of the way. At the beginning of the summer, the formidable material value of those pieces would have walled Lisa's perspective into a miserly smallness. Now she felt the tingling preciousness of time, and she could feel that the Duke's lack of it was transforming his kingside into negative space. Morphy didn't need to control it. The Duke's own overabundant resources blocked his escape. And she could taste the geometrical justice of the Duke's death, pressed up against the sweaty thighs of his inert vassals.

Lisa suddenly saw how this game was a reflection of Igor's better self. On move eight, Morphy and Igor decide not to grab the b7 pawn. Taking the material would be the safe path, to tax the world and use the proceeds to build armies of suppression. In Morphy's refusal to finish off his inferior opponent with workmanlike

---

[7] Morphy vs. The Duke 1. ♙e4 ♙e5 2. ♘f3 ♙d6 3. ♙d4 ♗g4 4. ♙xe5 ♗xf3 5. ♕xf3 ♙xe5 6. ♗c4 Nf6 7 ♕b3 ♕e7 8. Nc3 ♗c6 9. ♗g5 ♙b5 10. ♘xb5 ♙xb5 11. ♗xb5 ♘bd7 12. castles queenside ♖d8 13. ♖xd7 ♖xd7 14. ♖d1 ♕e6 15. ♗xd7 Nxd7 16. ♕b8+ Nxb8 17. ♖d8 Mate

LISA

opportunism, Igor saw his own refusal to allow his superior mind and physical body to easily win against an inferior world. And the geometrical mate of a lonely bishop and rook up against the vast remains of an uncoordinated army offered a sublimated hope to Igor's impoverished lifestyle.

♟

Igor met her outside the library. Lisa knew that it was his hidden chess board that gave the garbage bag tied to Igor's back its square shape. But her new classmates would not. Lisa feared their taunts, and imagined them saying, "Yo, Lisa, saw you with the homeless mutant ninja turtle. He showin' you some moves?"

"Igor, it's September, it's not gonna rain," she said. "Why do you have a garbage bag around your board?"

"Yes, is for truth. But board old friend."

"Are we going somewhere?"

"For truth," Igor said. "Arun give Igor and Lisa room. We now go there every day."

They again marched up the hill, toward the UC campus clocktower that loomed over the entire East Bay.

"Why do we need a room?" Lisa asked.

"We now look at Lisa's chess, need private."

Fear came to Lisa. She remembered the many times in Fresno and Lubbock that men had approached Igor to ask how they might improve their game. Perhaps they imagined the big man would offer them a minor adjustment, like a yoga instructor pushing a pose into proper alignment; they would walk away straighter, cleansed of all the niggling twistiness that worried their chess. But Igor's scarred face would always look down on their hopes and say, "You must study own game." The petitioners would walk away sadly. They would mutter "of course" or "you're right." But it was clear to Lisa

155

that they never would. They would never be strong enough to look at their chess. *Leave the presence of my master*, she would silently command these men. *You are neither worthy, nor capable of being taught. Go watch ESPN.*

But now Lisa felt the brutality of Igor's heartless inspection upon her. Dank orangutan hair spread from his forearms onto his hands. He was capable of killing. *Is natural*, he might say as he pulled arms from their sockets. He wouldn't remember his victims; to him they would be forgotten like grasses on the side of yesterday's road.

Lisa's nascent chess infrastructure had just been recognized with such an elevated form of praise that she had to sign for it. Her streets and avenues had dignity! Finally, there was something in her that others thought was good. The prosperous inertia that unfolded her streets should be allowed to create itself.

Lisa stammered, "But we haven't finished the Tal-Botvinnik match yet!"

"You know," Igor said. "I notice that when man and woman together they always wish for talk about another couple. How do they live? What choices they make? It is a pleasure for consider own self in lives of other. Is mirror without failure, guilt, and accusation."

Lisa followed Igor's worn sneakers into the Morrison Library. She avoided the contrast between the garbage-bagged chess board and the luxury of cork herringbone floors flowing up into fine wood paneling. If she just kept looking down, no human gaze could scald her conscience. Her eyes found the worn cherrywood tables. Easily incorporating generations of flaked skin into their soft durability, they reminded her of Polgar's chess pieces.

At the far end they turned left and ascended a tight staircase, which was like a ladder that had been left leaning for so long that it had grown into the building. With room for only one person at a time, each step had two precisely rounded footfalls gently massaged into the supple wood. Lisa imagined an age of wise women who wore wool socks. They left their shoes by the entrance, as she had done at Ruth's house.

Above, they found themselves in a narrow gallery, able to look down on the library. From bookshelves built into the dark wood paneling, quaint pages and bindings of an ancient tradition whispered reassurance to the earnest faces lit up behind computer screens. The students sprawled on leather couches in acrobatic gestures to an unconcerned and smug sense of belonging. They loved the upholstered bosom of this church so much they didn't want to go home to sleep.

Lisa tried to imagine herself underneath the green Morrison lampshades that softly caressed the natural beauty of their tables' grains. Her thoughts shouldn't have to burn underneath the stinging brightness of the Public Library and large tournament halls. She should also be natural, nurtured underneath this maternal light. The light she had known wanted her to hurry; it never encouraged her to stay. And this difference felt to Lisa like one of the irreparable scars on her arm. Those scars announced that she would never be whole, or one of the chosen. And that sense of weakness, of the inability to ever find completion, made her dread of the coming inspection of her chess all the more overwhelming.

Arun had promised that they would find a trapdoor right after the third bookcase. It was so small! Three feet by three feet, it looked like the opening to a garbage chute. Lisa was eager to get in there, worried that someone was going to come up the stairs and start asking questions. Igor said, "You open. Combination long: 43252003274489856000. Then hit pound." On her knees, Lisa hurried to set the numbers into the electronic pad and get inside. Igor had to unstrap his board and slip it through the hypotenuse of the entrance. He was too big there, like a rat who has to dislocate his bones to negotiate all the narrow spaces behind your cabinets, vents and heating systems.

Lisa and Igor felt with their hands along the greasy wall for a light switch. The room was musty, and smelled like a gerbil's cage. When Igor finally pulled on a string dangling from the ceiling, crinkly edges of candy wrappers caught the light of the solitary bulb as pieces of metal catch the rising sun: Kit Kat, Snickers, Jolly Rancher.

"What kind of place is this?" Lisa wondered out loud.

"Arun say only few mathematicians can break code. For normal is honor for come at late night, need also break Morrisson Library code." Amidst the trash they found snippets of paper with problems written on them like:

"Say you have a book with at least 100 pages, prove that there will be two pages, like say from pages 5 to 21, between which the total number of words is divisible by 100."

Lisa found a problem with an answer whose solution ended with: "Q.E.D. gimme a real problem you little bitch."

A chess board was set up in the middle of the room. Countless hours of blitz chess had rubbed the faces off the pieces, leaving them with the pleasing feel of rounded beach stones. Arun, or someone, had left a position for them. "White to play and draw," it said.

It would be easy. She would prove herself more than worthy of this room.

White to play and draw

She would show the composer of the problem to be a little bitch.

But she soon found the march of black's *a* and *b* pawns to be relentless; and that nothing much seemed to change with 1. ♖d1 ♔h2 2.♖d2 ♔g1 3.♖d1 ♗f1. Nothing. Lisa began anxiously banging her head against the lack of options to even consider. Nullity.

A half hour passed; Igor sat still. A full hour passed; tangy chemical salts from rancid potato chips floated like dust about the chessplayers. The problem was a door that wouldn't open for her. It was the SAT score she would never get. She wasn't smart enough. Cold and indifferent, the problem wouldn't even acknowledge the many times she had cruelly cast her delicate young body against its massive smooth marble.

"The problem's wrong." Lisa announced. "Fucking waste of time, these n00bs. And problems to draw are so lame. I want to win."

The interrogation light bulb dangled from the concrete ceiling. Igor said: "For me it is a pleasure for sit. No library clock make tick tock. You too young to remember, but we used to play the chess with such clock. They still wake in middle of night. You Americans put these clocks in every room; they look different, but little Chinese battery make same sound. Is anti-intellectual, time not clock. Dance many rhythm have. In this beautiful silence, I think: We come to special room for look at Lisa's chess. Your book, journal, seem like same thinking, but about Lisa's life. Each day new position for consider.

Lisa rolled her eyes. "The journal's pretty useless, Igor. You just write down your feelings and crap like that. Jan told me to write in it when I was a little kid. But she hasn't written in hers since forever. She's too stressed out with her store. And I'm too old for that kind of thing now."

"But you show me how, yes?"

"You mean you've known that the problem was wrong, and you were just sitting there, staring at it, wondering about my journal?"

Igor held his hands out in front of himself as if he were cradling a pregnancy. "Once big Russian belly, many fold, ecosystem of hair and sweat. When I your age not possible know that vodka make belly. Later, when friends all have proud Russian belly, we think is normal. Belly part of man we say; Body Mass Index big Jewish conspiracy to take man."

"You think you have the answer to the problem, don't you?" Lisa whined. "I don't believe you."

"Is horror," Lisa's coach said, "for repeat same mistake, over and over. You put unclean finger down throat, on cuticle furry bacteria play mariachi music. They have band. Here, in groove of finger—this how FBI can find Igor—in groove, feather-bacteria fly around like bird in valley. But all this not help. Usually only dry heave have. I repeat. But is same."

"What are you saying??" Lisa screamed. "Show me your answer. I bet you don't have it. How much you wanna bet? This is . . . this is bullshit!" As she had done in front of the liquor store, Lisa shouted at the problems. The word "fuck" was the electric cord; the other fury words supplicated this source like light bulbs and toasters.

Igor's posture became martial, and she felt the unfeeling shark eye on her, probing her. But he could not reach the deep sorrow underneath her anger.

♟

The following afternoon, Igor sat on the table with a green spiral-bound notebook, the kind Lisa knew could be had for $4.37 at Walgreens. The following rune stood of the top of the page: личное вертуально. Это не путь мужчины. Журнал—это для женщин и педиков. It was the entrance into chess wisdom. Lisa's time of initiation had come, in the special math room at UC Berkeley.

With her voice full of wonder, Lisa asked, "What does it say?"

"Personal not truth," Igor answered. "Not path of man. Journal for woman and faggot."

"Why is the journal only for women?" Lisa asked. *But it was true,* she thought. *The journal had come down from her grandmother through Jan, and she had never known a man to keep one.*

Her coach yelled at her, "You think I teach for money? Ha! Money for expensive vodka and crap American food. I not need that shit. I need journal. Need for know how Lisa look inside and make big jump."

Igor's great bald head glared like a polished helmet on an ancient noonday battlefield. His back was so straight, stretching up to the ceiling of the little room. Lisa couldn't look for long up into the cold shark eyes that wanted something from her. If she could just spit out all the things she didn't know, so that they could lie like tattered fabrics on the table between them—maybe then Igor would understand that she didn't have anything to give him.

Lisa brought her thick stupid legs up on the chair and drooped her head onto them. Igor had given her so much and she couldn't repay him. He wouldn't coach her once he figured out that the journal wasn't good for anything.

Igor remained silent until Lisa confessed. "Look," she said, "the journal is about all the small things that come and go, that no one cares about. It's like . . . it's like you're on the shitter in an outhouse, and instead of leaving the pot behind, you feel the need to start poking around in there. But you never find your shit. Yours is mixed up with a whole mess of other people's. The journal isn't like chess, or music. There's no truth in it."

Igor looked mournfully about the room, but said nothing.

"Why do you want to write in the journal?" Lisa didn't like to look at her master's face just then. He seemed so old and vulnerable, like one of those broken men she saw around Emeryville. Teardrop tattoos fell from their eyes, telling exactly how many men they had killed.

"I need for find," he said. "How I come here."

"But you had all the advantages," she said. "You grew up in Russia."

"Pioneer Palace," Igor remembered. "Was our chess school." He made a gesture to the table between them with no chess pieces on it. "Here was Soviet victory over bourgeois decadence. Money and gods not help capitalist here."

"But that not beginning. I enter into geometry as child, find harmony of pieces. Not remember who opponent was, probably one of my fathers. They few men who walk back from war with German. I construct first world against them, they true kings. First freedom, was road sign to intellectual life. Later, system force me say many obvious untruth, propaganda. You understand? But I always remember first moment. I think you I try for recreate this freedom when I get off plane in Gander. Now need woman secret. Freedom of journal."

"I don't get it," Lisa said. "You have the Russian tradition. There isn't even a tradition of the journal."

Igor again gestured at the table between them without any pieces on it. "At palace we study game of grandmaster in magazine *Shakhmaty v SSSR*. Grandmaster game like religious text: Interpretation always favorable. We make big rationalization for mysterious move of our heroes. When GM lose to GM, game like fate, destiny, power of one god to overcome another. Grandmaster know something higher. He not make simple mistake. Was no computer for say: He is wrong. No computer for cut umbilicus. In old time, grandmaster have ladder into elegant world, out of all the shit."

"Chess was about strength," he continued. "I tell you already. Chess about becoming man. Chess one man breaking will of another.

"I have coach in old times. When not think, he shout at me, he say, 'Is problem, Princessa?' He say, 'If you not control mind, you become slave.' He say, 'If you not man, you somebody's bitch.' But OK, your swear words not translate. Russian more powerful. I thank this man, my coach. He teach mind run creative and free under pressure. He teach smile when dance kazachok.

"From him I learn: Strength happen on other side of pain." Lisa's coach leaned back in his chair thoughtfully, as if he were gently caressing the virtue of self-torture.

Lisa asked him, "So the journal is painful and there is something on the other side?"

"Must be," he said. "I one time see catfish. 1997 Gulf Coast Classic, tournament organizer take fishing after tournament. Everyone help pull seventy-four-pound creature out of Alabama swamp. White, unseeing eyes. Scales color of Chernobyl. I understand. That was beast living at bottom of soul. He eat my best thoughts, rotting on bottom of dark emptiness. He grow bigger, more confident.

"Long time I think this fish my big belly. My fat. Unclothed belly hang like tumor, foreign thing, sometime growl, always hungry, complain about sunburn. I see pretty people stare, they can go fuck themselves.

"Then fat kill Wojo. You understand? For him I kill belly. But catfish still there, for truth. He not go. Because I have no journal for pull out. No way for study own games."

"WHAT?!" Lisa screamed. "You don't analyze your own games?" Instantly, her mind put Igor up onto a scroll of adults who didn't do what they wanted her to do: Jan couldn't keep a journal, Frohlich didn't go to therapy himself, Laynee's teachers didn't study the stuff they taught. Like goddamn Mr. Reese. Even Ruth, she didn't play in tournaments anymore. The conspiracy was now complete.

"Number of game I play since Gander uncountable," Igor confessed. "Like thread in Afghan rug, cannot take apart."

It hurt Lisa to think of Igor as just another broken man, tumbled from the shrill roughhouse of romper rooms into the unreflected compromises of half-lit adult spaces. She again remembered the tournament in Fresno, where several older men had asked Igor how they could improve their game. They smiled at her coach and graciously shook his hand. They acknowledged that he must surely be right: *They must analyze their own games.* But they wouldn't. And without that reflection they would disappear back into the most worn paths of their existence. *Why had she believed that Igor was any different?*

Igor continued, "I have called to brothers, living and dead. I say: 'Inside me, brothers, beast chew light and meaning. Is catfish. You know him? Help me!' These men embrace me. We kiss, is Russian way. You understand. They say: 'We have shed blood together, Igor. You are my brother. Together, we look out into meaninglessness. Is nothing else. We are men, strong enough for admit senselessness of the life, of our battles. Blood of slain our purpose.'

"I stand with them, Lisa. Every day we look into the nothingness. Is summit of strength and man. Now I must travel back. No place else for go.

"But each time I begin walking, friends call to me: Of course you have bourgeois pain, everyone have. But you big Russian man, you have place for put. Small man no place have for hide. You already know! Personal not truth. Not path of man. Journal for woman and faggot!"

♟

The next day, Lisa crawled through the trapdoor like a four-legged animal to again find Igor behind the table with his journal, no set. She clapped her hands like a madman, sending the dust she had picked up into a cloud about her. Then she announced: "Listen, Igor, I don't know why you think I can help. I don't have a secret. I don't even keep a journal anymore."

"Not truth," Igor replied. "Lisa find who she want for be, make big think in journal. Like salmon, you think about same currents that fathers swam, for whole life. Then you jump from anti-intellectual stream of big forget. You make escape with woman secret."

Igor's demand pained Lisa. But she thought of Arun, and how his generous spirit had risen up to meet Igor's need for mathematical beauty. "Pretend that life is chess," Lisa said. "You are in control, you are responsible for your own moves. Try to find clear truths." Offering this exhausted Lisa, and she cherished Arun even more. Her master began to write in his Walgreens notebook. And she was left alone.

"Umm," Lisa said after about a minute of listening to Igor earnestly scratch his Cyrillic thoughts onto the lined paper of his notebook. "What am I supposed to do?"

"You know already."

"Damn." Lisa had spent her day in the drowsy half-light of Project Darkness. She had begun by trying to do one of the Kasparyan problems Igor had made her. But they were hard. And she started skipping from one to another, trying to find an easy one. That's how she fell asleep.

When the school's final bell rang, Lisa woke to a really nice drool that connected her lip to a viscous puddle. It was her best ever, hard as a stalactite. This artistic creation was the acknowledged goal of Lisa's fellow inmates, for it meant that the black wool of sleep had readied them for the mayhem of midnight.

"Igor," Lisa softly said. "Would you show me your answer to the problem?"

"Nyet."

"Whaddaya mean? I just helped you."

"Russian tradition say you must sit 'til solve. Must face pain. Difficult moment make strong, able to make long think. Beauty on other side of pain."

Igor's wooden board was leaning against the concrete wall. Lisa unsheathed it from its black plastic bag and put it on the table between them. From underneath his chair she grabbed the purple felt bag that held the pieces. A yellow stitch embroidered upon it read: "Crown Royal. Canadian Whiskey." From her inner board Lisa recalled the position. She set the pieces up and then adjusted each to its most precise center, like someone who lights candles on an altar before praying.

Lisa moved in the catacombs below Paris, where tunnels continue to burrow for thousands and thousands of miles long after anyone remembers where they were going. All the colors of a black eye blew in from the sewers. In some tunnels, she saw the dried bones of millions whose struggles had nothing to do with her own. In others she found vagabonds and artists who had put up temporary camps. But most of the tunnels just looked the same. The thick air gripped her inability to tell one tunnel from another, and the bones pointed to her death. There was no way out.

The problem withered Lisa for two hours. Her mouth was dry, and she thought she now finally understood what real hunger was. Igor said it was time to go. Lisa forced herself to give up; she would put the problem away, as if into a drawer of a desk.

But the problem stuck around. Like a raccoon scampering about in the attic of an old house, it made unceasing little noises. A tireless animal, the critter kept trying the same thing over and over again, banging his head at the end of the same variation. Lisa commanded: *Dude, will you stop? You've been there before. Go to sleep.* But he would not stop. And he would sometimes misplace the pieces when he restarted the position.

That night, Lisa dropped two of Jan's Sleepitoffs. That was her only hope of smothering the anxiety of the problem. And her physical body did achieve something like rest. But the gathered energy of daytime sleep on a laminated school desk—that her Project Darkness cohort was now spending on the self-mutilating joy of every drug they could hurt themselves with—that power wouldn't let Lisa go. Her soul left her body and dropped into the mathematical world. Millions of positions sped through her with furious necessity. The pieces didn't talk in the human language. Knights did not ask their fellow men how they might best serve them, nor did they think about their own private aspirations (as they did in the analysis sessions with Igor). They spoke in pure shape and movement, and sounded like the march of speed metal chords. Lisa had never been to this overwhelming world before. But she thought she recognized it. She called it the real world, and the truth.

Then Lisa suddenly woke. She had seen the final position, the idea. She hurried to unpack her chess journal; she needed to write the answer: "1. Rb1 Kh2 2. Rd2 Kg1 3. Rd1 Bf1 4. Bg5! Bh6xBg5 5. Bg4 Pa3 6. Kg3 Pb2 (6. Pa2 Ra1) 7. Rb1! Pa2 8. Rxb2 Pa1 (Q) 9. Rg2! Kh1 10. Rh2 Kg1 11. Rg2 Bxg2 Stalemate! Gimme a real problem you fucking little bitch!!"

Lisa unfolded her plastic set and quickly assembled the final position in between her cot and the wall. The sublime beauty of the problem cut through the choppy crud of her life like a drop of lemony dishwashing soap in an oily pan. She would never have to deal with

Stalemate

any of that muck, ever again. She had solved a problem from the special math room of UC Berkeley. She felt the cold sweat as her body cooled. Her muscles were sore from writhing. The bed was wet. This was the beauty and the strength on the other side of pain.

Lisa looked up at her poster of Tal. He was the only decoration that could fit on her new narrow walls. A few straggling tufts of unkempt hair were pulled over his gaunt baldness. A satyr smile leapt out of the dying man, out from behind thin stumps of black cigarette teeth. Lisa called it his warlock smile. That smile would easily overcome whatever judgments people might have about his broken crust of a body.

To honor her hero, Lisa ripped a piece of paper from her chess journal, and wrote out her favorite Tal quote in her best calligraphy. She had never really understood the words before, though she had desperately wanted to. Now she felt like she had earned them: "In my games I sometimes found a combination intuitively, simply feeling that it must be there. But I am not able to translate this thought process into normal human language." This thought she pasted to the lower right hand corner of her poster.

Through the wall, Lisa could hear Spanish being softly spoken. She heard the steamy percolations of a coffee maker and the popping explosions of a frying pan. Though it was completely dark and silent outside, her neighbors were beginning their day.

♟

There wasn't much for Lisa to do when she ditched class. The Oaks Card Club was just a couple blocks away, and she went there a couple times. Igor said that Grandmaster Walter Browne worked there. All day he would sit at a Texas Hold 'Em table and beat n00bs who didn't have a basic understanding of statistics. The place was full of men whose lives had become so meaningless that they played games of chance. But Lisa never found Walter. Tattooed bouncers whose big bellies lurched toward Lisa's face shooed her out the door. They said she should be in school.

Everybody said she should be in school. They said it in the same commanding tone that Mr. Reese used to invoke his damning prophecy: *If she didn't pass her classes she wouldn't graduate. And if she didn't graduate she would be homeless.* And that always made Lisa think about the sad lady in front of the Berkeley Public Library who always had the same line: Miisterr, can you spare some change??

So Lisa wrote her apology. The administration said that she had to promise to never interrupt the class again. They needed to hear, in Lisa's own words, why it was not OK to interrupt. That was the only way she could get out of Project Darkness. In that letter, Lisa wrote about a vision she thought they wanted to hear. She talked about her friend Saheli, about the heavy backpack, and about who she wanted to be.

And they let Lisa back into Mr. Reese's class. It was the morning after she had solved the problem from the special UC Berkeley math room. She felt fresh, ready to face anything. *I'm gonna do the right thing; I'm gonna be good,* Lisa thought, as she sat herself in the front row and shut her trap.

Lisa soon found herself lost and powerless. The class had moved on to something about sines and cosines. Lisa wanted to participate. She wanted Mr. Reese to see the same kind of genius in her that the chess world saw. So she raised her hand and readily offered her most precious jewel: "Mr. Reese, can I demonstrate the Pythagorean theorem for the class?" The class gave a collective moan: *Why do you have to show off, fat chess bitch? We have our classwork, the test and a maximum number of absences. You're just making everything more difficult.*

Mr. Reese let Lisa come to the board. Maybe he had once suffered through a speech in the school gymnasium on *Student Initiative.*

As Lisa approached the board, Mr. Reese explained that what Lisa meant with her "Pythagorean thing" was the ninety-degree theorem.

Lisa started drawing her squares on the triangle. For the infidels, Lisa was ready to measure everything out with a stick, because they would never be able to see the pure shapes in their minds. "Hey, we doin' triangles here fatty!" someone shouted. Lisa felt the unpleasantness of her squaring upon the kids behind her. They were becoming a mob: *This is not some game. The class has to get to the end of the section before Winter Break.* But Lisa persisted; she would show her cohort this beautiful truth. Then came: "Órale, you so fat I can't even see the board." Lisa didn't remember much after that. And she found herself in Project Darkness once again, writing, "Fuck them, fuck them, fuck them . . ."

Lisa held her photocopies of the Kasparyan problems in front of her. She began with the first, and resolved that she would do nothing until she solved it. Through hardship, on a laminated desk in Project Darkness, with moldy boogers that stuck to its underside like gum wads, Kasparyan let Lisa into his world. He took her to the waterways underneath the city that everyone takes for granted. He showed her how to make bricks with her bare hands. He showed her the strength of a sewer arch. And he showed her how to find the underground peepholes into the seemingly private lives of others.

Å

That afternoon, Lisa tumbled through the trapdoor, clapped her hands free of the dust, and hurried to set up the final position of the problem on Igor's set. She found the scuffed scrap of paper that still read "white to play and draw." On it, Lisa wrote the answer and added: "Hi Quinn, Thank you for the problem! ☺ L.L.S."

The players sat across from each other, together with the accomplished simplicity of the problem.

"Who Quinn?" Igor asked.

"Remember the math problem addressed to Q.E.D.? Well, I'm pretty sure it's the same guy who set up the chess problem. There's really no other person with those initials at UC Berkeley. I found him on Facebook! Quinn Ernest Deveaux, but he hasn't responded to my friend request yet."

Igor laughed so hard his cheeks became rosy. He looked like his old Santa-face picture hanging at the Mechanics, from when he was a drunk. "Q.E.D. fancy way for say solution," he said. "Stand for *quod erat demonstrandum*."

In a solemn tone he then continued, "We give thanks. Composer is Alexey Alexeevich Seleznyev. After you suffer, I find in book *Энциклопедия Шахматных Окончаний*. Was member of pre-revolutionary players, with Bogolyubov and Alehkine. They imprisoned by German when First World War come to their tournament. Like me and my friends, they never make it back home. In this time, of wander, Alexey create problem."

Lisa didn't know when the wars were or why they were fought. She imagined war would happen if someone held the doors of the Oaks Card Club open for too long. An infinite stream of men who didn't care anymore would pour out into the streets. How they would kill each other didn't seem to matter much. They would do it with whatever they found.

"We do have friends, Lisa. Maybe we never meet. We pass on street, without knowing. Most gone like Alexey; we cannot say 'Thank you,' only possible share with him. Maybe we also make a beauty, somebody understand, someday."

With Igor, Lisa stared into the geometry. They fell into themselves, passed the traffic signals of language, and settled into an opaque stillness. There was no insight or revelation to be found there, only a numbing quiet that might occasionally tingle up the spine of the bustling world. From that stretching timelessness, Igor slowly arose and said:

"My life and chess become silly American ballgame, round and round bases. Is clear: No escape from circle except death. This loop make think that no opportunities are, always same. Only possible say: hit ball harder, run in stupid circle faster. I have made look into this meaninglessness. Once I even sit in stand, to watch stupid man run in stupid circle. Everybody cheer him; he same, like us. They yell, Go, stupidman, go!"

Lisa's hands were now on the wooden pieces, screwing them into their most precise centers. And her eyes held the board. Igor was supposed to be different, not part of all the lies around her. And now she wasn't sure if she could trust him. He told everyone to analyze their own games, and he didn't even look at his own.

"Each move chance for choose new world," Igor continued. "Deep well show seed sprout before happen, show mountain slow slide to ocean. Deep well reflect us, show multivariable calculus of soul. But I lose this, and run in circle like stupidman."

Lisa could tell that this was where she was supposed to say something about the journal. And she really did want to show him grandma Lena's path. But she didn't know it herself. All she knew was that Igor wouldn't be able to bullshit her over the board; because chess was pure. "Alright," she said. "Let's start with your last game from Fresno."

Igor laughed at Lisa, and made a little gesture with his hand that suggested: *Well, everything is meaningless then, because I'm talking to an idiot.*

"That's the game we need to study," Lisa said.

"You not understand. Game insignificant. Was formality. Enrico old friend. Easy peace allow both player share first place. Is better wait, 'til play new game. I not remember moves to this game."

But Lisa did remember, and she played out the first couple moves from that game to prove it. "It's your most recent game," she said. Igor laughed uncomfortably, and found himself forced to humor the pieces.

"You not understand," he sighed. "Back in old times, last round draw for first place would be arranged. Opponent come to hotel door.

He say, 'Igor Vasilyevich?'

'Da,' I say.

'Are you a fighter?' he ask.

'Nyet,' I say. 'Come in, we make big drink.'

This how you make tournament, Lisa." But then, as if he hadn't said anything much at all, Lisa directed her master's attention to the board, and began asking him about his opening decisions.

"Look," he said. "These are numbers of final round: Three thousand for win, 2122.56 for draw and 45.42 for loss. This money is then followed by 1099-misc form. That take more. Lisa, I must win big Church's Fried Chicken Grand Prix. Mr. Church must give Igor nice five-thousand-dollar prize if he win all the little tournament in one year."

Lisa knew that Church's Fried Chicken hadn't been the sponsor of the grand prix since forever. But she tried to imagine the cheap vodka Igor would have to buy if he lost his last round game. The plastic bottle had a screeching eagle on it; eventually that bird would make him blind. He would be kicked by other homeless people in the Greyhound station. Igor would clutch at the feathers of the eagle, hoping it would take him to the next town, to win Mr. Church's prize.

Lisa forced Igor to watch the moves he had forgotten. "You're building fortresses," Lisa said of her teacher's opening, "trying to protect yourself. Get some health insurance. Put an alarm on your house. Drive an SUV. This chess disgusts me, Igor. When are we gonna fight? When are we gonna prove ourselves? Knight f3? You know that's a bourgeois move! It's not who we are."

As the game progressed, Enrico's play seemed like a barrel of cheap fireworks rolling down Igor's sacred hall. Enrico didn't give a damn about Russia, he wanted to scorch the ancient tapestries that had hung for ages on the walls of Lisa's chess tradition. Enrico didn't respect the positional knowledge of her pieces! Like wounded children, they demanded punishment and vengeance, but they used the word justice. "Open him," Lisa repeatedly yelled.

But Igor did not open Enrico; instead he stepped back, as if saying, *Shhh, quiet now, great beast. You are young and want to kill. I retreat for a little bit, show many dangers in world: guns, rivers to cross, steel. You see, yes?* But Enrico did not want to hear Igor's paternalistic shit, and he continued to assault the idols of the Russian Church.

On day five of their analysis, Lisa looked up and shouted, "What The Fuck, Igor?! E6, e6! MAKE FOR PENETRATZ!"

For days, Igor had tried to explain his decision to offer Enrico a draw in a better position like this:

Syracuse is folly: The motley forces there will join together when we attack; our supply lines are fragile, and the Spartans will be emboldened by our adventure. But worst of all, the Egesteans, our supposed allies, have misrepresented how much treasure we will find in the temples if we are victorious.

Igor had elaborate rationalizations for the compromises he made. He especially liked to talk about some Ancient Greek word called *phronesis*. "Is big experience, not in mind, is in gut," he said. "Tell you when to play safe, when to make draw."

To Lisa, all this bourgeois shit sounded like a trench Igor could no longer climb out of. It probably began as a playful path through a flowery field; he enjoyed it so much that he walked there every day. The clean air of rivers and great forests had promised broad possibility. But millions of his heavy footfalls had slowly opened a crack in the soft earth. Now the trench was so deep that Lisa could only see the top of his bald head. Igor could no longer see over its

rim, to view the desolation of the shoveled landscape that surrounded his rut.

Fallen into the phony compromises of the adult world, Igor was
no different from the tired men in Fresno—they also could not
study their own games. Wooden beams, coated with words like
phronesis, held the hard-packed earth back. Fooling with it invited
structural collapse. And so the trench got deeper, and marched Igor
into the mindlessness of repeating the same moves over and over.
He was somehow still travelling around the country in a Greyhound
bus, trying to win the Church's Fried Chicken Grand Prix.

♟

That evening, the patterns rose up easily into Lisa's consciousness, as
if they were old friends coming to see her. At the old photocopies of
the mate-in-twos Ruth had made her, she shouted: "Not so easy, Mr.
Bambeezy!" And: "Are ya in the lurch? Take that, Mr. Church!"
These patterns shot Lisa upward, and she sped ever faster through
the transparent likenesses of a more pure self.

When she came down, out of the geometry, Lisa began to notice
the many physical histories of Ruth's old photocopies. Oily
thumbprints showed how rigidly she had grasped the pages. She saw
the exclamation points next to her favorite problems. And she came
to the page still stained with her angry tears, permanently smudging
the play of the pieces within the little black box that had brought so
much grief. Such a long time ago! Jan had not wanted the problems
in her house, and had stolen them from her. But Lisa had been a
novice then. Now she was strong, and properly owned them. Stupid
Jan, she would never get it.

The analysis of her chess would begin the next day. Lisa was
sure. For they had finished Igor's game. Lisa knew that Igor would
want to examine her struggle with Zarra. They would need the

carbon copy of the game score. Russian tradition demanded that they have it with them, which was really pretty old school, because the Polgar Championship had been the one tournament where all of her moves, along with the time she had spent on each one, had been electronically transmitted to the internet, for everyone to see.

From the shoe box where she kept her game scores, Lisa took out the painful memory that was now a crinkly wad. She had angrily mashed it after the game. Oblong, it looked like it had been hewn together in the wash.

♟

"You have?"

Lisa understood what he meant. And she placed her wad squarely between herself and the board. But she couldn't open it.

The strong and hairy forearm reached across the board to pick up the crusty spitball. He worked patiently, turning the papier-mâché, feeling for a hook with which he might unfold his student's game score. But it was difficult; Igor's fingernails were short. As Igor tried to untangle her game, Lisa said matter-of-factly, "There was nothing I could do. She played a perfect game." Igor was so lean that she could see his veins and tendons bob with the delicate motions of his fingers.

Lisa remembered her loss to Zarra like this: *Emma Woodhouse has all the advantages—her father is rich; she knows how to play the piano and sing; her manners are so much better than mine. My language is poor. Mr. Elton and Mr. Knightley want her. I am a low-born Smith of uncertain parentage. She pretends to be my friend, and says that I can rise as high as her. But I can't marry those great men. I must learn to content myself with the farmer boy.*

Lisa watched Igor use his massive palm like a clothes iron, smoothing the sheet. And she remembered what the analysis of a move should be. She should let the opponent's move fall like a

176

pebble onto the surface of her well. The rippling should be a sensual reflection of all her prejudices. In the most complex of positions, this first splash might be the only thing she could know. That's why Lisa had to remain pure, to accept and know the pebble.

The pebble would continue to fall through a spectrum of light. If she could be strong, and wall off the trivial chatter of the world, she would be able to stop time, and gently turn the pebble through her wavelengths. There would be nothing but her and the pebble. Lisa heard Igor's Soviet coach in her mind: *Igor Vasilyevich, turn all your intellectual aggression upon the pebble's future variations and intents. Dig, Igor Vasilyevich, and your well will grow deeper.*

The analysis lasted nearly two weeks. And in that time Lisa came to see that her pieces did lack manners, that their vocabularies were crude, and that she was in fact low born. Yes, she could occasionally shine with a youthful bloom, but that ruddy beauty would only gain her an introduction into the drawing-rooms of nobility.

In Zarra's thought, Lisa saw the nascent outline of ancestral elegance, like a charcoal drawing of a great masterpiece. And Igor pointed to this higher mind, upward from their current analysis, by offering Lisa moments from the games of Zarra's grandfather, a man known as Big Mikh. Groping in the unresolved ambiguity of that grandmaster's positions, Lisa was unable to give the pieces direction. And her pieces soon lost all measure of justice, pillaging for petty goods and throwing up rash architecture as they waited for imprisonment and death. Igor let her try again. But she could never find the deep baritone that would command the ennobling ambitions of all the pieces. And when Igor disclosed this voice, and the pieces suddenly knew themselves as if they had never forgotten, Lisa heard the divine mandate of kings.

It's so unfair! Lisa complained to herself. *Why couldn't I be born Jewish? Why didn't I grow up in Brooklyn? I'm branded by the low speech and thought of my school. And I'm cursed by Jan's low aspirations.* In the analysis,

Lisa didn't want to play her own position. She didn't believe in it. She wanted to play with Zarra's pieces, and prove her own pieces into the nothingness. Let Igor defend her side. And he did.

But he did so quietly. It was Igor's habit to forcefully envelop the heads of his pieces in the powerful flesh of his fingers and palm. He would shove and drill. But in this analysis, Igor lightly moved each piece from its base. Lisa was used to hearing the pieces shriek and growl underneath the violence of Igor's mind. But now everything was hushed, and the largeness of Igor suddenly vacated, as if he were channeling something without body or human disappointment.

In the beginning, Igor's suggestions were small bureaucratic hindrances to the destiny of Zarra's victory. *Yes, Igor, I see that she also has to file her taxes, and that her servants might give her some lip. But that doesn't change the* structure *of the game.* But Igor's softly spoken moves began to clear the brush from paths Lisa had not seen. She did not want to admit to these unseen opportunities. And she tried to refute them.

Once, after it seemed like both camps had bedded down for the night, Igor snuck over the demilitarized zone and rudely murdered all of Zarra's pieces in their sleep. "I kill like Odysseus!" he screamed with boyish joy.

Igor always let her try again, any position she wanted. Then he would crush Zarra's pieces again, and again. Days of this nastiness persisted, and the grime became more difficult to wipe away from the smoothness of Zarra's thought.

As the game progressed, and the position of her own pieces worsened, Lisa gathered the weight of Zarra's advantages and lustily pressed against the weak points of her own position. Lisa understood the principle of destruction: to press upon the frailty of one point, then *alternate* to another, waiting for the tired rubber band to break. But she was not prepared for the flexibility Igor and her own pieces demonstrated. She stood like an arthritic secretary with a repetitive motion disorder watching an advanced yoga class for the first time. She pushed on the kingside, and Igor performed the camel pose. She shot her cannons at the queenside, and he did the pigeon. With confident tanks Lisa came crashing through the middle, and Igor collapsed into the plough. At first, these deep bends seemed abject; they were chained to the black memory of her own fatalistic hopelessness. But Igor performed these defensive poses for days, and her pieces began to smile upon their oppressor, arching like wise trees to a storm that will water them and pass.

♟

The slamming bumpiness of SFO-LON-SKG and the bus to Chalkidiki battered Lisa. Voices came to her as if she were at the bottom of a pool. Igor sounded like he was shouting, trying to greet the other veterans in the hotel lobby. Lisa itched, and she was unable to find anything admirable in the new faces. She wanted her body to be translucent, the world entering her thoughts without diffraction.

Suitcases banged the white tile floor. Little boys squealed in languages Lisa couldn't understand. And parents kept coming up to Igor, asking him urgent questions about this and that, the when and the where—as if he would know! All this noise crowded in between Lisa and her teacher.

"This not your room, Lisa," Igor said. "I stay with head coach, GM Melikset Matikozyan. You with Zarra down hall, here key, room 517. Only couple hour rest before opening ceremony."

Lisa preferred to knock, not feeling entitled to put her key into the door. A gangly beanstalk of a man came to the door. He looked down on Lisa and called out: "כאן נמצא שלך לדירה, Zarra."

Zarra bounded to the door. With laughing smiles she cried, "Yelizaveta! Welcome!" Then she hugged Lisa. "Yelishka, this is my grandfather, Viktor. Viktor, this is my sweet Yelishka."

Lisa's eyed widened, but she was shy and didn't say anything at first. Sitting on her bed, prompted by the usual questions of travel, Lisa could only say, "Are you really Big Mikh?" Viktor laughed, and said that he was nobody special; that he was only a coach for the Israeli team. Lisa was very tired, but she had to ask. So she got out her board and set up one of his positions. "How did you find this move?" she asked. Lisa expected a deep revelation, but Viktor shrugged and said only, "It sometimes happen." That's all he said. "No, really, please tell me," she demanded. But Big Mikh only ever said, "It sometimes happen." And that is what Lisa fell asleep thinking: *It sometimes happen.*

The colorful dances of the opening ceremony were long over by the time Lisa found herself hurrying downstairs to the flutter of nervous kids and coaches who jostled around the long computer printouts that announced who would play whom in the first round. The European teams lounged nearby on couches. Their governments had paid for them to arrive early, to tour the ruins and play blitz chess on the decks of clear blue hotel pools. Lisa found herself mostly alone; Igor had to help the boys as well.

There was a security checkpoint at the entrance of the playing hall. A gruff man with ungroomed stubble slowly moved a black wand over Lisa's body as if it were a comb, checking for hidden chess computers or transmitting devices. Stoic voices announced that anyone not seated at the board within ten seconds of the gong would be forfeited, and that permission was required to use the bathroom.

An electric cord ran from Lisa's board to a cable underneath the long table. The moves of her game would be broadcast over the internet. An olive-skinned girl, wrapped in a black headscarf, came to the board. Her face seemed closed down, like a mummy. She didn't even look up. Lisa held out her hand. But her opponent wouldn't take it. Igor had taught Lisa that this ritual was sacred. He said that the handshake staged the violence and death of chess in a spirit of enlightened friendship. But her opponent would not shake Lisa's hand. She wouldn't even look at Lisa. Lisa knew that Igor would be scandalized by this offence against chess culture. A camera was on her; she could see it. And Igor would be showing an arbiter the offence in the coaches' lobby that very moment.

But no one came to help Lisa. Alone with her pieces, her first several moves were anxious. The unfriendly face across from her wanted to roll over her, joylessly and mechanically, like a bulldozer over a chicken coop. The girls on the neighboring boards were possessed by that same brutal determination. Lisa was startled. This was not the world that had been promised her. These girls were supposed to be her friends, her peers. They were supposed to show her something beautiful. They were going to show her something that would help her explain herself to Jan. Winning had not been the point, right? That you won was supposed to be a measure of the depth of your meditation. Isn't that what Ruth said?

Lisa's mind found itself up in the rafters of the playing hall, among hundreds of fanciful flags that shone like popular girls with bright colors and makeup. Up there, her mind squirmed, like a worm placed on an implacably large sheet of smooth plastic, unable to burrow. Playing for her country seemed as remote to Lisa as playing for her school and Mr. Reese.

Like a friend who comes to free you from prison, chess softly called to Lisa. *Come away! Let's leave this thoughtlessness.* Lisa watched her opponent's pieces leave the center to earnestly chase down a pawn on the side of the board. *You may have my pawn.* Lisa davened inside the mysterious weight of the center squares, and angry whips with flayed ends flew out to lick the walls protecting the enemy king. A fissure appeared; like fungi entering the leg of a weakened patient, the central power popped the king's fortress. The mate-in-twos rejoiced at the little naked man in the shower. "Dance!" they shouted.

♟

Lisa really needed to find Igor after the game. He had to hear about the center and her opponent's offence against chess culture (had he already filed a complaint?). But when she finally came upon him in the most removed room of the playing hall, it was obvious that he hadn't been following her game, either on the TV screen or on the computer. He was laughing with other old men, huddled around some plastic tables they had dragged from somewhere else. They joked about poisoned pawns and encircling maneuvers that came from behind.

The captain of the American squad, Melikset Matikozyan, introduced himself to Lisa. At the top of his loose shirt a silver cross clung to a clump of white chest hairs, like a baby kanga struggling to find its mother's pouch. Lisa dumbly stared at the mysterious symbol as she remembered what Igor had said about him. Melik had been the childhood coach of Levon Aronian, now the number two player in the world. Melik had been in his late twenties, his mind long initiated into a chess that could trace its lineage within the Russian and Armenian traditions. Melik had moved in with Levon's family, to suckle the young boy's mind. Igor said that American kids had no chance.

Melik addressed the old men as "The Senate," and told them a story of how a grandmaster named Dvoirys had taken a ballpoint pen to his forehead, crying "Idiota" with each stab, blood spilling all over his scoresheet and board. The men of the Senate nodded knowingly. Lisa too thought she knew what it felt like when the pieces no longer answered her commands. She already knew the terror of the gap between what she should be and who she was.

Into this circle of friendship, Igor solemnly submitted his earnest question: "You think we try for see something in the chess that we not find in the life?" But they laughed at him. And a chorus began: "Come on man, CHESS IS LIFE! CHESS IS LIFE! Fischer said that shit man, CHESS IS LIFE!" Then Julian, a coach for the Mexican team, broke into song with the Eastern European variation of this line: "No man, CHESS IS MY WIFE!" And they were soon swaying to the refrain as if it were the end of the evening, their liter-sized beers quickly refilled. "CHESS IS MY WIFE! CHESS IS MY WIFE!"

Lisa pestered Igor. She wanted him to be scandalized by the handshake that didn't happen. "Leave me, Lisa. I with old friends now," Igor said. But her opponent hadn't analyzed the game with her! And it was his job to help her. She hung about Igor's oversized knee as if she were beseeching an indifferent god, using the very brief interludes of conversation to complain.

"OK, OK, Lisa. Am I babysitter or something?" Igor took Lisa over to one of the coaches of the Iranian team. With fake solemnity he told his friend, "You know, Elshan, Ivanchuck say that if you wish for progress make in the chess you must realize that chess is everything. *Ab-so-lute-ly everything.*" Both men smiled at the childish beauty of this sentiment. And then Igor continued: "But you remember what chess told Chucky after he lose to child from Philippines and declare retirement?" Both men rose their heads and voices to deliver the well-known answer together: "Chucky can quit chess, but chess can't quit Chucky!"

As the entire Senate laughed, and even Lisa smiled, Lisa overheard Igor softly telling Elshan of her grief. Elshan only asked, "Is she a Jew?" Lisa was again disqualified, reminded of her low birth. But then Elshan said in perfect English, "Come Lisa, let us go find

Dorsa." And he led her off to the Iranian huddle while Igor remained with his friends.

"نظــركم لعبـــة نحلــل دعونـا," Elshan told the girl who had not shaken Lisa's hand, Dorsa Karimi. "One thousand years ago, before chess came to the west," Elshan told Lisa and Dorsa, "the queen was called 'ferz.' The ferz was the counselor, and that is who I shall be." As they played out the first moves of the game Dorsa muttered monosyllabic dissatisfactions to Elshan. Lisa didn't know what her words meant, but she recognized the guilt Dorsa's pieces felt: as if all of their moves had been wrong, and losing was inevitable. With Elshan, Lisa also became a ferz—originally a kind of powerless man who never moved more than one square from the king. Together they sought the true causes of Dorsa's defeat, lifting the ghosts and accusations from her pieces.

Then Dorsa started saying things in English, like "wtf?" and "Yolo." These phrases felt like a warm sun burning off the East Bay's morning fog, and Lisa laughed heartily. She imagined Dorsa learning English through Facebook posts and illegally downloaded American movies, where pop-up advertisements push sex with a lipstick lady popping out of a spandex suit. Dorsa soon trusted herself to complete sentences. And it turned out that her English was really good.

When they were done, and Elshan returned to the Senate, Dorsa told Lisa that she had not shaken her hand because Americans were Jewish. "Ha!" Lisa laughed. "I wish I was Jewish. I'd be so strong! Imagine, being a Russian Jew!"

But Dorsa told Lisa not to talk so loud. "It's not funny," she said.

Dorsa told Lisa of the ninety lashes a strong Iranian player received before the fatwa against chess was lifted in 1988. There were still fatwas against the game, even now, but they were not enforced by the theocracy. Many clerics called women who played chess in public whores. The coaches of the Iranian team wanted them to go further, to go abroad and play men. But leaving was difficult, and they were certainly not allowed to shake the hands of men.

To Lisa, Dorsa and her chess seemed imprisoned by plywood walls that hundreds of years of rain had soaked into fragile rot. Lisa expected the geometry of chess to push through that mush, as if the game were a higher language, an Esperanto of the true soul. Lisa said, "People who don't play chess don't get it. They never will. That's why we can never let them tell us how to live!"

Dorsa smiled at this. And it seemed true for several days. Nothing stopped Lisa from making friends. She could plop down next to strange boys playing blitz in the hotel hallways, she could visit with Igor and the men of the Senate, and she could bound up to her room to be with Zarra.

Lisa adored the older Zarra, and loved to hear how her tournament was going. Chess seemed so natural to her, as if it were simply there in her life. As if she didn't have to fight the world to have it. Lying in bed, Lisa would often think that maybe Zarra was the older friend she had always dreamed of, who would help show her who she was. But the weird thing was that Zarra didn't really show her anything new. She made chess seem ordinary. Zarra talked about chess the way Igor talked of his daily breakfast of raw oats, moistened with water and speckled with seasonal fruit.

Lisa's chess flourished alongside her new friendships. She looked forward to each day's 10:00 A.M. meditation, no longer overwhelmed by the flags and rules of the adult world. It no longer filled Lisa with emptiness when she thought she saw her opponent snarl, her lip pulled up just a little bit to reveal a tiny white dagger. Lisa knew that she would see the same teeth in just a few hours, flashing in laughter and joyful friendship. She would meet that girl's teammates, and learn something about the place their chess came from.

The blood of the girls Lisa slew no longer reminded her of her own death. Everybody was friendly, and that insouciance washed over her like a lukewarm Orinda wind. Of her next opponent, Gabriela Mecking from Brazil, Igor said, "True prodigy, arise from slum, to autodidact freedom." Melik said, "Is talent." Lisa came to the board as if she were come to propitiate the summer solstice, asking for true life.

Right as the game began, Lisa felt herself breaking free of the linoleum corridors that Jan and her school forced her to walk. Her pure self, high above it all, looked down on those old walls as if they were the flimsy partitions of a rat's maze. She would never be stuck there, ever again. Lisa didn't fear the warning signs she began to find near the mountaintop of her rational world—Park Boundary, Avalanche Danger. She followed them.

For each piece, Lisa unrolled its possible future and allowed them to stop the reel wherever they wanted. Her b-pawn talked at length about prediabetic conditions, her fear of lassos, and her dreams of backpacking though valleys and over mountains to reach the other side of the world. Her black-square bishop discussed her color blindness and the horrible sound her cane made when it tapped in the emptiness. She dreaded the rook; if the precious walls of the board ever fell the whole diagonal peek-a-boo thing would quickly lose its charm and get tanked by the rook's files and ranks. Like a witch, Lisa integrated these personal struggles through the great electric waves of time, the center and space that ran through the board. She channeled Igor and Tal.

An old woman appeared in the distance, underneath a redwood tree that stretched up into the cloudy sky above. She waved to Lisa. *Come up the hill to meet me.* She had a headscarf, like Dorsa, but her face looked like Ruth's. It was a long march. When Lisa arrived the woman was almost dead. She had waited. The lines on her face had grown deep, like a finger in an hour-long bath. These deep ruts in her face merged into the lines of the tree's bark. She pointed Lisa down to a narrow opening underneath the tree. Lisa gazed longingly at the wet tree roots poking the dark passageway. Maybe the old lady kicked her in, but the only thing Lisa could remember thinking as she lost control was *it sometimes happen.*

The pieces breathed with her. And she felt that whole, her whole, bending and wiggling through many textures. Her limbs inflated, like the sweaty tumescence of her legs' first climb up the hill, arriving at a vision. She squeezed Gabriela with all that love, and peacefully watched the contingencies of their thick embrace pulse through thick cloth, bristly towels and airy veils.

Lisa walked around like a Buddhist monk after the game, gently smiling at all the fallacies of the world. *Poor children, I can't help you in your state; all of my energy is contained within my spiritual quest, robed and mute. But follow me, follow me.* Lisa had not simply proved herself, she had gotten out of herself.

That night with Zarra, Lisa wouldn't let the delicate fabric of her spiritual experience escape out of her mouth, into words. Out there what was precious and true could never be held. It would rip and lose its color within the crude arrogance of boys and the falsity of adult compromises. Lisa simply gazed at her wonderful friend in the silence of their hotel room. Between them, with nothing being said, the ceremony Lisa had longed for was finally taking place: A chair was placed for her at the long table of intellectual nobility. She sensed the other girls around her and greeted them through a wick that drew the deep wisdom of Lisa's soul up to her eyes. They were pure.

♟

Then round eight came. She was playing Ulviyya Eyyubzada from Azerbaijan. Right away, Lisa couldn't see anything. Her face was pushed into a gravely sand, unmollified by water or life. Her legs were quickly bound. Something heavy landed on her right shoulder. And it broke. Why couldn't she see anything? A large ball was shoved into her left arm's socket and her face began to move. The bluntness of chalky stone passed from her lips to her mouth, feeling so large against her teeth. Red the color of Lubbock steak fell into the interstices of dirt and edge, to the forgetful place beneath the moving surface of things. Her life dripping, Lisa was driven in a circle, her body carving a path into the shifting rock.

Lisa was powerless. Again in Mr. Reese's class, she watched the clock move as his voice droned on and on. Soon she would be sent to Project Darkness. But she wouldn't accept her fate there. Feeling guilty before Jan and Saheli she would try to get out. She would apologize to the school that oppressed her, and she would try to be somebody else.

Lisa heard her opponent giggle, the heavy ball that had broken her shoulder was her opponent's head, driving her around like a bull. Lisa was about to be flipped. She would soon see Ulviyya's face, on top of her.

♟

Half-wake, Lisa felt ten gentle points gently massaging her scalp, underneath her ugly hair. Lisa's head rested against a small and gentle arm, a child's arm. Slowly, Lisa opened her eyes. "Thank you, Dorsa," Lisa told her new friend. Dorsa smiled back at her, and Lisa fell into a deep and nourishing sleep.

"How did you get in?" Lisa suddenly wondered.

"I saw you leave the tournament," Dorsa said. "You were so sad. After I finished my game, I found Zarra, and she let me in."

Lisa laughed. "I thought Zarra was the enemy!"

Dorsa smiled wisely and said, "Well, no one seems to care here."

This was something Lisa had wanted to hear so much, just a couple hours before. But now she said, "No, Dorsa; you were right. There are forces on us. They are real and strong. I felt them in my last game. The structures penetrate us. They tell us who we are. It doesn't help to pretend they aren't there. It was dumb of me to laugh, and expect you to easily overcome all your troubles. I can't even overcome my mom. She's like an iron wall separating me from my chess and everything I want to be." Both players contemplated. Then Lisa continued. "We only have a little bit of time to talk to each other. It won't last forever."

Dorsa nodded sadly and said, "It's only the tournament that brings us together?" Lisa nodded, and Dorsa then added, "Your name is Jewish, I could never bring you home to visit."

Lisa sat up and spoke in such quiet disbelief that it sounded like she was yelling: "MY NAME IS JEWISH? SCHMIED?"

Dorsa answered, "No, 'Lisa' is Jewish. I looked it up." The two young women were soon on the computer, discovering Lisa → Elizabeth → Elisheva → אֱלִישֶׁבַע meaning: My God is abundance → some woman who was married to a guy named Aaron in the Hebrew bible. Lisa was stunned. They even discovered that Yelishka was the Russian way to say her name. Then they read that her middle name, Lena, came from Mary of Magdalena (a place that means "palm tree" in Arabic), who was Jesus's disciple, but maybe also a whore.

Dorsa began a sentence with: "See, you are a Christian, and so you were baptized, but in Islam we . . ." Lisa was confused. Was she a Christian? What's baptism? Jan thought of herself as Christian. Or maybe not. She did do the cross thing at a funeral once. But they never went to church. And Lisa really knew nothing about it. Dorsa knew so much about Islam. She seemed to know even more about Christianity than Christians did. Dorsa said that the Muslims worshipped Jesus as a prophet, so Lisa guessed Dorsa was kind of a

Christian. Grandma Lena had once sang at a church. But which church was it?

Dorsa was mystified that Lisa could live without religion. Where did her strength come from? A man must have the Koran engraved in his heart, so that he can speak truthfully and offer direction. And a woman must know how all customs flow from the great book. If she did not know how the text incarnated itself in daily life it would be as if she didn't know how the pieces moved.

Dorsa said she didn't wear a headscarf at home; inside, she laughed and played with her mother. Together they made *Ash-e anar*, a soup covered in bright red pomegranate seeds. They watched foreign movies they found online. They wrestled. Indoors they could do whatever they wanted.

Lisa talked to Dorsa about Jan and Project Darkness as if she were a Russian: anti-intellectual conspiracies displaced Yelishka. Those inevitable forces were her and Dorsa's common enemy. It was only the tactics of the two worlds that were different. Yelishka's school and Jan used passive-aggressive thwarting maneuvers. They were harder to see, because the oppressors didn't have the guts to admit what they were doing. "At least the people in Iran are honest about it," Yelishka said.

And the two young women shared another question that no one around them seemed to ask: Why was there a separate tournament for girls?

♟

Lisa took second place in the girls U/14 group, behind Mo Guo of China. All of her new friends applauded wildly as Lisa went up to stand on the pedestal and receive her medal. And the American coaches whispered rumors about Lisa getting an invitation to the US Women's Championship.

Dorsa came over to the American clan for the first time at the closing ceremonies, but she only made eye contact with Lisa and some of the younger girls. She came to give Lisa a gift, a beautifully bound Koran with an embossed cloth that resembled jewels. It was in English, and must have been very difficult to find in Greece. Dorsa also gave Lisa the honor of a formal Persian goodbye. "La hawla wala quwata illa billah," she said. Lisa didn't have anything to say or give in return, and spent a long time simply looking down on her new book, holding it.

The end of the tournament was coming. Like chunks breaking off a thawing glacier, groups of children began to float away, back to their flags. And Lisa became desperate, thinking of how she would never see her friend again, and how she didn't have a gift for her.

"Give Dorsa your book," Igor said.

"My book?"

"Yes, your book."

"I don't know what you mean."

"Ha, you only have one book, Lisa."

Lisa sprung up. "But it's all full of my notes!"

"Is better," Igor said.

Lisa quickly ran up to her room to get it. But Dorsa was already gone when Lisa got back. Her only hope was to hand the book off to Elshan at the final meeting of the Senate. But Igor said she couldn't go. "We no longer coaches, you understand? We men, is momient. But I bring book to Elshan."

Bullshit! There was no way she was going to miss the momient. But instead of complaining Lisa grabbed a white sheet from her bed, put the medal around her neck as if it were some kind of amulet, and passed by all the parties and get-togethers that were being held on that final night. She threw her sheet over a plastic table about twenty feet from where she knew the men would gather. And she waited.

She heard Russian first. Then came a crinkly sound, followed by a small glass clink. In her soul, Lisa saw the brown paper bag and the elegant bottle of vodka. It wouldn't be the cheap kind, with the unkempt feathers of a nasty black eagle pasted onto it; it would be pure and translucent. "First big drink, zen big fuck!" Lisa yelled to herself.

More voices, speaking many languages arrived. Lisa heard El-shan accept her gift. "A divine book," he said. Lisa heard the soft rustle of her book as it passed through the coarse hands of the men. She felt their eyes on her notes.

Someone asked Igor what his favorite game of the match was. "Game twelve," he said. *That was the game where the bishops smiled!* Lisa remembered. "Psalm twelve, psalm twelve," someone cheered. Then Lisa remembered the screaming madness of that game. She had pushed it away. Igor had also been lost. He had no resolution to offer, no metaphor to at least put some stuff in shelves. Thickets of infinite variations tumbled over each other. That game had felt too much like life, too much like the hyper-aggressive evolutionary war that occurs in every warm puddle.

The pieces began hitting the board in a quick Russian rhythm; *tak, tak, tak,* they said. "I think you this momient not like, a lil' bit for coconut touch!" someone yelled. Shoving the pieces, the men quickly discovered many of the variations she had discovered with Igor over the course of many days. They found new paths too. Someone yelled, "I make penetratio!" Lisa knew that Botvinnik should have lost that game. Now she knew that he should have been fucked.

This was Igor's cohort. He had marched up Mount Vodka with them, where they had found obesity instead of Dionysus. Now they were old; the new prodigies of the game—who became younger every day—had no understanding for the cult of the grandmaster which had guided their early study. Karpov was losing games to just about everyone now, and the stern militarization of the Cold War had become a flowery memory of picnics and brunches.

♟

Lisa jumped from her window seat into the Arctic clouds. The enveloping oneness caught her fall, and held her so tightly that the clock no longer marched her around and around with everybody else, so tightly that her tiny body did not cast a shadow upon their sublime vastness. Lisa gripped the loose vapor as hard as she could, loving with everything she had.

Then she imagined stepping back, back into the tick-tock of the clocks that drove Igor mad, back into her window seat. From there, on the outside, she could imagine men like Arun forcing equations upon the shapes and slopes she was flying through. The less clever would see great white towers and hulls of overlarge ships.

On the falling curve into SFO, the clouds opened to reveal the steep glaciers of the Canadian icefields. There were no roads; the jagged land was barren of direction as far as she could see, like life would be when she got back home, without her friends. Teachers like Reese would want her to cage everything with their names, so she could graduate and not be homeless. *No!* Lisa thought. *I will never forget my game against Gabriela Mecking or the experience of the clouds.*

From his aisle seat, Igor stretched his oversized feet into the walkway, tripping up everyone as they followed their bladders to the bathroom. The man between them woke, and said, "Do your books get along?" Lisa looked down onto her Koran and Torah and said, "I don't understand anything. They're supposed to be everything, but I don't see what they have to do with me. My friend Dorsa gave me this Koran; isn't it beautiful?" The man nodded his appreciation.

"But when I brought it back to my room," Lisa continued, "my roommate Zarra hated it, even though she has never read it. I told her that Dorsa says that the Jewish Bible is also sacred to Muslims. And she said 'Well, you should take my English copy then. The Israelis say I have to study the Torah in Hebrew anyway.' That's how I got these two tomes."

The man introduced himself as Dan. Such a normal sounding name, Dan, like her own. So Lisa told Dan what her name meant and then asked about his. Dan answered, "It means 'God is my judge.' The first Dan was a slave who wouldn't do as his master said. Then he went crazy."

"Geez," Lisa said. "Religion is everywhere. Listen to what my friend Dorsa told me when we said goodbye. I've memorized it: 'La hawla wala quwata illa billah.' It means: 'There can be neither transformation nor power except through Allah.' Sounds nice, right? 'La hawla wala quwata illa billah.'"

Dan said, "That's very beautiful, Lisa. Even if the books don't make sense to us anymore. Take the word 'Goodbye.' So simple and clear, like our names. But the 'bye' is not 'good.' Goodbye is a contraction of 'God be with ye.'"

WATER

Jan had begun to use more makeup. And she looked especially cheap at the end of a work day. Her mascara ran a little into her crow's feet and a smudge of lipstick sometimes appeared on her cheek. Jan made Lisa think of what Igor had said of American chessplayers: "They like women, never know own power, put fancy clothes on outside—to hide from themselves. Make superficial play."

Lisa laid herself out on the short-haired Berber carpet of Jan's living room in Emeryville. From Jan's computer, Lisa's friends from Chalkidiki called her to places she couldn't yet go. Her third-round opponent, Hrund, wrote on her Facebook wall: "Lisa, come stay with my family in Iceland! It be crazy good time!" The spectacular TV was gone, along with the glass coffee table and the leather couch. A friend's garage had saved these treasures during the bankruptcy. And their deep imprints were still visible in the carpet. But they were now gone, along with Ted.

The memo next to her report card on the refrigerator read: "Dec. 22, 8:00 P.M., we talk." Lisa tried to imagine repeating ninth grade. But something would always go wrong; and she could never get through it. In some years, she would step over the maximum absence limit. In others, she opened her trap and spent all of her time stuck in Project Darkness. The kids kept getting younger and younger.

Jan was late; she had to work overtime with everybody else. Late December was the season for retail, especially for a home store.

When she finally got home, Jan tied her hair into a bun and came to sit next to Lisa on the carpet. They leaned their backs against the wall and stretched their socked feet out into the barren room. Lisa had known that this conversation was going to be her reckoning. But she hadn't expected Jan to speak to her as if she were an adult. From Jan's very first words, it felt like she was letting her go.

"I have also failed, Lisa. The business is gone; Ted is gone. And I have no means to help you. I don't have money for the antidepression drugs. I don't have money for Dr. Frohlich. And I certainly don't have money for Mens Conscia Recti; I won't be able to send you to college. I don't even have the time to look after you. I have to work, to support us."

Lisa's old school had cost $35,000 a year. That was one reason they were so poor now.

"When I was your age I had to go to my mom's office after school and wait until she closed everything down. There was a little loveseat hidden behind her desk where I was supposed to do my homework. It wasn't a good spot for math problems. So I read the books my mom gave me and I journaled.

"Your grandmother, Lena, sat behind a high metallic green semicircle. When you got off the elevator it looked like she was in charge of some kind of space ship, as if she had all kinds of hidden levers and buttons. The pixelated IBM logo and Lena's pretty smile welcomed people into the future. But from where I sat I could see that her desk was completely hollow. All she had was a phone and a notepad.

"Mom thought the world was kind. And she would try to write about that goodwill in her journal. She drew plants the same way. She wasn't interested in likenesses, to show other people and say, 'Hey look, this is a California Poppy, and this is a Magnolia.' She would laugh at men and all their phony objectivity, looking for unseen mechanisms that turn the color of a leaf and unfold a flower.

Mom wanted to behold beauty. She would see it and draw it. It seemed obvious to her that the power of everything was flowing out from the beauty she saw and wrote about."

Lisa had long wished that Jan would tell her more about her grandmother. It was like Jan was stingy with Lena, keeping her all to herself. Jan had given Lisa the journal, but not her grandmother's words, not the instruction manual that went with it.

"Beauty is a special kind of magic, Lisa, especially for those of us without power or money. We can make believe that it's all around us, and that no one owns it. But Mom was naïve. Men had made her life easy. A man she was dating got her the job at the office. They gave her things. And she accepted them as if the benevolent world were simply providing. She saw herself picking tasty nuts off a tree that nobody owned. And she would draw that tree. She would meditate on its goodwill in her journal. And she would see her own natural beauty reflected in it. So she didn't get a skill, Lisa. And she didn't fight for a place in the world.

"I watched her fade behind that desk. At first she was proud of her few white hairs. She said it was natural, and she called herself a Grayhair. That was a thing then, back in the seventies and early eighties. Lines began to show up on her face in the morning. They looked like tide lines on the beach, where the ocean has pushed its debris in the middle of the night. Men stopped looking at her. That's hard for every woman, Lisa, when you start becoming more and more invisible to men and the world. Imagine what it's like when they pass you by and flirt with your underage daughter.

"The red lipstick came first, as if she needed just a dash of color. Then her loose, earth-toned clothes began to peel away, and tight fabrics began to grip her body. It was like she was naked in public, like she was trying to point to her body, away from the age on her face. She went to *jazzercise*, Lisa, every day. It was so demeaning, and, you know, I thought about *jazzercise* every time Ted tried to get me to sweat, that hypocritical fucker. Then the jewelry and heavy makeup came. She bleached her hair blond. Her place behind the desk was no longer an easy job that slipped in and out of her benevolent contemplation. The world was no longer nice. And she had to fight.

"I wasn't there to see her get fired, Lisa. I had just gone off to UC Davis. I hadn't really thought about why I went to college. I guess it was because I saw my Mom at her most beautiful when she was alone, thinking. And because I was supposed to. But Mom never told me to study.

"Mom accepted her unemployment. She gave her power suits, her makeup and her jewelry to Goodwill. She told me it was OK to be poor, Lisa; there were a lot of poor single women then. Together they made yogurt, sauerkraut and even mead. They knew how to garden, and grow the best vegetables. They would steal from the orchards that used to be all over the South Bay—apples, lemons, pears, oranges, pomegranates, figs and grapefruit.

"Mom was crafty. She would invent things in her journal while she was dreaming of the small kindnesses she could do for others. When her neighbor and friend Judy said that her garden slug problem was so bad that it seemed like phalluses were crawling all over her backyard, destroying everything beautiful, Mom cut a hole in a plastic yogurt container, put some beer in it, and yelled, "Free Beer, Boys!" and nearly two hundred slugs drowned themselves that first night. She figured out how to make sauerkraut in big Mason jars. And she was one of the first to use hydroponics to grow pot in her closet. She was very good, and that went on for a couple years. But she didn't want to know anything about money. And she couldn't afford health insurance."

Lisa had never seen Jan cry before. She had always been so stoic and strong that Lisa never really questioned why she had the shop, why she traded false smiles with fake friends, why she had married Ted. Jan continued, "That's when your grandmother got breast cancer, Lisa. She must have felt the lumps, but hoped they were benign. Because she couldn't afford cancer. I think she knew something was wrong for a long time. It was only after she was shitting and coughing blood that she walked through the Emergency Room door. That's the only hospital door a poor person can walk through.

"So I quit school and came home. We had a routine where I would take her in for chemotherapy once a week. Then I would sit with her at home. I applied cream to the areas of her skin where the chemo had burned her. I watched her lose all her hair, all her strength. I helped her eat with a tube; cans and cans of liquefied baby food. I felt so helpless, Lisa. I knew there were better treatments, but we didn't qualify for them. Everything was so routine at the hospital, like they were just waiting for her to die.

"On one of those days, I went back to her old office. I wanted those men to apply the cream to her dying skin. They should connect the tube to my mother's stomach. They should put her clothes on. But when I got there everything was so clean, and I was so dirty. Only there could I smell the sickness on me, all of the little creatures that come to eat the dying covered my body and clothes. And the new pretty woman behind the same metallic green semicircle wouldn't let me pass.

"She already had the makeup, the dyed hair and some fitness routine. I could see part of the armrest of my old loveseat behind her. She made me wait in one of the lobby chairs. The fancy African art was still on the wall, great warriors with shields and oversized penises. Finally I saw Pete, Peter Schulte was the name on his door. He came in with his big tennis bag, jangling the keys to his Porsche. 'Pete!' I said. But he acted like he didn't remember me or my name. He was so flush and tan with health. 'I'm Lena Schmied's daughter,' I said. He nodded at me as if I were a bothersome groupie, a fan of his band. And he just walked on by, past my mom's old desk.

"I jumped up and grabbed his hand. I didn't know what I was going to say. I didn't have a plan. I just knew that he owed me something. 'Please,' I said. 'Lena needs help. She's very sick and needs better treatment.' Mom's replacement started yelling at me, 'MISS! MISS!' Pete tried to wrest his hand away. But I held on, Lisa, with everything I had. I wasn't going to let him get away. Then the new girl pulled my pointer finger all the way back, really hard. The new girl, Mom's replacement, she was fighting for Pete.

"Mom died a couple weeks after that. The hospital stopped doing the chemo. They said the cancer had metastasized and that there was nothing they could do."

Jan got up to put the kettle on. Lisa watched her as the room became silent. There was a new pot, black and earthen, and new teacups too, with raised red and green flowers glazed upon them. The set must have been from the store she worked at. Maybe it had been returned with a chip and Jan got it for nothing. Lisa watched Jan assemble everything carefully on a large silver tray with handles, as if she were adjusting her pieces to their most precise centers. Then she brought her elegant arrangement to their humble spot on the carpet to continue her story.

"I thought I was following my own path when I was on that couch behind her. But I was writing it all down in a journal. And I was reading the books I found on her bookshelf. She had all the Jane Austen books, and I became obsessed with them. I knew all the characters by heart; I could plot their lives and genealogies. I thought I was so smart, maybe even British. And I had teachers who encouraged me. They praised my book reports, and said I should study English in college.

"I know it will sound weird to you, but I often see my own Jane Austen phase when I look at you playing chess. Austen didn't want to talk about the whole world. She cut away politics and the ships of the English Empire. She cut away business and the world of men.

She wanted to talk about the development of a few people inside of their relationships to one another. That's how she became precise, by making the world smaller. I never really thought of it as a mathematical thing, but in my imagination I did see scenarios playing themselves out, people unrolling with the passing of time. And I guess that's what you're doing in chess, only instead of a drawing room and a few people you have a board and a few pieces."

Jan fell silent, and a long quiet slipped its arms around Lisa and Jan. Thin drywall separated them from their neighbors and the rushing Pacific Ocean fog. The microbial world beneath them starved; Ted and his take-out food were gone. *O bejeweled lake of golden curry, where we swam and baptized our children. O breadcrumbs where we harvested the green fungi. O sizzled bit of hamburger from whose bowels came the ever-so-delicious little worms. The apocalypse is upon us, and we must kill each other over the scant oils of feminine feet and the dry flakes of downy skin.*

Lisa remembered Igor's summary of life: "Is great paternity uncertainty." He had talked to Lisa of his fathers, the few men who had returned from the war. Women wanted these precious men. Even the drunks and chessplayers got to be kings. Jan's story about Lisa's biological father and the car accident was probably bullshit.

Lisa imagined Jan again walking into grandma Lena's old office, this time on the fifteenth anniversary of Lena's death. A new girl sat behind the same hollow desk. Everything was the same, except the African art was gone. Now signed musical instruments hung on the wall: guitars, drumsticks and a Zildgian cymbal.

The men needed to pay. Jan wasn't sure how yet. But they would pay for the health insurance and stock options they didn't give Grandma Lena. And they would have to finally give Jan access. As a girl she had sat for too many afternoons on the loveseat behind her mother's metallic green semicircle; they had never let her any further in, back to see the machines. Now they would.

Jan walked out of the elevator and faced the new secretary with the breezy confidence of a virago. With its stern lines down the side of her body, Jan's power suit already knew how to gently command underpaid women.

Jan pretended to have business with the company, and easily took control of the new girl behind the desk, Jenna. In the same way that Lisa had seen Jan have light conversation about the cruel life of retail with her employees, Jan now got pretty Jenna to tell her everything. Peter Schulte had made it to the top. He now sat on the board of IBM. Such a nice man! He donated some of his wealth to keep the local parks clean, where Jenna jogged.

Jenna told Jan about the company's new math whiz, Zak Zilber. Summa cum laude from Stanford, the young man had developed some equations that had sent stock soaring. And Jenna said yes, Jan could pass by the great metallic green semicircle and knock on Zak's door.

Peter Schulte's keys jangled so effortlessly. Men like him waltzed through life, spawning South Bay pools and parties with iced tea. From the first moment she saw Zak, Jan beheld his power, to create the mysterious gadgets that led to the money and stock options. Jan would take it. She would put his mathematical prowess inside her body. *It had to be true*, Lisa thought. *That was the deep power she felt when she played chess. That was where her Jewishness came from!*

Back at his expansive apartment without enough furniture to claim the emptiness, Zak sat Jan down in a lonely chair and took out his tenor recorder. Jan tried to politely refuse his concert, but he insisted. He played Sarastro's air from Mozart's Magic Flute, slowly walking in a circle around Jan. She felt suffocated, slobbered upon, especially when he stopped to explain the mathematical beauty in the harmony of the piece. This song was his love and lovemaking. But Jan couldn't approach this world, and she had to wait with a fake smile.

But Lisa had not turned out like she was supposed to. She was fat, like him, ugly like him, socially awkward like him. Like Zak, and Igor, Lisa wanted her glasses to be overlarge, as if the extra surface area would help them capture something everyone else missed. Back then they didn't have words like "autistic" or "Asperger." That's why Jan hadn't seen it in Zak. Now it would be obvious. And that was one of the reasons Lisa wouldn't make it where her father had. Everyone could see that there was something wrong with her. She wasn't going to make it in the world. She wasn't even going to make it in school.

"Jan?" Lisa asked. "Did my father really die in a car crash?"

Jan said that he did. But she looked away when she said it, like when Ruth confessed that she had done nothing to help Bobby through his madness.

Lisa imagined that Jan would never tell the truth. Jan feared that her daughter would demand a name. Lisa would walk up to whatever South Bay mansion he now lived in, looking for her biological identity. Then she would knock on his door, with the same intrepid stupidity with which she had knocked on Igor's door, uninvited.

But Zak wouldn't open the door. Lisa would be held waiting. Zak would look at her, but only from a hidden distance, from his security camera. He wouldn't trust himself to see his own procreation in her face. He would only trust the machine. So he would take a piece of Lisa and give it to the machine. And the machine would tell him that he was the father. He would then declare himself outraged with Jan, and his lawyers would take Lisa away from her. No. He had been Jan's tool. And that tool might not have performed as she had hoped—but Zak Zilber would always be only a tool.

Jan interrupted these thoughts of Lisa's, and said, "I know I haven't been easy on your chess, Lisa. And I know you think I hate it. But you were losing yourself in it. I didn't want you to become shut out. I wanted you to be armed, to never be as defenseless as my mother was and I now am. See, we're now like the people who didn't make it into Jane Austen's books. Her characters all had at least some prospect of access, of money. She understood that a life without money is bestial. That kind of life is undignified and uninteresting. Look at me: I'm alone, I don't have health insurance, and I'm too old to ever make it again.

"I wanted you to have money like the men in the South Bay have. They own the world. They have the say. They send their sons to chess class. That's why I sent you. Chess trains their sons to climb up mathematical boulders. Chess trains them in the art of hostile takeovers. But it's just practice, Lisa. You're not supposed to get stuck there.

"After your grandmother died, I realized that I had to face the real world. Reading and journaling only means debt. So I got a job at a kitchen store, not very different from the job I have now. I was good at it. In those early days I learned that people need distinguished forms of primitive household technologies. And I knew the primitive from my mother's poverty. When I opened my own store I designed a metal slug trap, and had thousands made in China. I imported beautiful Polish sauerkraut crocks. And I marked those babies up.

"I know how to help people buy the expensive cutlery and tools they will never use. Each customer is trying to buy the domestic life they never had. They think that if it's expensive it will fill the empty space, the way people put gold frames around ancestors they didn't care to know while they were alive. I have always understood that pain, trying to reclaim my mother."

☖

Igor got Lisa to pause her chess during the Holidays. The Russian needed her mind to take everything in before moving forward, like the way silt must sink to the bottom of a lake before its waters can become clear. And he wanted Lisa to somehow mark her great achievement, something personal. Of his own attainment of the grandmaster title he said, "I should have put stop to the life, put title on arch of back. For understand momient." On the long and sleepy train ride back from the airport, Igor drew this tattoo which should have connected his shoulder blades: **ГРОССМЕЙСТЕР**.

But Lisa didn't understand what Igor wanted her to do in this dark time that he called Winter Solstice. The chessless told long stories that somehow always said: *These are the things you have to do— right now!* Like the way Jan demanded that Lisa return to school, even though Lisa would now have to repeat the ninth grade whether she went back after break or not. But for everything Jan said, she still didn't tell Lisa the truth about her father. That was the naked duplicity of the chessless.

The rains returned to the windows. And Lisa tried to think about all the failing grades Jan had posted to the refrigerator door. But her narrow cot didn't give her any room to flop about. She tried to imagine sitting through Mr. Reese's class. But she could never pass the ninth grade. Again and again she failed, and the kids got younger. For days, Lisa stuffed this emptiness with the white bread, packaged meats and frosted cakes that Jan brought home from Trader Joe's. Then Lisa got marked—only not with a tattoo, but with a picture.

Lisa sat in a high wicker chair. Someone must have returned it to Jan's new store, along with the two great vases filled with flowers that flanked it. The chair filled the place on the carpet where Jan had talked to her, the place that Ted had left empty. Jan was bringing in the outside world to freshen up the shame of her small apartment. A photographer from the *Oakland Tribune* was coming to take Lisa's picture. And Jan made her ready.

Slip into this red sundress, Lisa. Feel the simple straps on your bare shoulders. Look at how these cheap glass earrings sparkle like diamonds. Rub your lips together, and smack the red lipstick. Hold your eyes open while I bring this little mascara brush terrifyingly close to your eyeballs. Let me scrub your doughy cheeks with rouge. Jan's stiff movements said what Lisa already knew: There was nothing inside her that had value, nothing that she could offer the world. So, like Grandma Lena and Jan before her, Lisa also had to learn to use makeup.

The black and white photo that came out in the *Tribune* piece, under the headline *Local Girl Masters Game of Kings*, seemed pretty harmless, even a little flattering. And Lisa kinda liked reading her own answers to the dumb questions that the chessless ask. "What's your favorite piece?" "The queen, obviously." "When will we have a woman world champion?" "Any day now." Maybe Mr. Reese would finally understand that she was a genius, and do something to help her pass ninth grade.

Then a color version of the photograph surfaced on USchess.org as part of their coverage of Chalkidiki. The girl Lisa saw on Jan's computer screen was scared. She looked away a little, as if she were afraid of something and didn't want to look at it. Jan had taken the girl's overlarge glasses away from her. They had been her last line of defense, stopping the chessless from ever seeing how moist and blind her eyes really were. In the photo, Jan's makeup met the camera with a laughing smile; the girl did not.

The photographer had wanted the white queen in the shot. Lisa hadn't thought much about it at the time; she had just grabbed the plastic piece from her travel set. Cupped in her hands just beneath her chin, the queen looked like a gift she was offering. Was she, Lisa, the white bitch? The rest of the scene was photoshopped into a blur, Jan's wicker chair and vases paintbrush dabs of blue, yellow and brown.

Lisa began finding the photo all over the place, on Chessbase.com, Chesscafe, Chessdom, Echecs, superajedrez, and 64.ru. All her friends from the tournament were there too. But why? Why were there so many pictures of them? Lisa did a Google image search and found Chessbabes.com. Her photo had four out of five stars. In the comments section below the picture, poisonpawn27 said:

"I'll give this hottie a WIM."

Poganinaissohot answered: "You can tell, right? She wants the WPhD real bad."

Luvsglasses3 said: "I'll give it to her, if she's ready to fuck her way to the top."

Allaboutjudit added: "That bitch would fuck Bobby Fischer's corpse."

Lisa closed the window and Jan's computer as fast as she could, before she could read the rest. Warm, the computer continued to hum on her thighs, the bluish tint of the screen still in her eyes. Lisa sat behind grandma Lena's metallic green desk. The men came up behind her, from the back offices, where the machines were. Their hot red peckers were already out, poking at her. Everyone said this was going to happen. Her leg, her stomach, even her eyeball—they had to find a way in. Lisa had wanted them to do it too, that's why she had put on the makeup.

Chessbabes found Dorsa's naïve smile behind her dark blue headscarf. Zarra was rated a five. Lisa wanted her friends to tell her: "Listen, Lisa, they aren't real chessplayers. Luvsglasses3 for example, his real name is Joe Schleimowitz, he sits behind a computer all day spooning dog food out of a metal cylinder, wondering why he's only rated 1132. He's not one of us, Lisa. He's on the other side."

But Lisa knew what they would say. They would talk to her about God. That was always their final answer to every difficult question. And there would never be any way to reach Joe Schleimowitz, to fuck him up. He was anonymous.

Lisa turned to the one book that both Dorsa and Zarra said was true. Lisa davened over *Genesis*. In her study, Lisa sometimes yelled up to her ceiling, "Oh Jesus Christ! Help me, show me a way!" But

no one in the book had mentioned that guy yet. Little made sense to
Lisa, but she knew how to sit inside a murky position until the pieces
begin to speak. Like a black-square bishop, Lisa groped at the half of
the board she couldn't see. For there had to be an answer; she hadn't
made such a bad mistake for her position to be so completely
unplayable.

During that Winter Solstice, Lisa discovered that God only made
men in his image. Only men were given the power to name things.
Woman was so insufficient she had to be created twice. The second
time she was derived from a man's rib, like the way scientists made
human ears and fingers grow out of rats.

Lisa called out to her friends, even if they were trapped inside
Jan's computer. They were good, and they would show her how the
Word of God didn't mean what she had read. Lisa wrote to them on
her Facebook wall: "Genesis I:27; II:23, WTF? #Dorsa Karimi
#Zarra Mikhalevski."

Zarra was the first to respond. "I called my rabbi and he quoted
his rabbi: 'At first He created her for him and he saw her full of
discharge and blood, thereupon He removed her from him and
recreated her a second time. Hence he said: *This time she is bone of my
bone.*' And that is the line right after the one you quote. Maybe that's
why my Rabbi won't shake my hand :-("

Dorsa added: "The Holy Qu'ran reveals that the beginnings were
not so complicated. But this is not ours to publicly discuss. 4:34: 'So
good women are the obedient, guarding in secret that which Allah
hath guarded.' Eva's true name is Hawa, which comes from the word
'life' (*haiy*). Allah is All-Embracing, All-Knowing."

It was obvious that this discussion was actually about Chessbabes. But no one had the guts to say it. Lisa didn't either. It hurt too
much to write it out on Jan's keyboard.

A chessplayer named Tim, from England, continued the thread
with "Let a woman learn in silence with full submission. I permit no

woman to teach or to have authority over a man; she is to keep
silent. For Adam was formed first, then Eve; and Adam was not
deceived, but the woman was deceived and became a transgressor.
Timothy 2:8–15; :-)" Lisa had never even met Tim. Her Facebook
friend count had jumped from 356 to 703 in the weeks after the
tournament in Chalkidiki. If someone had at least ten friends in
common with her she would accept their friend request. Because
these were real people, chessplayers.

Then Alexander, from the Ukraine: "Genesis, 3:6 'And the
woman saw that the tree was good for eating and that it was lust to
the eyes and the tree was lovely to look at, and she took the fruit and
ate, and she also gave to her man, and he ate.' Yo Lisa, why you
trying to seduce us? :-)"

This was the way it was then, from the very beginning. She
wasn't supposed to talk back. She couldn't name herself. She was the
hot bitch in the red sundress. She seethed with sex, the whole damn
thing was her fault. How did the men at Chessbabes know she wore
cotton panties?

Laynee continued Lisa's Facebook thread with, "Ummm, is this
why there is a separate tournament for girls?"

Lisa had met so many men at her summer tournaments. Were
they the men who wrote stuff underneath the pictures of her friends
at Chessbabes? The same men who gave her rides and free advice?

♟

Lisa met Igor in front of Berkeley Public on the second Saturday of
January. That's how long she had to wait for the end of Igor's
solstice. The Morrison was still closed for winter break, and Arun
hadn't told them how to break that code. It was unseasonably warm,
one of the seventy-degree days in January that cruelly command trees
and flowers to bloom. Lisa and Igor arrived in shorts, like pagans.

Igor said he had stashed his board behind the bookcases of the children's room. But the carved pieces of her master did not call to her. In her mind, Lisa could already hear the sounds of people screaming at each other on the first floor, the screeching of chairs, children whining, the green flatulence and the musty dusty of homelessness. None of that had bothered Lisa before. But now she feared it, and she missed the serene quiet of Arun's secret study.

Not so long ago, Lisa's one wish had been to enter this library. Now she asked Igor if they could run. Igor lifted his eyes. He looked up to the mountains, and then down to the water. "Yes," he said. "We run." Did Igor know about Chessbabes? Lisa couldn't bring herself to ask. He wouldn't understand the pain and betrayal she felt. Maybe he used the site himself.

Without intent, Lisa found herself descending the gentle slope to the water, rolling downhill, like she had done on Jan's bike before it was taken in the bankruptcy. The sweat began, and Lisa encouraged it to flow; she wanted it to wash over her like a cold Pacific Ocean wave. Mile one. Lisa was not fast. The capillaries in her bouncing roll of belly flesh demanded the same oxygen that her legs needed. But she never stopped. She had learned from Igor to hope for strength and deliverance on the other side of pain.

They passed over the freeway on the high University Avenue bridge, briefly inhaling the prehistoric animals whose carbon burned as gas below them, and soon found themselves in a dog park. Mile three. Humans whose ideal of friendship was canine had driven there so that their dogs could smell other dogs. And when they talked with other members of their cult, they did so through the medium of the dog, commenting on breed and how good they were. Paved paths, erosion barriers and grass cut so short that it poked like lesbian hair; these were the minimalistic gestures to a tamed nature that called the dog-worshippers to prayer. Lisa hated these people. So they kept running, to the kite park. Mile four. There Lisa saw people forcing the same fake smile which had made her face sore for days after the photo shoot, their kites celebrating the sleepy rewards of a forgetful life.

Igor tried to play up the place. He told her it was not real land. It was landfill, a trash heap from a faraway time that tried to extend land into water. He told her about the mice, skunk, possum and raccoons who live there. Then he talked about the coyotes and burrowing owls who come to hunt them at night. He told her about the halibut fishermen on the pier who once in a lifetime pull up that sideways fish from its foreign planet. He tried to imitate the celebratory dance they would do around the captured alien. He told her about the amazing health insurance that the leashed dogs have, and the basic help that his friend Wojo didn't have. He told Lisa about the kite runner who would come to this very spot to artfully cut down the dreamy air buoys. But Lisa couldn't see any of that. She only saw false smiles crowding her, as if their deceit could break the wind off the water, temper the sun and stop their own sweat. "I wanna keep running," she said.

So they headed north, and the prettiness ended beside a strangle of low-tidal muck. The stench was like a physical barrier they had to pass through. Yellow ammonia and proteins rose from the dying microbes and awakened the slumbering creatures inside Lisa's body. *Has our time come?* the larvae, fungi and bacteria inside her asked. *Will we now feast upon you?* Lisa briefly sensed that she was not alone.

Then they climbed a hill to a horse track; to her right, Lisa saw the horse penitentiary, narrow stalls filled with flies and shit. At the top, Lisa saw the betting men whose dollars no longer smiled when they won. Mile six.

On the northern side of the hill, Igor pointed to an obtuse peninsula beneath them. "Is trash from another time," he said. "Forefathers make land in water. You wish for go?" Lisa thought of the mounds made by the Indians in Emeryville, that she now lived on. "Da," she answered. "We run."

The main trail brought them to a dirt clearing and the unplanned beginnings of at least eight paths. Many didn't seem to lead anywhere; and everything was brown, as if the plants didn't want to paint themselves. Like a witch, Lisa sensed the red and blue ores beneath the dwarf trees and the broken hunks of concrete that the roots of the prickly shrubs ran up against. A syrup of pink and gold chemicals slithered through it all, like the way Equinox had once made its way through her brain. This land was her heritage. This land was what her forefathers had left behind. The chessplayers kept running down, toward the water, as if it were the only sensible direction, their bare legs lightly lashed by the itchy tendrils that wanted to reclaim the anarchic trail.

An overgrown concrete structure greeted the chessplayers as they arrived at the water. Maybe a massive WWII gun had once swung on its turret here, prepared to meet a Japanese assault. Generations of graffiti extended back into the walls, like light from a distant star. Lisa admired the recent layers of angry artwork. She petted the flippant expressions, and felt that she was not alone. Others came here, like her, to find the truth.

They had to keep running, to keep their sweat from drying into a cold salty crust. So they headed north along a coast of lost concrete and rebar jabbing up into the air, no longer knowing its original purpose. They came to the sculpture garden. Figures of fishermen, philosophers and misfit animals were wedged together out of the found metal, driftwood and concrete that littered the place. Unfinished, they called out for an author.

Underneath a low sun, the chessplayers came to the great warrior. She was twenty feet tall, and her hair hung down low in fat chains, each link the size of Lisa's fist. Knotted driftwood formed the many delicate bones of her powerful face. Woven chainmail armed her.

They had to keep moving, and ran up the path over which the woman looked, inland. Sad to think her adventure over, Lisa turned back to her, as if she were an oracle and could tell her something. Lisa said, "They do not name her here. She is the Guardian, the Cherubim." Lisa decided that if there were a boy up in the sky, who had created the earth and people as some kind of science experiment, she would not pray to Him.

Lisa wasn't ready to go home. There wasn't anything there for her anyway. She wanted to bushwhack her way to some metal objects she saw flashing in the setting sun. So they followed the shine like magpies on a quest, and discovered a sprouting rebar fern, each metal reed crowned with found treasure: a spinning bicycle wheel, a large green glass bottle, a lion sewn together from filmy metal strips. "This is the tree of knowledge," Lisa announced.

Next to Lisa's tree stood a shack that had been cobbled together out of driftwood and repurposed two-by-fours. Lisa approached the humble structure, but Igor called her back. His voice even shook a little, as if he feared an armed and angry hermit. "Don't be so scared all the time," Lisa said as she walked in. To her, it seemed natural that she should find a library. A couch, a couple chairs and a roughly cut section of carpet covered the earthen floor. On a shelf, Lisa instantly spotted a cheap plastic chess set, the kind that's hollow inside and doesn't have any weight in your hands. The books were different. They weren't filled with stuff that teachers like Mr. Reese expected you to study but had never even read themselves. These books were all gifts, each brought by someone who wanted to share their experience.

Igor was nervous. He said that if he left anything outside his house—the plywood carcass of a stereo case, a slouching bookcase decorated with mold—that shit would disappear immediately. It would leave on principle, Igor said. That was the American freedom he had known.

The sun dropped and strong winds began to rattle the wooden boards of the library. Dogs started barking, some distant, some very close. They had to move. Running. Salt stung Lisa's eyes and her legs quickly felt like rubber. The lights of the city were too distant to swallow the blackness of the water. Bouncing thoughts began and ended like the animal paths she had seen, without direction or the need of a connection. Up on racetrack hill, the last rays of sunlight caught the top of the UC Berkeley clocktower.

They came to the aquatic park. Lisa was picturing waterslides and screaming children, but it was just another cesspool of dying algae. Mile ten. At the southern end, Lisa saw men in dark clothes wait in a narrow parking lot. Flesh-colored motions flashed in the thin bushes. They ran through streets filled with wide warehouses from another time. Mile thirteen, Lisa was almost home.

"I have a special request," Lisa said as she finished her first half marathon. "Can we do our next lesson at the library?"

♟

Igor met Lisa close to Jan's apartment the next day. Her teacher had strapped his board to his back without the protection of a black garbage bag. The soft mahogany and maple squares faced outward. As Lisa walked with Igor, she imagined the maple squares enlarging first, and cracking, unable to expand in the tight grip of the mahogany. Tiny particles of salt and sand would pockmark the board's veneer; spores would travel through those cracks, and a fungal mycelium would burst inside the wood. Igor's beautiful board would soon be just as ugly as the rest of the world. Lisa thought about her own uncleanliness, the tampons and her dark mess. She remembered that God had sacrificed Jesus to atone for what Eve had done. The Lord's bloody death atoned for her contamination of Paradise.

Lisa and Igor slowly walked back through their run of the day before. The sounds of heavy machines and clanging metals came from the warehouses. The southern shore parking lot was now empty of cars, only a few sticky condoms baked upon the pavement in the morning sun. They went over the high bridge. They were about to skirt the dog park, to then climb the mound that held the racetrack and descend to the Bulb. But Igor stopped.

"Is time," he said. And he started walking into the dog park, next to the Berkeley pier. "I tell you now about good friend. Name, Aleksander Wojtkiewicz. American chess fan gentrify him, call him Wojo, as if he cuddly bear. They never know beauty of mind that travel from one small tournament to another in big Greyhound bus. When he drink self into sickness, they not get doctor."

Igor got down on his knees and started to shovel up the manicured grass with his bare hands. From his pocket be brought forth what looked like a large friendship bracelet to Lisa, but the string was covered with worn wooden beads. Igor placed this in the ground. Igor said, "Was his. From time in Soviet prison. He not let us help. He not take morphine. He not wish debt, you understand? When sick he hide, holding these beads, forever alone."

Igor covered the mound and both players continued their walk in silence. Lisa imagined hordes of Eastern European boys. She had seen some of them in Chalkidiki. They carried heavy packs and sought the ascent. The sublime was up there. They could see it as they approached. They would molt their personal pasts and all of their infantile fallibilities at the mountain's peak. And they would be reborn as men, strong enough to perceive and wield beauty, strong enough to not need women, to not need money. The complex harmonies they played together spoke of this coming truth. And their aspirations were flattered by the echoes that resounded from the nearby peaks of math and music.

Each of these men did travel upward, and chess rewarded their sacrifices by allowing them to manipulate the power of the transparent world. But they did not find peaks on which they would slough their lower selves and jump off into the higher with their noble spirits. They found themselves on plateaus. There they would struggle with one another, and prove their strength. They pushed each other down to reach for the higher.

Years of battle ensued. They did not have the physical space, or breath, to pause. Fresh challenges called out to their manhood and demanded struggle. Igor had told her of the rabbit, the guy who was always getting beaten down. He was probably the one who showed the others the ledge of their tabletop plateau. Together, they then looked out into the meaninglessness below. And they were strong enough to concede the nothingness and untransparency of the world from which they had arisen. Up high, they were isolated in a sad and lonely world of men. So they huddled together and drank.

Now Igor was on a journey back down. He buried his friend's wooden beads, and would soon give his set to Lisa and the homeless library of the Bulb. He would return to the unclean and opaque thought of daily life. The path Igor had used to get up to his plateau would now be completely unrecognizable. Year-round snow covered everything above the tree line. Igor would fall through that snow, the ice would cut his legs. Then he would have to bushwhack, the thorns would tear at him. That would be his practice for the long bike ride into the emptiness.

As they approached the library, dogs began to charge them from the shrubbery. Lisa huddled close to Igor's thigh as long fangs snapped just inches from her face; frothy drool dripped onto the nice leather shoes Jan had bought her when they were still rich. Then three worn faces began to approach. Covered in uneven whiskers, their skin looked like uncured animal hides. Lisa thought they were noble, that they must have undergone some kind of rugged enlightenment. Igor said something about Stalin and camps.

The veterans gathered around Igor's board and carved pieces, amazed to hear that such a beautiful piece of art would soon belong to the library. The tallest, a man named Clint, challenged Igor to a game. But Igor refused, he said that Lisa would play. The other two enjoyed the awkwardness of Clint's situation. They saw that he was now obliged to beat the girl, to tear her clothes and give her a bloody lip, right in front of her old man. Clint would have to fulfill the silent accusation they saw in the fearful eyes of civilization whenever they left the Bulb. His friends jeered him, "Go on Clint, don't ya got any napalm left?" "What's wrong, monkeys coming down out of the trees?"

The second man, Carl, used the space created by Clint's mumbling dissatisfactions to ask for a game against Igor with the library's plastic pieces. Then the third, a big black guy named Ronnie, said, "Shiiit, who am I supposed to play then?" Lisa unpacked her own plastic set that she always had with her and said, "I'll play all of you, at the same time." They laughed at her, "Shiiit," "No, lil' darling'," "Ah, c'mon she jus' foolin' you man." But Lisa wasn't fooling. "And I'm gonna play all of you blindfolded." The trio was all laughing and having a good time at the silliness of the whole thing. "Twenty bucks a game," Lisa said.

All eyes turned to Igor, as if he were the arbiter of this strange event. They followed him to the wide plush chair near the entrance of the library. A wealthy house might have found a small tear in the upholstery unsatisfactory, and released this lounge onto the sidewalk. Then a man like Clint had pushed the chair in a shopping cart down the hill to the shore. As Igor fell into the chair he said, "Is decadence. I like." Then he just sat there, quietly, waiting for the event to happen. The men started setting up the pieces outside the library;

Lisa sat in the half darkness of the library, behind Igor, ready to call out her moves. Igor closed his eyes and told Lisa, "You wake after big fuck."

Lisa taught the men how to call out their moves. And she made them write the moves down, so they couldn't screw up the position. Her blindfold would be the walls of books inside the library. She would call her moves out from there.

Each book had been worn into pliancy, not only with notes in the margins, but with a mind that had appropriated its ideas, to fight in the world. Each had been honed, in a personal way, like Igor's board. Lisa felt like she was in the middle of a pile of ancient weapons, like the way men in violent societies used to disarm, placing their daggers and bows in a common heap so that no one would die when they came together to discuss matters of importance.

Lisa was only disturbed once, when one of the dogs came into the wooden shack. A red cock came out of its sheath and viciously poked at Lisa's pant leg. He whelmed her with his unwashed smell and sexual appetite. Lisa screamed, but the men laughed. "I think he likes you!" they hollered. Ronnie had to come in to pull the dog off her; Igor didn't help—he was fast asleep. Lisa had to pause, to rediscover the positions after the disturbance, without looking at the boards. Lisa fell into her well and found the early structures of each game. Then she quietly unrolled each of them to their current position.

The men had no money to pay Lisa with. In the midst of their embarrassment and shame, Lisa began petting the dog who had humped her. They told her his name was Johnny. "I'll take him," Lisa said. The men started hooting, and thought it an agreeable way out of their financial disgrace. Especially since no one really owned Johnny. "But here's the thing, Lisa," Clint said. "Any dog who leaves the Bulb has to have his balls cut. Those are the rules the man has made." The men nodded agreement. Then Charlie said, "And we can't allow that. There's been too much ball-cuttin' already." Lisa stared at the mutt. They said he was only around six months old, but he was already huge. She thought of the old men in Igor's Senate, and couldn't imagine being friends with any of them after cutting their balls off. So she said, "Alright, I'll come out every day to take care of him. He can sleep with the other dogs at night. But his name isn't Johnny. I'm naming him Cherub. He'll protect me."

Lisa returned to the library; Igor snored and flies slowly droned in a shaft of sunlight. She found *Emma* on the library's shelves, by Jane Austen. It was water-stained and soiled. But she could read the words and the book was hers to borrow. Lisa remembered what Jan had said of her grandmother: that she thought the world good, that it would provide, that she didn't need money. Lisa also remembered the day Ted brought his spectacular TV home and yelled, "Ya get what you pay for!"

Lisa woke Igor from his slumber and shoved *Emma* in his face. Jan said Austen talked about the world as if it were a chess game. Igor would tell her if that was true. "Known momient," her teacher said as he dragged himself out of the deep chair, "is about people who wish for be married and have money. No one understand." The rain had already begun, and Igor said it was time to start running. Lisa left her plastic travel set at the library alongside Igor's. She said goodbye to Cherub and they ran.

♟

The following day Igor marched Lisa to some place called the Berkeley Bowl. It was a big and sprawling grocery store, with aisles and aisles of stuff to choose from, like every other supermarket Lisa had ever known. But it was as if her master didn't see any of that. Undistracted, he made a direct line to the back of the store.

There, on a few wooden shelves, was a huge pile of fruits and vegetables. Squished under the weight above them, many of the skins broke and released slicks of orange, purple and yellow. Seeking a leak, these colors crept up the sides of the plastic bags that held them, like slurpees and sherbets, like Lisa's own spit after she had stuffed nearly twenty Mike and Ike candies into her mouth.

"Best always cheap," Igor said. "Rich people not understand ripe, they leave for us. If no money have, look for fruit in dumpster." Igor bought three bags of oranges, two bags of apples, two bags of pomegranates and one bag of red onions. Each bag cost ninety-nine cents. Then they ran up to Hillegass Street and picked lemons from a tree.

Back at his cottage, Igor gave Lisa a pair of scissors and told her to cut some of his kale. Lisa wandered through Igor's forest, and carefully cut from the Siberian dwarf, dinosaur, rainbow and perennial walking kale. Then Igor had Lisa strip the kale leaves from their stems while he put thin slices of red onion into the lemon juice.

"Put all together," he said. "Push lemon juice and onion into kale leaves. Squeeze!" Igor oversaw Lisa as she macerated the thick leaves, and the lemon juice burned her soft hands. "Now we let sit for momient, let lemon talk to kale. Eat fruit outside." Igor sat on the ground with his plants and took his shirt off. With his bare hands he started to twist a huge pomegranate, looking for a seam. Overripe, the fruit exploded like a grenade and splattered his hairy chest with dark red. He handed the halved fruit to Lisa and broke his own. Lisa watched him take huge chomps, his chin stubble catching the exploding spritz. Her master was cleaning the whole fruit out, eating the white interstices that everyone else worked around. Dreaming of the pomegranate soup that Dorsa made with her mother, Lisa began to carefully pick each kernel out of its bed. She patiently gathered a handful, and held the springy kernels up to the light. There she saw shimmering purples and blacks hidden inside the red. She threw them all in her mouth, and they were the best thing she had ever tasted.

Lisa's eyes followed the red from Igor's mouth as it dripped down his torso. There she noticed something truly remarkable: Stretch marks were etched into Igor's lean body like ancient stratifications in an exposed layer of rock. An excess skin hung about his belly, loose and papery, like the slough of a snake. Igor had really once been a fatso.

"Eat, Lisa, eat!" Igor exhorted her. They moved onto the kale salad. And as he sprinkled some quartered almonds into Lisa's bowl he asked her, "Today we go for Walden Pond?" Lisa said she didn't know where that was. Igor explained, "Is American tradition; for find self and truth in nature, alone. Is big make-believe. Thoreau go only three mile from home. Ha! Big journey. Is like your journey. Like way Fischer lock self in Pasadena apartment for big training."

Lisa was startled to think of herself as an American. More than anything she was Russian. She sprinkled some of her own hard-won pomegranate seeds into Igor's bowl, onto the kale her own hands had mushed with lemon and red onion juice. The men who looked at her online. All of Jan's hypocritical expectations. Lisa never felt any of that when she was Russian, with Igor. No one ever told her she should be in school when she was with him.

A feral cat named Laska visited them. The walking kale stretched up high above her, into the pleasantly warm noonday sun. Like a lullaby, Igor told Lisa of the brisk air that came from the vast Pacific, scooping out the pollution of the cars. He told of the many hills he rode his bike over, reaching the top in a sweaty bath of manhood. He told of the fruits and nuts of the Central Valley, growing effortlessly in a sunny paradise.

Then he said, "Today final lesson."

☖

"Jump, Lisa, jump!" Igor's head disappeared and then reappeared, bobbing in the three-foot swells just off the shore of the dusty brown peninsula that held her library. The tide brought in the salt water that had been up in Alaska just a day or two before. That brackish water mixed with the pure mountain waters of the Sierras that the Sacramento River washed down. Dolphins, crab and sturgeon swam in there. Thick rain clouds suffocated a pale sun.

Cherub whimpered beside her. He didn't like this momient. Lisa had stripped down to a cotton T-shirt and some athletic shorts—the kind grandma Lena wore when she ran on a gym treadmill to stay perky for the men who passed by her metallic green desk. Igor was practically naked. It seemed he always was.

This was the final lesson. Ruth had wanted her to follow this man. What was she supposed to find out there? But she already knew. She was supposed to go to the other side of pain, to find someone stronger, to find someone else. It was an atheist's baptism.

"Jesus Fucking Christ!" Lisa screamed as she surfaced. The January cold bit the papery shell of her body into a blue numbness, and she began to die. From the world of the living, Lisa heard Igor calmly call, "Put head in water, Lisa, swim!" She was furiously dogpaddling a couple feet from the rock she had jumped from. Cherub yelped in terror, and then dove in after his new master.

Lisa scrambled back onto the slippery boulders that lined the shore. Igor called to her, "Today one minute. Tomorrow two." Lisa shivered all over. Her teeth chattered and she rushed to get completely naked so she could dry off and put her layers on. Cherub kept spraying Lisa and all of creation, violently convulsing his body in quick revolutions. Lisa heard Igor call, "Is time for earn nihilism!" Then he was gone.

In the far distance the Berkeley Pier floated on the horizon like the kind of insignificant stick Cherub wanted to fetch. That's where Igor was going. He would swim around it, over the lines of the fishermen. Lisa didn't know where he would go after that. But it seemed he was going off to write in his journal. And, in some strange way, he was doing it for her.

♟

That evening, Lisa stitched together two garbage bags that she had cut to fit her body. In them she would become an it. No one would see her as she ran out to the library every day. Igor's board and her chess trophies had disappeared into that black plastic; now she would too.

At first it was real cool, to run to the water and the library. She could do anything she wanted. For several days, Lisa flipped through the books that others had given. In them, she expected to find some vision or path that she could follow. There had to be a manual on how to play life well. There had to be masters whose lives she could study. But Lisa always came back to Jan's apartment, leaving Cherub to bed down for the night with Clint and his dogs.

Jan and Lisa pretended that Emeryville High was still part of their lives. They had conversations like, "What the hell are you wearing?" "My school uniform." And, "How was school today?" "Fine." Lisa had a line of defense ready if Jan started poking her. She was going to shout, "You haven't even been there! Why don't you go to Project Darkness for a day! Igor came to see it." But Jan never tried to rip that scab off.

Most of the library's books were about conspiracy theories, some structure out there in the world that prevented us from being who we really were. But Lisa could do anything she wanted. Nothing was stopping her now. And Chessbabes was a world away, on the other side of the black plastic, in some place with an internet connection.

Clint and the other veterans offered Lisa their histories of the world. "Yep, I'm just sittin' here, waitin' for my patriarchal dividend," they liked to say with a laugh. "Check's comin' any day now!" Lisa's skin hardened and cracked in the salty wind. She nailed driftwood and two-by-fours onto the library.

Lisa felt most lonesome when the books couldn't hold her interest. She tried reading the library's weather-beaten copy of *Emma*, but it was like digging a hole in wet ground. Obscure words like "valetudinarian" and "drawing room" were soppy shovelfuls of mud that just led to more water. Those words belonged to Emma Woodhouse's foreign and petty world. Igor was right. It was just a dumb book about some hottie who wanted to get married and have lots of money. So what if she could never get over herself.

Lisa couldn't focus on anything; the drip-drip of a leak would lead her into daydreams of how she would rebuild the library, with towers and many special areas to study. A whimper from Cherub made her think about what Clint had said, that Cherub was often scared at night, when the coyotes came out to hunt. He could smell them, Clint said. Cherub could also smell Lisa, and would always come out to greet her before she was even close to the library.

Lisa's days were often just a collection of these threads that didn't lead anywhere, when she and the mildewy smell of the carpet became trapped in the little wooden structure, rain pouring all around. Igor's immaculate board was right there; all she had to do was unpack the pieces from the purple bag that said Crown Royal. Where the hell was he?

Dorsa had also lost her chess practice. Back in Emeryville, on Jan's computer, Lisa read: "I've been studying your book, Lisa, in my quiet room in the suburbs of Tehran. A vase of purple and white fritillaries sits on my window; they bow their heads and smell like wet fur. Behind them I can see the long ridge of Mount Tochal. I understand now how you became so strong. You went up there, with the Russians. And I went after you. Every day I washed away my sweat in the clear mountain streams. And I felt pure. I climbed all the way up to the majesty of Game eleven. But then, sad news. They took the book away from me. They said it was inappropriate, and that I was obsessing over it. I'm so sorry, Lisa. I fear the book and your notes are gone."

Lisa hadn't even finished studying all the games from the Tal-Botvinnik match with Igor. Chess never made any sense without him. And jumping in the water alone always seemed so pointlessly cold. She wasn't making any progress in her swimming—it was always just a quick plunge and then a very long shiver. Cherub didn't jump anymore. He just came to the rocks and watched his master's painful routine with an air of grave disappointment.

Lisa decided that she would wander from the library. The gun turret was so close. She would let all her tightness go, and release everything inside her that had ever said no. Getting fucked up with her fellow runaways would be like Russian boys drinking vodka before the final day of the tournament; it would cleanse her. Lisa planned to tell them that her name was January, "Cuz my mom knew I was gonna be a cold cold bitch." She would show them the cut marks on her arm.

The truants and the loiterers allowed Lisa to enter their circle and participate in their ritual. Her new friends held the false world above their heads as if it were one of Jan's precious vases. They laughed at it and bonded in their deep hatred of it. Upon the concrete floor they would then dash that stupid world—though it was usually just a beer bottle. Then again, and again.

Afterward they would sit down in a state of drowsy melancholy and startle each other in the spray-painted shadows of the turret. All they had at hand were the shards of the vases and bottles they had broken. Lounging around, they would pick at themselves with those sharp edges. Then they would leave, saying something about getting back to their fifth-period class, and Lisa would again be alone.

♟

Jan had no right to compare Jane Austen to chess. She didn't have access to the three dimensions that flowed through Lisa's soul. She had no idea how to talk to her pieces, to unroll their fates through time. And she certainly didn't know anything about the crisp precision of the problem Lisa had solved inside the special UC Berkeley math room.

Lisa decided she would refute Jan, by disproving the life of Emma. Lisa wasn't sure yet how the proof would go. But it would be conclusive. Lisa scanned the pages of the book for weaknesses and began building a scaffold around Emma's life. She slithered down the poles and clambered up to the many wooden planks of her construction. It felt great to stick lusty swords and drive long lances deep into Emma's flesh. The more Emma bled, the freer Lisa became.

The execution gave Lisa something singular to do. And that was a great relief. For there were too many things for her to study. Carl tried to teach her how to play Go. "It's way deeper than chess," he said. Clint showed her some chords on the library's guitar. And she was supposed to be studying chess. But it sucked without Igor.

Lisa's construction wound itself around Emma like her pieces had once encircled Davidson. She stabbed at Emma and shouted, "You know you're gonna have to get out of there. Your small talk and small expectations are like Mr. Reese's math problems. Page after page, like all the stuff Jan wants me to do."

Emma's life seemed so thin, as if she couldn't see the mountains, or seek the ascent. Lisa shouted at her as if she were talking trash in a school yard: "And why do you always have to be such a bitch? Cuz you didn't have a mommy and a daddy?" Lisa looked around. Cherub wasn't there, only the sound of the raw wind whistling through the fragile wooden boards of the library.

I'm like Emma, Lisa thought. *We both didn't have a mother or a father. We didn't have anyone to tell us what was important. So we had to create our own worlds. That's why everything revolves around us. That's why everybody thinks we're arrogant.*

♟

In early May, the hard rains began to turn into short showers and Lisa took her garbage bags off. The water was a couple degrees warmer and she had worked her way up to a three-quarter mile swim. She was aiming for three miles. That was the distance the guy Igor called Pondboy had walked to escape society. The final swim would feature going around the Berkeley pier, those were the last waters Lisa had seen Igor swim toward.

Lisa had run to and from the library every day. She bought the bags of soft pomegranates, mushy persimmons and brown bananas that sold for ninety-nine cents at Igor's grocery store. She picked up the apples and plums that dropped into Berkeley streets from the yards of wealthy houses. From dumpsters, Lisa selected the most wonderful pineapples and figs—fruit that was too delicious for rich people. Her tummy was hard; only when she looked close could she see the little lines that had once held her fat. Her mind could now go the distance.

Lisa again won the Northern California Girls Championship, and she got some students. She gave them Ruth's old photocopies, closed her eyes, and told them to tell her where the pieces were. It was part of her training for the Polgar tournament at the end of the summer. Lisa felt free without the board, like being without a car, a bike or money. Like being in the water. "It is a pleasure," she told them. Lisa especially liked it when they protested.

In an email titled "The Journal," Lisa wrote:

"Hey Igor, you always wanted me to tell you something about the feminine tradition of the journal. That was the deal. Back then I selfishly took from you without being able to give you anything in return. I want to try now:

"Journals were created when women were beaten so far back that all they really had was their most private self. That's where we learned to talk to our pieces. You have to figure out what they really want. But you can only do that by listening to all the pieces around them. Their stories are your stories. Have you ever seen old ladies gossip? It's kinda like that.

"But let's look for examples of what we're talking about, like Arun would want. For the Polgar tournament at the end of the summer I am mostly studying my own games. I get it now, why it's so hard. You have to look at what you are running away from. Here's some of my analysis:

—"Mr. Reese is not my enemy. Every day he has to contain the sexualities of thirty-some kids, like the cardboard around a cheap box of wine. His struggle is not mine.

—"Botvinnik is not my enemy! He's not The Man, as Clint likes to say. Botvinnik's chess is careful and wise.

—"Vlad is not my enemy. Dr. Frohlich is not my enemy.

—"Not even the men at Chessbabes.com are my enemy. I can hear their girlfriends and mothers say, "You're a grown man and you still play with dolls?" It always sounds like my mother's voice. They feel like they have to explain chess. Again and again, these men violate the beautiful, trying to put chess into the words of the chessless. It's like trying to get past ninth grade. Eventually they give up and walk away. Like wolves without a pack, they mourn their loss in the forests on the edge of town, where the scent of the people

LISA

they came from mingles with the rawest nature. Or maybe it's a shack next to some cold-ass water, ha!

"To them, my picture seems like a way back. It's like I'm whispering: 'Odysseus, come home. Tell me about your struggle.' But I can't bring them home from the edges. Because I'm already there, with them. That's why my picture makes them so angry.

"But I do have friends. You, Ruth, Saheli, Zarra, Dorsa and hopefully my mom. I know you're out there, analyzing your games. I'll be here, whenever you're ready to come back. —Lisa"

♟

Lisa had written this letter out in her chess notebook, which was also her journal, and she had to type it all into her mother's computer. Jan was home more often now, as the evening light began to move toward the summer solstice. No one was buying anything until Mother's Day, still a couple weeks away.

For months, Lisa had imagined sending her mom a letter. She was going to put it on fancy paper and send it in the mail. Because that's what they did in the Jane Austen novels. But Lisa changed her mind. She would take her mother to the place in the living room that Ted had left empty and read to her aloud, as she once had to Igor.

For the occasion, Lisa got some of Ruth's Green Snail Tea. She picked out hundreds of pomegranate kernels and made Dorsa's *Ash-e anar* soup. Her mother's tea set, bowls and tray had little scratches and dents. They were the same imperfections that had sent the library's luxurious chair down toward the water, in whose seat she had spent so much time studying and thinking.

Lisa approached her mother with her journal in her hand. Jan opened her eyes as Lisa led her to their spot on the carpet. Her face reminded Lisa of her own. That's how I looked right before I studied the Morphy game with Igor, Lisa thought, prepared to attune myself

229

to the choir of the pieces and to then take responsibility for my own moves.

This is what Lisa said:

"Dear Mom: I've been trying to come home. I just didn't know it, even when I stole your Jane Austen collection out from under your bed. Now I think of those books as my inheritance.

"I remembered how you and Ted met at a home show. You had been looking for things to sell at your store. He was looking for things he could put into his hotel rooms, to make travelers feel cozy. He asked you for advice. And then you rehearsed the ancient ritual, from faraway Austen time. You married him. I think you wanted someone to be one your side, maybe even love. But I never let myself see that. I never thought about your pieces. It was always only me, me, me.

"I think I understand why we fought so much over the journal and chess. You saw my journal as a retreat into a private feminine world, where we had to go because we were powerless in the real one. Good for little girls, but not for young women. In a kind of similar way, Domestique wanted to bring the household gods out of their private places and make them the real gods. You never wanted to see us cast aside again, like Grandma Lena was. That's why you sent me to chess class, to get a piece of the South Bay's power. You wanted us to have a place in the world, to not have to depend on men.

"A man named Arun is helping me with math. He's a former chess prodigy who teaches at UC Berkeley. He's teaching me the fundamentals, no phony bullshit. Remember when you said that you can only see what's important after you've taken something away, like the way Austen took away the world of ships and men? Physics takes the dirt away and pretends that everything is mathematical. That's how they discovered the bend in space/time. Arun promised I will be able to feel the bend in space/time around a Kleenex tissue in a couple years. My friend Saheli says that I'll be able to see the bend even sooner than that, but I have to do the problems Arun gives me. It's the same bend that all good chessplayers know. You know it too. Jane Austen showed me how I bend around you.

"I made sauerkraut in the kitchen. I got the big mason jars at a yard sale, so cheap! Have some. For the slug problem in my new community garden plot I made some beer traps out of plastic yogurt containers. I yelled, "Free beer, boys!" You know, just for old times.

"I've got some teaching gigs. Every Saturday I lead a chess workshop for Indian girls down in Fremont. They all think I'm a rock star or something, ha ha! It pays well, but I don't really need the money. I'm working so you can have health insurance. It's important to me. Online, it said that it would cost around $400 a month for you to have it. That's how much money I've enclosed. Please take it, for me.

Love,
Lisa Lena Schmied"

Made in the USA
Lexington, KY
15 October 2013